Sincerely

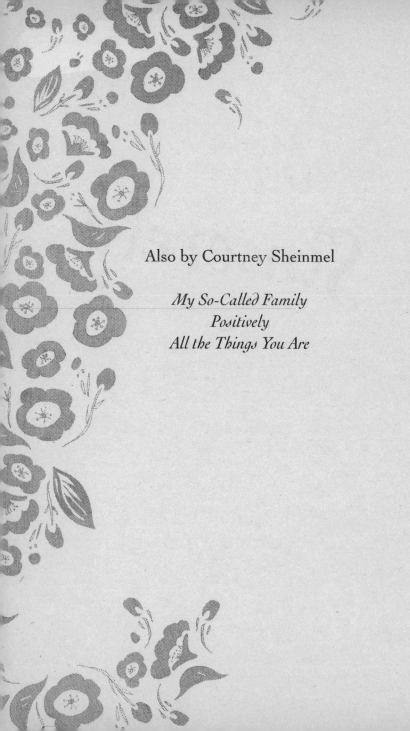

Also by Courtney Sheinmel

My So-Called Family
Positively
All the Things You Are

Sincerely

✳ ✳ ✳

Sincerely, Sophie
&
Sincerely, Katie

✳ ✳ ✳

by Courtney Sheinmel

Simon & Schuster Books for Young Readers

NEW YORK   LONDON   TORONTO   SYDNEY

SIMON & SCHUSTER BOOKS FOR YOUNG READERS
An imprint of Simon & Schuster Children's Publishing Division
1230 Avenue of the Americas, New York, New York 10020
This book is a work of fiction. Any references to historical events, real people, or real locales are used fictitiously. Other names, characters, places, and incidents are products of the author's imagination, and any resemblance to actual events or locales or persons, living or dead, is entirely coincidental.
Copyright © 2010 by Courtney Sheinmel
SIMON & SCHUSTER BOOKS FOR YOUNG READERS is a trademark of Simon & Schuster, Inc.
For information about special discounts for bulk purchases, please contact Simon & Schuster Special Sales at 1-866-506-1949 or business@simonandschuster.com.
The Simon & Schuster Speakers Bureau can bring authors to your live event. For more information or to book an event, contact the Simon & Schuster Speakers Bureau at 1-866-248-3049 or visit our website at www.simonspeakers.com.
Also available in a Simon & Schuster Books for Young Readers hardcover edition
Book design by Chloë Foglia • The text for this book is set in Cochin.
Manufactured in the United States of America • 0511 OFF
First Simon & Schuster Books for Young Readers paperback edition June 2011
2 4 6 8 10 9 7 5 3 1
The Library of Congress has cataloged the hardcover edition as follows:
Sheinmel, Courtney.
Sincerely : sincerely Sophie, sincerely Katie / Courtney Sheinmel. — 1st ed.
p. cm.
Summary: Brought together as pen pals by a school assignment, Sophie and Katie, eleven-year-olds living on opposite sides of the country, find comfort in their growing relationship when problems at home and at school disrupt their lives.
ISBN 978-1-4169-4010-4 (hc)
[1. Pen pals — Fiction. 2. Friendship — Fiction. 3. Family problems — Fiction. 4. Schools — Fiction. 5. New York (N.Y.) — Fiction. 6. Redwood City (Calif.) — Fiction.] 1. Title.
PZ7.S54124 Si 2010
[Fic] 22
2007044488
ISBN 978-1-4169-4022-7 (pbk)
ISBN 978-1-4424-0664-3 (eBook)

Acknowledgments

With thanks to all those who made this possible—my agent and dear friend, Alex Glass; my editor, David Gale—three books later, and I still can't believe I'm lucky enough to work with you; Justin Chanda, Paul Crichton, Kiley Frank, Navah Wolfe, and everyone else at Simon & Schuster who worked so hard to make this book better than I ever dreamed it could be; Elizabeth Law, for her invaluable editorial skills; and my family and friends for reading all those early drafts and cheering me on.

Sincerely, Sophie

For Alyssa Sheinmel,
my little sister

One

Everything changed last fall when I started sixth grade. For one thing, it was the first time that the teacher wasn't the tallest person in the class. Jillian Harris came back from summer vacation and looked like she had grown a foot taller. She was at least two inches taller than our teacher, Ms. Brisbin. Then there was Jessie, my best friend. She started acting differently, too. All of sudden all she seemed to care about was boys.

And me, well, I think I started to become a grown-up. Well, maybe not a grown-up exactly. It's not like I had to get a job and pay my own bills, but I definitely didn't feel like a little kid anymore. It all began on the first really cold day of the season. That Friday I woke up to my sister Haley's voice.

She always woke me up before I was actually ready.

"I'll just wear pants under my skirt!" Haley said to herself excitedly. Even when Haley talks to herself, she's loud. I hadn't opened my eyes yet and wondered if I was still dreaming. I rolled over toward the wall and squeezed my eyes shut tighter. "Hey, Sophie," Haley called. "Time to wake up! Should I wear leggings or jeans?"

I groaned and rolled over. I hated sharing a room with Haley. I never got any privacy or peace and quiet. "What are you talking about?" I asked. Haley bounded toward my bed with two pairs of pants.

"Mom said I have to wear pants today because it's going to be really cold, so which ones?" she said.

"The jeans, I guess," I said. Usually Haley and I wear uniforms to school—gray skirts with white blouses. But on Fridays we're allowed to wear whatever we want. I like to wear jeans every chance I get, but Haley hates wearing pants. She's four years younger than I am, and she likes to wear a skirt or a dress every day, even on Fridays.

Haley climbed onto my bed. "I think I'm going to wear my purple skirt over them," she told me.

"Haley, get off my bed," I said. I stretched out my arms and legs so there wouldn't be any room for her. "That skirt is going to look really stupid over your jeans."

"No, it won't," Haley insisted. "The jeans will be just like tights." She jumped off the bed and went to the closet. "Oh, purple skirt, where are you?" she called. She moved some hangers aside noisily. I was sure she was making a mess, and I was already preparing to complain to Mom so that I wouldn't get blamed and have to clean it up myself. "Oh, there you are!" Haley exclaimed suddenly. She yanked on the skirt and the hanger crashed to the ground. Even though Haley's only in second grade and pretty small for her age, she makes a lot of noise and takes up a lot of space. You always know when she's in the room. Haley's good at being the center of attention, but I like things to be quieter.

"You better clean that up," I told her.

"I will," she said. "After breakfast. Mom said I could make it myself."

"Where's Dad?" I asked. Dad usually made breakfast. Mom called him the family chef.

"He went to work early," Haley said. I watched her pull her skirt on over her jeans. "Now it's waffle time," she said, and she skipped out of the room.

I got out of bed after Haley left. I knew exactly what I wanted to wear: my favorite jeans and a pink long-sleeved shirt. I had pink Converse sneakers that matched the shirt perfectly. I like things to match, even though Jessie told me that pink is a babyish color. A month before, pink had been her favorite color too.

I finished tying my shoes and then I looked at myself in the mirror behind the closet door. I thought I looked okay and not too babyish. People always think I'm younger than I really am because I'm small for my age. I've always been the shortest girl in my grade. Jessie's the second shortest. She's just a little bit taller than I am, plus she has curly hair so that adds a bit to her height. We both have light brown hair, but my hair is straight and flat. I really wish it were curly like Jessie's. I tried to puff it up a little with my fingers. It worked a little bit.

Jessie and I met in kindergarten and have been best friends for five and a half years. We go to the Anne B. Victor School for Girls, but everyone just calls it Victor. Anne B. Victor was a real person who started the school more than a hundred years ago. It's a private school, which means we have to pay to go there, and which is why we have to wear uniforms. Victor goes from kindergarten all the way through twelfth grade, so you can stay at the same school until it's time to go to college. I'm perfectly happy not to have boys in school, but the way Jessie had been acting, you'd think the fact that there are no boys caused her actual physical pain. She was all excited about the school dance the next month because there were going to be boys there.

Victor is on the corner of Eighty-Ninth Street and Madison Avenue in New York City. There's a boys' school across the street from our school. It's called the Dorr Day School, and Jessie liked to hang out on the corner after school to talk to the Dorr boys. They get out of school about fifteen minutes after we do. Jessie waited for them to come down the block and cross the street, especially to see one boy in particular: Madden Preston. She never just called him by his first name. She always said "Madden Preston." At lunch the week before she'd said, "Oh my God, Soph! Did you see what Madden Preston did with his hair yesterday?" Madden Preston's hair had looked the same to me every day I'd seen him, but Jessie went on and on about how he must have started using gel in it. "He has the most beautiful eyes, too," she told me. "Sometimes they're blue and sometimes they're gray. It depends on the way the light hits them." I told Jessie that I hadn't noticed. She said that was because I never paid attention to details.

I didn't really think she was right about that. Details have always been important to me, which is part of the reason why I remember most things. I remember people's birthdays, and the day I won the writing award at school, and the day my sister Haley broke her wrist, and the day my teacher Ms. Brisbin caught Jessie and me passing notes during math—that was also the day Ms. Brisbin started hating me. I had even noticed plenty of details about Madden Preston— like how he'd looked at me sort of funny that day when he'd crossed the street to where Jessie and I were waiting. I don't think Jessie even noticed, which proves that I was paying more attention to detail than she was. Frankly, sometimes I wondered if maybe she was just making up her crush on

Madden Preston because she wanted to be cool. She even started blowing her hair dry in the mornings and putting just a little bit of glitter on her eyelids. If she put on too much, she'd have to wash it off. You're not allowed to wear makeup at Victor until high school, and that's three years away. But Jessie was smart. She put a tiny dab over each eye, so you could only really tell if you were looking for it. She thought it made her look exotic, but I think glitter is kind of silly and certainly more babyish than the color pink.

Lunch was right after our math period, which was a good thing because math is my least favorite subject and it was nice to have a break afterward. Jessie and I went down to the lunchroom together. Friday is always leftovers day, and I wanted some of the macaroni and cheese from Wednesday. Jessie refuses to eat leftovers. I stood in line while she went to pour herself some cereal. "Save me a seat," I called to Jessie, even though I knew I didn't have to tell her that. We always sat at the same table, just left of the center of the room. It's a good table to sit at so you can see what everyone else is doing, and it is far enough away from the teachers' table on the far right-hand side of the room.

I balanced my tray on one hand and carried my orange juice in my other hand. Jessie was across the room at our table. Three other girls from our grade, Amy, Lindsay, and Melissa, were also sitting there. I'd never been that friendly with them, but because there are only about forty girls in our entire grade, you get to know everyone pretty well. Even so, I didn't really want to eat lunch with them. But Jessie always did, so sometimes I had to put up with them.

Jessie was sitting in between Amy and Melissa. It's not like I *needed* to sit next to Jessie every day, but I did anyway, unless one of us was sick. I put my tray down next to Lindsay. "Oh, gross," she said as I sat down. "I can't believe you got the leftovers. That's from like Monday."

"Wednesday," I said. "Monday was beef Stroganoff."

"Whatever. I don't exactly memorize what I eat each day," Lindsay said. The other girls laughed, even Jessie. And Jessie had said I was the one who was bad with details. Anyway, I don't know why Lindsay thought leftover macaroni and cheese was gross. She was dipping two fingers into a mound of cottage cheese and sucking it off her fingers.

"So anyway," Lindsay said, "my mom is determined to be one of the dance chaperones."

"Oh, that's terrible!" Melissa said.

"I know," Lindsay said, and she paused to slurp on her fingers. "But she did promise that if she's there, she won't try to talk to me for the whole night, and if anyone asks, she'll pretend to be someone else's mother."

"I don't know why mothers always want to be such joiners," Amy said. "My mom said she wanted to come too. She thinks it's so cute that we're having a school dance. But I told her she couldn't come and ruin my night just because she wanted to relive her childhood."

"I know what you mean," Jessie said. But I knew she was lying. Jessie's mother never comes to anything. It's not because she doesn't want to, but she works a lot. When we were younger, Jessie would get really upset about her mother not being around. Jessie's mother is a researcher at a news station and she also teaches three nights a week at NYU. The only field trip Jessie's mom ever came on was the one we went on in third grade to the TV station where she works. They pulled up the morning's news stories on the teleprompter, and we got to read into a camera and watch ourselves on the monitor. The producer told us to ignore the monitor and just speak into the camera, but it's really hard not to get distracted when you see your face staring back at you on the screen. Jessie and I got to be the anchors and sit next to each other on the couch in the front of the set. We read from the teleprompter in unison. Jessie's mom had a tape made of it, and we watched it a couple times at her house.

Jessie used to tell me I was lucky because my mother is almost always around. My mom works too. She's a head-hunter. I hate the name of her job because it sounds like she is out chopping off people's heads, but really it means she finds people jobs. She interviews people in a room in the back of our apartment that is set up as an office. It should be a bedroom, but Mom has a desk, some chairs, a bulletin board, and a bunch of file cabinets in there. My dad even built shelves for her into the back wall behind the desk. My dad's a lawyer but he likes to build things too. He made bookshelves for Haley and me, too. They are a little crooked but they work just fine.

The reason that Haley and I had to share a bedroom was so Mom could keep her office. By the time sixth grade started, I thought I was getting too old to share a room with a second grader, but at least if something important happened at school, or if there was a field trip, Mom could arrange her schedule to be there. Jessie's father died when she was a baby, so her mother has to work an extra amount. He had a heart attack in his office. They rushed him to the hospital, and hooked him up to all sorts of machines to try to fix it, but he had another heart attack in the hospital, and he died. Jessie never talks about it, and she doesn't remember him because she was so little, but my mom told me about it. My mom said that Jessie's mother sometimes gets very angry with her husband for dying and leaving her all alone.

At first it was hard for me to understand why Jessie's mom would be angry with someone for something that was absolutely not his fault. I mean, it's not like he wanted to have a heart attack and die. But my mom told me that being really sad can make you angry. The thing is, Jessie's mom never seems really sad. She's pretty, just like Jessie, she likes her work, and she has a lot of friends—and of course Jessie. She even lets me call her Liz instead of Mrs. Adler, even though I have to call all of my other friends' parents by their last names.

I never met Jessie's dad, but I've seen his picture a lot. There are a bunch of photographs of him in Jessie's apartment, and also, Jessie keeps a special album of pictures underneath her bed. It's a secret album, but she showed it to me. All of the pictures are of her dad and her when she was a baby.

Lindsay swiped the last bit of cottage cheese off her plate and slurped on her fingers. She pushed her tray away. "I'm stuffed," she said, and turned toward Jessie. "Hey, did I tell you I decided to get that dress from Bloomingdale's?"

"The blue one?" Jessie asked.

"Yeah. My mom's taking me tomorrow. You should totally come. You have to get something to impress Madden!"

"That sounds good," Jessie said. Lindsay is one of the wealthiest kids at Victor, and her parents get her whatever she wants, but I wondered if Liz would really let Jessie get a new outfit just because Madden Preston was going to be at the dance.

"And after you guys finish shopping, you can come over and hang out with Amy and me," Melissa said. Amy and Melissa live pretty close to Bloomingdale's. Actually, Amy and Melissa live in the same building, so they're always together. Lindsay lives in another building on the other side of the city, on the West Side, so she doesn't always get to hang out with them, but Lindsay doesn't strike me as the kind of person who would care about that or feel lonely. Amy and Melissa both really looked up to Lindsay, so I'm sure she knew she was invited to their homes anytime she wanted to be included.

I listened to the four of them make plans to meet at Melissa's after Lindsay and Jessie finished shopping. Nobody said anything to me at all, as though I weren't even there. I noticed that Lindsay, Amy, and Melissa had the tiniest bit of glitter on their eyelids, just like Jessie. I wondered if they had done it to be like Jessie or if Jessie had done it to be like them—probably Jessie had copied them.

"You guys can even sleep over," Melissa said.

The five-minute bell rang, and we picked up our trays and walked over to the conveyor belt where we have to put our trays when we're finished eating. If you get caught leaving your tray at the table, you have to wear your uniform on Friday, so I always make sure to clear my tray. Usually I hate hearing the five-minute bell, but this time I was relieved to get back to class. It felt strange to hear Jessie make plans that didn't include me. In fact, it just didn't make any sense. We were best friends, so we always included each other.

Jessie had even come with my family to Florida a few times over spring break when we went to visit my grandmother, because Liz usually has to work over vacation. I decided to talk to Jessie about it. Maybe it was just a misunderstanding and I really was invited.

Two

Jessie was ahead of me as we walked upstairs to our class-room, and I took the steps two at a time to catch up with her.

"Hey," I said, pulling at her arm. She turned around.

"I didn't do the reading for English," she said. "I really hope I'm not called on. Can you tell me what the chapter was about?"

Jessie never read our English homework, so I was used to filling her in on what the books were about. Whenever we had book reports to do, she would come over and I would tell her what to write down. I didn't mind because Jessie always brought snacks with her. Besides, she was my friend, so I was supposed to help her out. That month we were reading *Little Women*. It's a book about four sisters. They don't have a lot of money and their father is off fighting in a war. Parts of it are pretty sad, but I liked it a lot. The sisters made up plays and acted them out, which is actually something Jessie and I used to do. Sometimes Haley wanted to play with us, and we always made her be the pet. She would roam around on all fours while Jessie and I acted out the real parts. Anyway, I had already finished the whole book, even though we were reading it chapter by chapter and we only had to be up to the ninth chapter at that point. I had reread chapter 9 the night before, so I knew it really well, but I didn't really feel like helping Jessie.

"How come you didn't invite me?" I asked.

"What do you mean?"

"When you go to Bloomingdale's tomorrow," I said. "How come you didn't invite me?"

"What's the big deal, Soph?" Jessie asked. "We don't have to do everything together. You don't even like shopping. Besides, I'm going over to Melissa's after and I can't just invite you to someone else's house."

"I guess," I said.

"Maybe I can see you on Sunday," Jessie said. "Now can you please tell me about the chapter from last night?"

I filled Jessie in, but she didn't get called on during English. I didn't get called on either, which was a good thing because I was pretty distracted for the rest of the day. I wondered what Jessie would do at a sleepover with her new friends. I bet they didn't know she was scared of the dark. Whenever she stayed at my house, we always left the light on in my closet so she didn't get scared. Haley liked it better that way anyway.

The afternoon dragged on. I kept looking up at the clock at the front of the room to see how much longer we had to go. Finally, there were just fifteen minutes to go before three o'clock. Just fifteen more minutes before the final bell and I could go home. I had to meet Haley in the lunchroom, where all the second graders go for dismissal, and walk home with her. It's kind of a pain to have to walk home with Haley, but my parents said if I wanted to be able to walk home without one of them or a babysitter, I had to take Haley, too. Haley had ballet after school on Mondays and Wednesdays, and I worked on the school paper on Thursdays. But on Tuesdays and Fridays we walked home together. Haley loves walking home with me, because I like to stop at the deli next to school on the way home and buy a cookie or a doughnut, which Mom never lets us do.

Ms. Brisbin was saying something about our country's geography, but I wasn't paying attention. I looked over at Jessie. She sat across the table from me, and I could see the glitter on her eyelids sparkling. On second thought, it wasn't altogether babyish. It did look kind of pretty. Maybe I would start wearing some myself. I needed a new look, anyway. I pulled the cap off my pen and started a list of things I thought

I should buy over the weekend: glitter eye shadow, lip gloss, dangly earrings.

Suddenly someone kicked me underneath the table and I looked up. Jessie was looking at me funny. "Sophie Turner, do you care to join us?" Ms. Brisbin said. A few people started to snicker. My face got really hot, the way it does whenever I get embarrassed or upset. Why do teachers always feel the best way to get your attention is to humiliate you? I muttered "Sorry," lowered my pen, and folded my arms over my paper to cover my shopping list. Ms. Brisbin turned back toward the front of the class.

"As I was saying," she said, "the sixth grade scored very poorly on the state geography test last month. We don't want you to go through sixth grade without knowing the geography of the United States, so we're going to start a grade-wide project. It's pretty exciting, and I hope you will all enjoy and learn from it."

It already didn't sound too exciting to me, but I knew I had better pay attention since I had just been caught. Ms. Brisbin explained that the other sixth-grade teacher, Mr. Warren, had read about a nationwide pen pal project. Schools could sign up to participate, and then all the students' names were entered into a big database, and everyone was matched up with someone from another state. Once you were matched up with a pen pal in another state, you were supposed to start writing to each other once a month about what it was like to live wherever you live, and what things were in your neighborhood, and what you and your friends did. Mr. Warren had signed up our entire grade to participate. I thought the whole thing was pretty silly. Our state tests had been four weeks before, and I'd gotten only one question wrong. I thought the capital of Texas was Dallas, but really it's Austin. Why should I get extra homework if I wasn't one of the people who'd done badly on the test?

Ms. Brisbin said we had all already been matched up with a pen pal and that we should write our first letters over the weekend. We weren't even supposed to have homework on the weekends. That doesn't start at Victor until seventh grade. A few kids groaned.

Ms. Brisbin forgot all about being angry with me. She seemed really excited about this new project. "Come on," she said. "This will be fun. I know you girls are used to instant gratification with e-mail, but when I was young we didn't have computers in our homes and you got letters in the mail. Trust me, getting something in the mail can be very exciting."

Grown-ups are always telling kids about the things they didn't have when they were young, like remote controls, and DVD players, and cell phones. If you ask me, it doesn't sound like it was much fun to be a kid back then.

Ms. Brisbin said we should think about what kids in other places would want to know about New York City and what makes it different and interesting. "Any ideas?" she asked.

Lindsay raised her hand. She always has something to say.

"Yes, Lindsay," Ms. Brisbin said.

"We mostly live in apartment buildings instead of houses, so we live closer together to a lot more people."

Ms. Brisbin nodded. A girl named Alyssa called out. "It's pretty noisy here, even at night," she said.

Jessie said, "A lot of really famous buildings are in New York."

Ms. Brisbin said we should think about how some of the kids we would be writing to might never have been to New York. They may have misconceptions about it being danger- ous and a bad place to grow up. She said we should write about the things that are great about New York, like Central Park, and the views from skyscrapers, and our class party at the ice-skating rink at Rockefeller Center.

As far as I am concerned, one of the greatest things about living in New York is that you can pick up the phone and order food from restaurants and they will deliver it to your house at any time, just like room service in a hotel, but I didn't think that was what Ms. Brisbin had in mind.

Ms. Brisbin started calling our names and handing out the forms with our pen pal assignments. "Samantha, here you go. You were matched with someone in Arkansas. Claire, your pen pal is from Pennsylvania. And Amy, your pen pal is from Washington, D.C." I thought, *Washington, D.C., is not even a state*. Ms. Brisbin walked over to our table and I looked at the stack of papers in her hands. They looked very official. In big block letters at the top of the page were the words: "PEN PALS ACROSS AMERICA." Ms. Brisbin said, "Here you are, Sophie. Your pen pal lives in California." She handed me the piece of paper. A couple inches below the heading, I saw my name and address, and right beneath that was the name of my pen pal and her address: Katie Franklin, 40 Ridgewood Court, Redwood City, California.

The first thing I noticed about Katie Franklin was that she had two first names. My dad's boss is named Ed Simon, and Dad doesn't like him very much. Once I asked him why, and he said he didn't trust anyone with two first names. Even though I knew he'd been teasing and that was a stupid reason not to trust someone, I still wondered about Katie Franklin. Did it count that Katie was a girl, and that her last name was a boy's name, so it couldn't be her own first name, anyway? There is a girl in the grade below me at Victor named Jordan, which can also be a boy's name, so maybe Franklin could be a girl's name too. Either way, I wasn't sure I had much to say to Katie Franklin. I love writing, especially writing short stories, but writing to a perfect stranger all the way across the country is completely different.

The final bell rang. Ms. Brisbin reminded us to write to our new pen pals over the weekend. I packed up my bag and put my jacket and scarf on. Mom had made me bring a hat with me too, but I don't really like wearing hats, so I left it in my backpack. As long as Haley and I were walking home alone, my mother wouldn't have to know, and I wouldn't get in trouble.

I met Haley in the lunchroom. She ran over to me when she saw me and threw her arms around me as if she hadn't seen me in a year. "Sophie, you're here!" she cried. "It's my sister Sophie!" Haley loves to show me off to her friends.

I helped Haley gather up all her stuff. Besides her jacket and backpack, she had a few paintings rolled up to take home. "I even made one for you," she said. "It's a portrait. It really looks like you. Do you want to see it now?"

"It's all rolled up," I told her. "We can look at it at home."

"Please can we look at it now?" Haley said. "I made it just for you." Sometimes she can be very cute and I don't mind having her around. I pulled the rubber band off her paintings and she unrolled them.

"Here," Haley said. "This is it." She held out her painting and looked up at me. It didn't look like me at all. Haley painted my skin too dark and my hair too light. There was a big bow on the top of the head, even though I don't think I had worn a bow in my hair ever in Haley's lifetime. The lips took up half of the face and she had forgotten to paint in ears. I hoped she didn't expect me to hang it up on my side of the room. "Do you like it?" Haley asked anxiously.

"It's really great," I told her, and she beamed.

"Come on," I said. "Let's go to the deli."

I rolled Haley's paintings back up and helped her with her jacket and backpack. We went to the deli and decided to get a black-and-white cookie to split. I broke the vanilla part of the cookie off for Haley and kept the chocolate half for me. We had to eat it on the way home, because if Mom saw us, she would want us to save it for after dinner. Our apartment building is only four blocks away from school. We ate quickly and got crumbs all over our gloves, but it was worth it. I shoved the last bite of cookie into my mouth and we walked into the building.

Three

I didn't get to see Jessie on Sunday because we went shopping for pumpkins so we could make jack-o'-lanterns for Halloween the next week. Even though eleven is a little too old to be interested in carving pumpkins, I still like going to the pumpkin farm. The weather had warmed up, but Mom told Haley that she still had to wear pants because we would be outside for a while picking out pumpkins. Luckily it was warm enough that we didn't have to wear hats, because I would have hated that. Haley put on her jeans and a sweater with puppies on the front. Then she pulled her purple skirt back over her jeans. I was getting used to her new look.

I decided to wear my pink shirt again, but I couldn't find my pink sneakers anywhere in my room. "Look under the beds," I told Haley. "I'm going to check the living room."

I walked out to the hall and heard my parents' voices, louder than they should have been. "You're right. There's no reason to come," Mom said, her voice thick with sarcasm.

"Don't try to guilt-trip me, Andrea. It's not going to work this time," Dad said.

"Of course it won't," Mom said. "You don't think about anybody but yourself anyway."

"There you go," Dad said. "You don't know how to talk without trying to make me feel guilty. Well, I'm not giving in this time. You're just going to have to accept that it can't always be what you want. Some of us have to go to work."

"I work too, Jack," Mom said. "This isn't about your work, and you know it."

"What's that supposed to mean?" Dad asked.

"You know exactly what it means," Mom told him.

"That's right," Dad said. "I can read minds." I heard him starting to walk toward me, and I stepped back so he wouldn't see me. I went back into my room even though I hadn't had a chance to look for my shoes.

"They weren't under the bed," Haley told me.

"That's okay," I said. "I'm just going to wear my brown boots." I hated hearing my parents argue. It happened a lot, but it was the kind of thing I never got used to. Whenever Haley and I fight, Mom and Dad tell us to behave and apologize to each other. I doubted that would work if I tried to tell them that, and I felt a little shaky as I bent down to get my boots from the closet. Haley didn't notice that anything was wrong. "You look like a cowgirl," she said once I had my boots on.

"Girls," Mom yelled out a few minutes later, "let's go." Her voice sounded sharp and mean. Mom's voice always changes after she fights with Dad. I knew it would go away after a little while. Dad is just the opposite. Whenever he fights with Mom, he acts extra cheerful and happy in front of Haley and me, like nothing at all is wrong.

We go to the same place for pumpkins every year. Without traffic it takes about an hour to drive there, and you need to take the highway. Dad usually drove because Mom hates driving on the highway. That's part of the reason why she loves living in Manhattan. Most things you need are right in the city so you don't have to use a car.

The four of us rode down in the elevator together. Dad turned to Mom. "So you know where you're going?"

"Of course I know where I'm going," she said. "We've only gone to this place every year since Sophie was two." I could tell she was still angry with Dad.

"You're not coming with us?" Haley asked Dad.

"No, sweetheart. I have to go in to the office," Dad told her.

"Then where's your briefcase?" Haley said.

"I guess I forgot it," Dad said.

"If you're going to work, how come you're not wearing a suit?" Haley said.

"Because it's the weekend," Dad said.

"What if Ed Simon is there?"

"You ask too many questions," I complained.

"That's all right, Soph," Dad said. He turned back to Haley. "If Ed is there, he won't be wearing a suit either."

We got to the car and I opened the door to the front seat. Haley stamped her foot. "How come Sophie gets the front?"

"Sophie is old enough," Mom said. "Seven years old is too young to sit in the front." Mom opened the back door. "Come on, Haley, get in."

The thing about Haley is that once you give her a reason for something, she usually accepts it and stops complaining. She got into the backseat. Dad bent down and helped her put her seat belt on, even though Haley was old enough to do it by herself. "You know, Sophie," he said, "you were never this pliant."

I turned around in my seat and glared at him. "Do you know what 'pliant' means?" he asked.

My dad always tries to make every conversation a vocabulary lesson. It can be very annoying. "Yes," I said, even though I had no idea what "pliant" meant. I just knew it was something he thought I should be but wasn't.

"Use it in a sentence," Dad said.

"I don't feel like it," I told him.

"Come on," he said. He was smiling a goofy smile.

"I wish my dad was not obsessed with the word 'pliant,'" I said. "There you go. There's your sentence." I turned back around so he would leave me alone. Dad laughed and patted my shoulder.

"All right, girls," he said. "Have fun." He closed Haley's door and walked around to Mom's window. She rolled it down.

"I know how to get there, Jack," she said.

"What will you do if you get lost?" Dad asked.

"I won't get lost," Mom said.

"Well, I have my cell phone," Dad said. "Drive safely." Dad slapped the side of the car and Mom turned the ignition key. Mom shook her head. I knew she was still angry. I turned around and watched Dad standing on the sidewalk, waving to Haley, until we turned the corner and I couldn't see him anymore. "What does 'pliant' mean?" I asked.

"It means someone who listens to her parents," Mom said.

"Come on," I said. "What does it really mean?"

"It means someone who's willing to go with the flow," Mom said.

"Oh," I said.

We drove through Manhattan and then got onto the highway. Another car zoomed in front of us and cut us off. My mother cursed softly, but I heard her. "Mom!" I said. I hate when she curses.

"I'm sorry," Mom said.

"You shouldn't do that," I said. "What if Haley heard you?"

"I won't do it again," she said. I glared at her for emphasis. "Sophie, I promise," Mom said. Haley was singing in the backseat about pumpkins, so I doubted she'd heard Mom anyway.

"Hey, Sophie, do you know this song?" Haley asked.

"No," I said.

"That's because it's brand new. I'm making it up now," she said.

"Can we put on a CD?" I asked. Mom nodded, and I opened the glove compartment. I picked out a Tori Amos album and slipped it into the CD player. I don't think many girls my age listen to Tori Amos, but I do. Mom loves her, but Dad doesn't like her at all, so we only get to listen to her when Mom drives—and that doesn't happen too often. The music started and Mom said, "Good choice."

Haley told us that she wanted to get a tall and skinny pumpkin. "I'll name him Bill," she said. "Do you think Bill is a good name for a pumpkin?"

"Bill is an excellent name for a pumpkin," Mom said.

I sat back and listened to Tori singing. I know most of the words to her songs, even though I don't always understand what they're about. Sometimes I sing along, but sometimes I like to listen silently so I hear only Tori's voice. Dad says she sounds like she's whining when she sings, but Mom says her voice is powerful. I agree with Mom.

My favorite song is called "Winter." It started playing, but in the middle of the first verse my mother cursed again. This time she was louder. Haley heard and repeated it from the backseat. I hated that they were interrupting my favorite song. "Mom!" I said angrily. She had promised she wouldn't curse again, but she doesn't always keep her promises. Sometimes I feel like my mother is the child and I am the grown-up.

"Give me a break, Sophie. I don't know where we are," Mom said.

"Give me a break, Sophie," Haley repeated, and then laughed to herself. I could barely hear the music over her giggles.

"Shush, Haley," Mom said. "I need to concentrate."

"Are you going to call Daddy?" I asked.

"I'm going to get off at the next exit," Mom said. She turned down the music because it was distracting her, so I couldn't hear it at all. We got off the highway at the next exit, but Mom didn't call Dad. She pulled into a gas station instead and went into the convenience store to ask for directions.

Haley kicked the back of my seat. "Stop that," I told her.

"What if the pumpkin place closes before we find it?" Haley said.

"Then Bill will have to spend the night alone," I said.

"Oh, poor Bill!"

Mom came back into the car with a bag of chips for Haley and me to share. "Okay," she said. "We're not too far."

We hadn't even finished the chips when Haley called out, "Look!" I turned to look out the window and saw the pumpkin farm up ahead. Just beyond the carved wooden sign that said PUMPKINS, there were thousands of pumpkins on the ground. From the distance it looked like a solid orange blanket that was stretched out for miles. Haley sighed. "I don't know how I'm going to pick," she said.

Mom parked and we got out of the car and walked toward the pumpkins. Up close there were paths between the pumpkins so you could walk around without stepping all over them.

It's hard to find pumpkins that don't have scrapes or marks on them, and sometimes the stems are too long or too prickly. We took our time going through the rows of pumpkins to make sure we found the best ones. Haley picked out Bill, and then she picked up another pumpkin that she said was Bill's twin brother, Charlie. Charlie was a little plumper than Bill, but Haley explained they were fraternal twins, not identical. Haley was obsessed with twins because there were two sets of twins in her class. Mom agreed that we shouldn't separate the twin brothers, so Haley got to keep both pumpkins. I picked a small round pumpkin. Haley said its name was Oscar.

After Mom paid for the pumpkins, we went to a little restaurant called Susie's Nook that is just down the road from the pumpkin farm. We go there every year. Susie herself takes our order. She wears her hair in a long gray braid hanging down her back, and there are wrinkles all over her face. The wrinkles in her forehead are so deep they look like they were carved that way. I wondered if they hurt. When Susie saw us come in, she said, "How are my favorite customers?" She calls us her favorite customers whenever she sees us, even though we're there only once a year. I can't believe she really even remembers us, but she gave us free cupcakes for dessert and she knew to give Haley a vanilla cupcake and me a chocolate one, so maybe she does know who we are.

On the way home we stopped at a couple of antiques stores because Mom wanted to get a new end table to put next to the couch in the living room. The prices are better outside of Manhattan, but Mom didn't buy anything because everything she saw was either the wrong color or still too expensive. Haley sang her song about pumpkins as we walked through the store. She had added a few new verses about twin pumpkins.

We didn't get lost on the way home but it was still already dark out when we got back into Manhattan. Haley was really excited to introduce Bill and Charlie to Dad. She ran into the apartment as soon as Mom unlocked the door. Dad was stretched out on the couch. He looked like he had just woken up, but he sat up when he saw Haley bounding toward him.

"Dad!" she called.

"Hiya, Haley," he said. "Hey, Thumbelina," he said to me. It's a nickname he gave me when I was younger, because I was the tiniest girl in my class. I tell him not to use it, but sometimes he does anyway.

"Don't call me that," I said. "I hate it."

"But it's such a great name," he said. "You know Thumbelina from the Hans Christian Andersen stories. There's even a song."

"I don't care," I said, before he could start singing. "I still hate it."

"One day you will love being small and looking young," Dad told me. My dad is always so sure about what I will think or want when I get older, but usually I don't think he's right.

"*I* like being small," Haley said. "You can call me Thumbelina. And look, Dad, I got two pumpkins. They're twins. This is Bill and this is Charlie. You can tell them apart because Bill is the tall and skinny one."

Dad turned to Haley, the pliant daughter. "He's a very lanky pumpkin," he said. "And he's a pilgarlic."

Haley tried to say the word, but she couldn't. "What does that mean, what you just said?"

"A pilgarlic is a bald man," Dad told her.

"He's not bald," Haley said, pulling on Bill's stem. "See his hair."

"How could I have missed that?" Dad said.

"Sophie only got one pumpkin," Haley said.

Dad looked over at me. "Poor Thum—Poor Soph," he said. I wondered if he had messed up on purpose.

"You could have had two pumpkins if you wanted," Mom said.

I told her I didn't mind. "My pumpkin's an only child," I said. "He's so lucky."

"No, my pumpkins are lucky because they're twins," Haley said. She leaned back against Dad and sighed. "I wish I had a twin."

"One of you is bad enough," I said.

"Mom!" Haley whined. "Did you hear Sophie?"

"I was trying to ignore Sophie," Mom said, and she turned to me. "Apologize to your sister."

"I was just kidding."

"It wasn't funny," Haley said, and she sniffed so my parents would think she was going to cry.

"You're such a drama queen," I complained.

"Sophie," both my parents said at the same time. They always agree when they think I've done something wrong.

"Fine. I'm sorry," I said. I didn't really mean it. "I'm going to go do my homework now."

"Homework on a weekend?" Mom asked.

"It's this stupid thing Ms. Brisbin wants us to do," I said. "We have to write letters to pen pals in different states. I think sixth grade is too old for that."

"I agree," Mom said. I know some mothers would pretend to think it was a good idea just because a teacher was making us do it, but my mom isn't like that. She said she was sorry I had homework to do and we could carve the pumpkins when I felt like taking a break.

I started to walk down the hall to my room, and Dad called out from behind me. "Jessie called you a little while ago, by the way."

"Really? Why didn't you tell me?"

"What do you mean?" Dad asked. "I'm telling you now."

"Never mind," I said. I went into my room and put Oscar on the windowsill near my side of the room. Then I took off my coat and draped it over the chair beside my desk, even though I'm supposed to hang it in the closet.

I called Jessie back before I wrote to Katie. She said she'd been bored at home all day. "That's too bad," I told her, even though I was secretly glad that she hadn't spent the day with Lindsay, Amy, and Melissa. After all, she'd already seen them on Saturday. She didn't have to spend *all* her time with them. "Well, I better go," I told her. "I still have to write to my pen pal."

"Oh, I did that already," Jessie said. "I sent my pen pal a postcard so I wouldn't have to write as much. It's not like

Ms. Brisbin has a way to check on how long our letters are anyway."

After Jessie and I hung up, I pulled open my desk drawer and took out the light blue stationery Grandma Vivian had bought me for my tenth birthday. It's custom made and has my full name, Sophie Lauren Turner, written in script across the top of the page. I liked it because it's very professional-looking, but I hardly ever used it. I had written letters before only to thank Grandma Vivian when she sent me things for my birthday or for Christmas, so I still had almost the whole box left.

I got a pen and sat at my desk. It was hard to think of what to write to Katie Franklin. "Dear Katie," I started. "My name is Sophie Turner." Then I realized that was a dumb thing to write because my name was already across the top of the page. I crumbled up the paper and threw it into the garbage can under my desk. Even though I had a lot of it, I didn't want to waste my stationery. There's exactly the same amount of envelopes as there are sheets of paper, and now I would have an extra envelope. But I also didn't want to sound stupid.

I remembered Ms. Brisbin telling us to write about what it was like to live in New York, and I started again: "Dear Katie, I am sitting at my desk in my apartment in New York City. The window above my desk looks out toward another building. I can see lights on in other apartments across the way, and people moving around inside. But it's too far away to see what they look like, so they just look like shadows." Ms. Brisbin had once told me it was not grammatically correct to start sentences with the word "but," but I had actually seen a lot of books with sentences that began with "but." I asked Dad about it, and he said it was one of those rules they teach you in school that are not always applied in real life.

I was in the middle of the next sentence when I felt sticky hands pressed over my eyes. "Guess who?" a voice said. "It's time for a break so we can carve the pumpkins!" I was so startled that I jerked my hand and ripped the letter I'd been writing to Katie. Now two sheets were ruined.

"Haley!" I yelled. "You ruined my letter!"

Haley stepped back guiltily. "I didn't do anything," she said.

"Yes, you did, and you're going to be sorry. Mom!" I called. "Mom!"

Mom came into the room. "I'm going to kill Haley," I told her. I held up my letter with the rip right down the center. "Look what she did!"

"I didn't do it," Haley said.

"Oh, shut up," I told Haley. "Get out of here."

"It's my room too," Haley said.

Now I had to start my letter all over again. I never got anything done with Haley around. It made me really hate having a younger sister. "Sometimes I wish you would just disappear," I told her.

"That's a terrible thing to say, Sophie," Dad said, walking into the room. "Say you're sorry."

But I was sick of apologizing to Haley. All I wanted was to be alone in my room so I could do my homework. Why didn't anyone understand that? Why did they always automatically take Haley's side without even hearing what I had to say first? I didn't feel sorry about anything that I'd said. I felt the tears start behind my eyes. My face felt hot. I bit my lip to try to keep from crying. Dad looked at me. "Sophie, I'm waiting," he said. Haley went to stand next to Mom. She reached out and took Mom's hand.

"Not so fast, Haley," Mom said. "You apologize to Sophie, too."

"But I didn't do anything wrong," she said. "Sophie ripped her own paper."

"I can't even do my homework without her messing me up," I said. "I really need my own room. It doesn't have to be your office. We can close off the dining room. We don't need a kitchen table and a dining room table. I won't care if it's a small room as long as it's my own."

"If Sophie gets her own room, then I want a dog," Haley said.

"Haley, you're so stupid. If I get my own room, then you get your own room too."

"I don't want my own room! I want a dog!"

"That's enough!" Mom said. "Sophie is not getting her own room, and you're not getting a dog."

"You're so mean!" Haley said, and I agreed. Haley went up to Dad and hugged his waist. Dad patted the top of her head. He usually took Haley's side.

"Go finish your homework in my office," Mom told me.

"What about the pumpkins?" Haley asked. Mom told her it was getting too late and that we would have to wait until after school tomorrow to carve them, and Haley started to cry. I stood up and opened my desk drawer to get the box of stationery. Then I closed the drawer with a bang and stomped down the hall. "You didn't apologize yet," Haley called after me. Her voice was thick and syrupy from crying, but I ignored her. After all, she hadn't apologized to me, either. I went into Mom's office and closed the door behind me. I would have slammed it, but then I would have been yelled at more. My parents have a thing against slamming doors. My mom doesn't even like me to close my door, although Dad says it's okay to do when you really need privacy. I definitely needed the privacy just then. Still, it just wasn't the same as having my own room. Mom's stuff was everywhere, and her computer took up so much room on the desk that I barely had room to write my letter. I didn't feel like writing it anyway. I couldn't think of anything good to say about New York, although I could think of a lot of things to write about younger sisters, particularly what it felt like to be four months away from my twelfth birthday and still be sharing a room with a second grader.

It wasn't like my letter would ever be graded. Ms. Brisbin would never even see what I wrote, like Jessie said, so really I could write about whatever I wanted. It didn't just have to be about New York. It didn't have to be about New York at all. "Dear Katie," I wrote. "I have a sister named Haley who is seven years old. I don't know if you have any brothers or sisters, but sometimes it is very hard for me to be an older sister. My parents tell me that I should set a good example for Haley because she watches everything I do and likes to copy me. But when someone is constantly watching you and copying you, it can be very frustrating." I told Katie about how Haley tried to hang out with Jessie and me, even when we didn't want her there. "My parents try to make me include her a lot," I wrote. "Then they get mad at me when I want privacy. I don't think Jessie minds as much as I do."

I finished my letter and wrote, "Sincerely, Sophie," in my best script. Then I pulled an envelope out of my stationery box and folded up my letter to put it inside. I wrote "Miss Katie Franklin" across the envelope neatly, and admired my handwriting. I would mail the letter on my way to school in the morning. I hoped Katie had already written to me.

Four

Halloween was on a Saturday, which was great because we didn't have school. I told Mom we shouldn't have to go to school on Halloween even when it falls during the week. It would make a much better day off than some of the other boring vacation days, like the presidents' birthdays.

Haley put her costume on as soon as she woke up. My parents told her she should save the costume for later, but Haley insisted that Halloween lasted the whole day, and so she wanted to wear her costume from beginning to end.

Haley was dressed up as a piglet. She wore her pink leotard from ballet class, pink tights, and a rubber pig nose and ears. Mom had tried to find a pig's tail to pin onto the back of Haley's leotard, but the costume store didn't have any, so

Haley had made one herself out of a pink pipe cleaner. Every time she sat down, she crushed it. Mom told her that she should at least leave that part off until it actually was time to go trick-or-treating, but Haley wanted to wear the full costume. "Whoever heard of a piglet without a tail?" she said.

"Maybe you're a deformed pig," I offered.

"You're not helping, Sophie," Mom said.

Dad made pancakes for breakfast. He tried to make Haley's and my pancakes in the shapes of our initials, but it is hard to make an *S* or an *H* in pancake batter. They just looked like blobs. It didn't matter to me because I still got to flip them, which is my favorite part. I'm pretty good at flipping pancakes. I can't flip them in the air like they do in restaurants, but I know just when they are done enough to take the spatula and flip them over without the batter oozing out from the sides. The trick is to watch the edges and make sure they are browned enough. When the edges are browned and the middle part starts to bubble, the pancake is ready to be flipped.

We finished cooking and Dad brought the pancakes out to the table on one big plate. Haley reached across with her fork to spear a pancake.

"Hold on a minute," Mom said. She put her hand on Haley's arm.

"I can do it myself," Haley insisted. "I think that one is the *H*." Haley shook free from Mom's grasp and moved toward the plate of pancakes. Her forearm knocked over her glass of orange juice. It spread across the table and dripped off the edge onto Haley's leotard. "Oh, no!" Haley cried. "Look what you made me do!"

"I told you that wasn't a good idea," Mom said. I don't know if she was talking about Haley wearing her costume at breakfast or her insistence on serving herself. Haley just cried harder. Mom took a napkin and started to mop up the table.

"Daddy!" Haley moaned, and Dad got up to help Haley.

"Oh, Jack, you baby her," Mom said. But then she reached across the table for my napkin and took it to wipe up Haley's shirt.

"It still smells like oranges!" Haley said.

"I can't get the smell out like this, Haley. Why don't you let me throw it into the washing machine?"

"I wanted to wear my costume the whole day!" Haley whined. She sat limply on Dad's lap while Mom peeled the leotard off of her. If you ask me, they both babied her. Mom took Haley's costume down the hall to the washing machine. "Sophie, can you bring me the towels in the laundry basket? I may as well do some of the laundry now." I didn't think it was fair that I had to do work just because Haley had spilled juice all over herself. The day wasn't starting out very well.

Mom made me help fold the towels when she was through with the laundry. Haley came into the living room in her underwear to get her leotard, and she rolled around on the floor in the warm towels. "That's gross," I told her.

"I'm clean," Haley said.

"You just spilled juice all over yourself. Now you're going to make everything smell like orange juice," I said.

"I don't smell like orange juice," Haley insisted. She spread her arms across the towels and rubbed her palms against the towels. "I wish they stayed this warm all the time," she said. "It feels like a blanket."

"All right, Haley," Mom said. "Get up now. Take your leotard." Haley obliged. She rolled over and pulled her leotard out from under a towel. Mom rubbed her back as she crawled away from us toward the bedroom, oinking.

"She gets away with everything," I complained. Mom ignored me.

Haley's friend Jennifer came over a few hours later. Even though Jennifer is Haley's friend, I think she likes hanging out with me best. She doesn't have an older sister, and she likes to pretend that I'm her sister. Jennifer never argues with me or acts annoying. She just likes to sit next to me when we watch television and lets me braid her hair without screaming that I'm hurting her. I wish Haley liked me as much as Jennifer did. My parents always say Haley worships me, but I know they just want to make me feel better.

Haley was back in her piglet costume. I had my costume on too. Even though we were really too old to dress up for Halloween, Jessie and I had decided to do it for one last year. We were going as Tweedledee and Tweedledum. We'd read the Alice in Wonderland books for our summer reading. Well, actually, I don't think Jessie really read them, but I did. When we started to think about Halloween back in September, we decided to get matching costumes. Tweedledee and Tweedledum were my idea. I went on the Internet to find a picture of them, and Jessie and I figured out what we needed to buy to look like the picture. We bought fat suits from a costume store, and then we went to Bloomingdale's to get red pants that fit over the fat suits, short blue blazers, white shirts, and red suspenders. Mom also bought us miniature red baseball hats. I wanted a beanie cap, but we couldn't find them.

I pulled my hair back into a tight ponytail and twisted it into a bun. Then I put my baseball hat on and used bobby pins to secure it to my head. I looked in the mirror and I knew I looked pretty silly, but it would look better when there were two of us. Dad said it was a very well-executed literary idea.

Jennifer had brought a face painting kit with her, and I took her and Haley into the bathroom to do their makeup. Haley sat on the toilet and I knelt in front of her. It was hard to stay steady in my fat costume. I should have waited to get dressed up until after I had finished doing their makeup. Haley bounced up and down excitedly. "Hurry up, Sophie," she said.

"Do you want me to do this or not?" I asked Haley.

"I want you to," she said.

"Okay, then, be patient for a minute." I pulled the towels down from the back of the door and piled them up in front of where Haley was sitting. Then I knelt back down and rolled back onto them. Haley and Jennifer laughed when I landed on my bottom with a thud. Finally I was ready to get to work. I put pale pink paint all over Haley's face, and blended some red in with the pink on her cheeks to make them rosier. There wasn't much more I could do to make her look like a pig. Pigs don't even have whiskers, so I didn't draw them in. Haley twisted around and studied herself in the mirror. "I still look the same," she said. I told her she needed to put on her nose and ears. She went out of the room to get them, and I sat Jennifer on the toilet to do her makeup. Jennifer was dressed up as a clown. Her costume was white with colored polka dots all over it, and she even had big red clown shoes on and a rainbow wig.

"Do you want to be a happy clown or a sad clown?" I asked.

"You decide," Jennifer said.

"Okay, I'll make you a happy clown," I said.

I put white paint on her face first. Then I drew purple triangles around her eyes. I made her cheeks bright red, and then I outlined her lips with the same red paint. I made the edges of the mouth turn way up like a big grin and I colored it all in. Jennifer looked in the mirror admiringly. I have to admit I did a good job. When I was finished with Jennifer, I drew bright red circles on my cheeks too. Jessie could do the same when she came over, if she wanted.

The doorbell rang and Haley ran to answer it. She wanted to give the candy out to the trick-or-treaters while she was still home. Mom had a basket of mini-bags of M&M's by the door. I had wanted to get the regular-size bags, but Mom had said that would be too expensive. Every Halloween, Jessie and I keep track of which apartments give out the big candy bars, and we try to hit those apartments more than once.

I followed behind Haley in case it was Jessie at the door, but it was just the kids who live down the hall dressed up in Star Wars costumes.

"Cool sword," Haley said.

"It's a light saber," one of the boys corrected.

"Oh, yeah," Haley said. She gave them each a bag of M&M's and closed the door. "Hey, Mom," she said. "Can I have some M&M's now?"

"You're going to get so much candy tonight," Mom said.

"I'll just split a bag with Jennifer," Haley said.

"Just one bag," Mom told her.

Haley said she wanted all the M&M's that were primary colors. She had just learned about primary colors in school. Jennifer got the orange, brown, and green ones.

"If I eat a yellow M&M and a blue M&M at the same

time, do they make a green M&M inside my mouth?" Haley asked.

"You are so dumb," I said.

"No, I'm not. Yellow and blue make green!"

"Not in your mouth. It's candy. It will dissolve before it mixes colors."

Haley popped a yellow and a blue M&M into her mouth and started chewing. "I'm going to look in the mirror," she said, ignoring me.

I was getting restless, waiting for Jessie. She was always late, and it was usually Liz's fault. My costume was getting too hot. I wasn't used to feeling so big and bulky. I sat down on the couch next to Dad, but I couldn't get comfortable. "I hate always having to wait for Jessie," I told him.

"Why don't you just start going to the apartments on our floor," he said. "Jessie will probably be here before you're even finished."

"I don't want to go without Jessie," I said. "It won't look right to be Tweedledee without Tweedledum."

Haley skipped through the living room with Jennifer at her heels. "Careful there," Dad said.

"I can't help it," Haley said. "I'm so excited. I wish we could go now!" She hopped back and forth from one side of the room to the other. "When will Jessie be here?" Haley asked.

"Soon," Dad said.

Finally the intercom buzzed. Mom picked it up and

called to me. "Jessie's on her way upstairs," she said. I went out into the hall and waited for her by the elevator. I could hear the sound of the elevator beeping at each floor, getting louder and louder as it got closer to our floor. When the doors opened and someone stepped out, I heard Jessie's voice saying my name, but for a split second I didn't even recognize her. She was wearing the witch's costume she'd worn last Halloween. The hat was bent awkwardly at the top, probably from being stored at the bottom of her closet for a year. Instead of the fat suit, she had on tights and a skirt. Her face was heavy with makeup.

I looked her up and down and gasped. "What happened to your costume?"

"My mom made me return it," Jessie said.

"That's so mean! Why did she do that?"

"She said I was spending too much money on clothing and if I wanted to keep the black skirt for the dance then I had to return the costume."

"So you returned it," I said.

"No offense, Soph," Jessie said, "but what am I really going to do with a Tweedledum costume? I mean, after tonight, it's completely useless."

"I can't believe you didn't tell me before now," I said.

"It's not that big of a deal," she said, sounding annoyed. I couldn't believe what was happening. Jessie had known me practically her whole life, and she had had barely ten conversations with Madden Preston, so why was he so much more important to her than I was? How come she cared about how she looked to him instead of caring about hurting me? The worst part was that she didn't even seem to think she had done anything wrong.

I turned back into the apartment. I knew I was going to cry, but I didn't want Haley and Jennifer to see me. Haley especially would want to hear all the details about what was wrong, and I didn't want to talk about it to anyone. I walked straight into my room and slammed the door shut, even though I knew that would make my parents angry.

Sure enough, Mom came into my room. "What is going on?" she said.

I was lying facedown on the bed and my red cheeks had rubbed off on my pillowcase.

"I can't go as Tweedledee if Jessie isn't Tweedledum!" I said.

"If you keep talking into the pillow, I can't hear you."

I lifted my head up and looked at her. "I can't be Tweedledee if Jessie isn't Tweedledum," I said again. "I'll look stupid!"

"Sophie, it's Halloween," Mom said. "Everyone looks stupid." She sat on the edge of the bed and rubbed my back. "Come on, they're all waiting for you."

"I'm not going," I said, and I put my face back down into the pillow.

"Oh, Sophie," Mom said. "Now you're being silly."

I heard footsteps, and I looked up to see if it was Jessie coming in to apologize, but it was just Dad. "She doesn't want to go," Mom told him.

Dad said I was keeping everyone waiting and making Jessie feel bad. It figured that they were concerned with everyone's feelings but mine. Jessie was the one who had started the whole problem.

"I just want to be alone," I told them.

They didn't argue with me; they just walked out of the room. I heard Dad telling the other girls to start without me and to check back in once they had gone to all the apartments on the fourteenth floor, which is the floor we live on.

I sat up on my bed and wiped my eyes. My fingers looked pink from the remains of the face paint. Jessie and I used to be alike in almost every way, but now she needed to hang out with Amy, Melissa, and Lindsay, and she needed to look good for Madden Preston. I didn't think there was much room left in her life for me. I took off my costume, put on jeans and a sweater, and walked into the living room. I was too old to dress up anyway.

"What are you dressed as now?" Dad said.

"A parent taking her kids around on Halloween," I said.

"So you're going to go," Mom said. "I think that's good."

"I want the candy," I told her.

I waited until Jessie, Haley, and Jennifer came back

to the apartment after they had finished all the apartments on our floor, and then I went with them through the rest of the building. Haley said I shouldn't get to have any candy because I wasn't in a real costume. Jennifer said she would share her candy with me.

We went up and down the halls of the other floors and I watched Jessie carefully. She didn't seem too happy to be with us. I wondered if maybe she felt bad about the costumes or if she was just bored.

Our building isn't very tall. In fact, for an apartment building in New York City, it's pretty short. The fifteenth floor is the top floor, and really there are only fourteen floors. That's because our building doesn't have a thirteenth floor. Some buildings in New York skip the thirteenth floor because thirteen is an unlucky number. We actually live on the thirteenth floor. The sign by the elevator says FLOOR 14, but we're right above twelve. Anyway, we were done trick-or-treating pretty quickly. We rode back up in the elevator to our apartment. Jennifer and Haley made deals about splitting up their candy. Anything with nuts in it was for Jennifer, anything with caramel was for Haley, and anything with both they decided to share.

The elevator doors opened and I stepped out to go home. "Hold on a second," Jessie said. "Why don't we hit the building next door before we go home?"

The building next door is twice the size of our building.

It's also very fancy. The doormen wear white gloves and the lobby is all marble and gold. There are even a couple of famous people living there. I had been there a bunch of times when I was little. This girl Abigail who I went to preschool with used to live there, and our mothers took turns picking us up from school. I always felt like I was walking into a museum when I went into that building. Abigail would run into the building and never feel bad about having mud on her shoes or making too much noise, but I was always scared of getting in trouble, so I walked slowly behind her and held my mother's hand.

I wasn't sure we could just go there without being invited by someone who lived there. "I'll go tell Mom and Dad," Haley said. But I knew my parents would say no. Jessie looked at me. It felt like a test. I wanted to make sure I did the right thing.

"No, Haley," I said. "It's okay. Let's just go." I stepped back into the elevator and Jessie pressed the button for the lobby.

Five

It was freezing outside and we didn't have our coats, so we ran down the block to the other building. I was nervous because I thought the doorman would ask us where we were going, but we were in our costumes, so maybe he didn't realize we were strangers. He just opened up the door and let us in, and the four of us walked toward the elevator banks in the back, pretending that we belonged there. While we waited for the elevator, Jessie suggested that we start at the top floor and work our way down.

"I bet they won't let us up to the penthouse," I said.

"Do you think someone famous lives there?" Jessie asked.

"I don't know."

"We can just start with the floor right under that," Jessie said.

The elevator doors opened, and the elevator operator stepped forward. He wore the same uniform and white gloves as the doorman. His name was embroidered across his chest. HUGH, it said. We don't have an elevator operator in our building, just a regular doorman who stays by the front door of the lobby and opens the door for you if you are carrying something heavy. When we use the elevator in our building, we get to press the button for our floor by ourselves. But Hugh was waiting to push the button for us. "Where to, young ladies?" he asked.

"The next-to-the-top floor," Jessie said.

"The next-to-the-top floor it is," Hugh said. We stepped inside and the doors closed. There was a small bench at the back of the elevator and Haley and Jennifer both sat down on it. "So, what do we have here?" Hugh said. "A witch, a pig, and a clown. And what are you supposed to be?" He leaned toward me.

"I'm just supervising," I said.

Hugh laughed. "You girls know someone on the twenty-seventh floor?"

"We're friends of the Johnsons," Jessie said.

Hugh nodded and laughed again. The doors opened. Hugh held up his arm and motioned for us to go out. "You girls be careful," he said. "Crazy things can happen on Halloween."

When the elevator doors had closed, I turned to Jessie. "Who are the Johnsons?"

"Oh, I don't know," she said. "I just figured it's a pretty common name. There has got to be a Mr. and Mrs. Johnson somewhere in this building."

Even though the building was really tall, there were only four apartments on the floor. A couple of other kids were trick-or-treating down the hall. I thought maybe we should follow them and try to blend in as part of their group. I was going to tell Jessie that, but she had stepped forward and already pressed the doorbell of the apartment closest to the elevator. "Come on, you guys," she called to us impatiently.

Behind the door someone said, "Who is it?"

"Trick or treat!" Haley and Jennifer called. They weren't scared of anything.

A woman opened the door. "Oh, hello, girls," she said, like she'd been expecting us. She gave us each a small bag of Hershey's Kisses.

"It's Mrs. Johnson," I whispered to Jessie, and she smiled. Jessie looked so familiar all of a sudden that I almost forgot that she'd returned her Tweedledum costume. She seemed just like the old Jessie.

It took us only a couple minutes to go to the four

apartments. "How come there aren't more apartments?" Haley asked.

"Because the people who live here are very rich," Jessie told her.

"What do you mean?"

"Their apartments are very big," I explained.

Jennifer went to press the button for the elevator, but I didn't want to get in it again. What if Hugh starting asking us more questions? I could tell Jessie was thinking the same thing because she suggested we take the stairs.

"We're too high," Haley complained. "I don't want to walk down all those stairs."

"We'll just walk down one floor at a time," Jessie said.

We walked down the hall to the stairwell. The door was solid and heavy. It didn't even have a window. I held it open for the other girls. They walked in and I let go of the door. It slammed shut behind me and I heard an ominous click. I knew what that meant—the door was locking into place. Jessie, Haley, and Jennifer were already running down the stairs to the twenty-sixth floor, but I decided to check the door first. My heart was starting to beat faster and I tried to turn the knob to reopen the door. The knob wouldn't move. "Jessie," I said, but she didn't hear me. "Jessie!" I called louder.

"What?" she said.

I ran down to the next landing to meet her. "The door locked," I told her.

Haley and Jennifer had already reached the twenty-sixth floor and were pulling at the door. "It's too heavy," Jennifer said.

Jessie reached in front of Jennifer to open the door. She tugged on it hard. "It's not heavy," Jessie said. "It's locked."

"We're locked in?" Haley said. Her lower lip quivered beneath her rubber snout. Jennifer ran over to me and reached for my hand. I squeezed her hand back.

"Don't worry," I said. "We can just bang on the door. Someone will hear us and open it."

Jennifer dropped my hand and went to the door. She and Haley banged their fists hard against it. "Help! Help!" they called. Jessie and I stood behind them and banged our fists too. I pounded until the side of my hand started to hurt.

"This isn't working," Jessie said. She rubbed the side of her hand. We stepped back from the door. Haley and Jennifer looked up at Jessie and me.

"Maybe no one has walked by yet," Haley said.

"The doors are probably soundproof," I whispered to Jessie.

I guess I was too loud, because Jennifer heard me. "You mean they'll never hear us?" she said.

"I don't think so," I told her.

Jennifer leaned back against me and started to cry.

"What if I never see my mom again?" she wailed.

Haley started to cry too. Jessie rolled her eyes. "Don't worry," I said. "We'll just head downstairs. One of the doors is bound to be open, and if not, someone has to come into the stairwell eventually. We'll get out."

"Are you sure?" Haley asked tearfully.

"Yes," I said. I tried to sound confident. Haley and Jennifer seemed to believe me and stopped crying, but really I was scared too. The fluorescent lights were flickering overhead and there was a cobweb in the corner. I doubted that any of the doors would really be open, and it could be a long time before anyone came into the stairwell. My parents thought that we had just been trick-or-treating in our own building. If we took too long getting back, they would get worried. They wouldn't even know where to look for us because we hadn't told them where we were going. We hadn't even brought a cell phone with us because we weren't supposed to leave our building. Jessie had grown quiet. It was all her brilliant idea, and she wasn't even doing anything to help now.

We started to walk downstairs. Jennifer reached for my hand again. "It's cold in here," she said. "Do you think we'll freeze?"

"It'll get warmer as we keep walking," I said.

"What if we starve before anyone finds us?" she asked.

"We have plenty of candy," I reminded her.

Haley was a couple of steps ahead of us. She pulled out her bag of Hershey's Kisses and handed it up to me. "Can you open this?"

"No," Jennifer told her. "You should save it until you're really hungry."

"Give me a break," Jessie said from behind me. I didn't think it was right of Jessie to give Jennifer a hard time when it was Jessie's fault we were in the building to begin with. I turned around to look at her, but she didn't look familiar anymore. Sometimes I had a hard time recognizing Jessie. It was like she had two different personalities—the old Jessie who was my best friend, and a new Jessie, who I didn't know at all. It was very confusing.

I turned back around to Haley and Jennifer. "We're almost at the next floor down," I said. "Let's try the door."

The door was locked on the next floor, and on the floor after that. Jessie said maybe we should walk back up and check the door to the roof, but I told her I'd rather be trapped in the stairwell than on the roof. She seemed annoyed that I didn't like her idea, but she kept following us down the stairs. She was eating her candy and dropping the empty wrappers onto the floor. "You better pick that up," Haley told her.

"Why?" Jessie asked.

"Because littering is against the law."

"So arrest me," Jessie told her. I turned toward Jessie,

and she rolled her eyes again. Jessie used to be nice to Haley. In fact, she was nicer to Haley than I was, but she had changed so much. Part of me was so angry with Jessie that I didn't care if Haley gave her a hard time, but I also knew that if Jessie got really upset and angry, she might never want to hang out with me again. I already felt like I was losing Jessie, so I told Haley to be quiet.

"But, Sophie," Haley said, "she really shouldn't litter."

"Oh, Haley, be pliant," I said. "You're driving us crazy." Haley pouted and looked like she might cry again, but I ignored her and we kept moving down the stairs.

We weren't racing down the stairs anymore like we had at first. Now we had slowed to a walking pace. It was kind of dizzying to keep walking down and down and then circle at each landing. Haley pulled off her pig snout, leaned over the handrail, and shouted "Hello!" Her voice echoed, and she giggled. "Hello, Haley," she shouted even louder. Her voice reverberated around us again. "Did you hear that? Did you hear that, Sophie?" Haley said. Her face was flushed with excitement and she forgot to be scared.

"Come on, Haley," I said. Haley stepped down from the rail and ran to catch up with me.

"Sophie?" she said.

"What?"

"I have to go to the bathroom."

"Why didn't you go at home?" I asked.

"I didn't have to go then," she said.

"You're going to have to hold it," I told her.

"My feet hurt too," she said. "Will you carry me?"

"You're too heavy," I told her. "We're almost there."

Jennifer had not let go of my hand since the twenty-fifth floor. Her palm was getting sweaty. Usually I liked having Jennifer around because she listened to me and thought I was great even if I wasn't friends with Lindsay, Amy, and Melissa, but I was starting to get impatient. I dropped her hand to wipe my palm on the side of my pants. Jennifer reached for it again.

"You know, I bet the door to the lobby is unlocked," Jessie said suddenly.

"You're right," I said. I tugged at Jennifer. "Come on, you guys. We're almost there!"

We ran down the last few flights of stairs. The door at the bottom was a different kind of door from the ones on the other floors. It had a small window at the top and had a big red sign in the middle of it. It said: DO NOT OPEN. ALARM WILL SOUND. Jennifer dropped my hand and walked up to the door, sounding out the words. I stood on my tiptoes and looked out the window. "It doesn't go to the lobby," I said. "It looks like it opens to the alley behind the building."

"Now what do we do?" Jessie said. She sat on the bottom stair with her witch's hat in her lap.

"Is it breaking the law if we open it?" Haley asked.

"I don't think so," I said. I had never heard of anyone getting into trouble for opening an emergency door, and besides, I was pretty sure that this was an emergency. My dad's a lawyer, so I thought if we got into trouble, he could always help us.

"I think we should open it," I said.

Jennifer started to cry. "I don't want to go to jail," she said. I wished Jennifer would stop crying. I didn't want Jessie to get more upset than she already was. But Jessie didn't say anything when Jennifer cried. She didn't even roll her eyes. Maybe she was nervous too.

"Don't cry," I told Jennifer. "Remember, you're a happy clown."

"Go ahead and open it, Sophie," Jessie said.

"You do it," I said. I thought it was only fair since it had been Jessie's idea to come to this building, and Jessie's idea to take the stairs.

"No, you do it," she said.

For a split second I thought of saying something back to her, like it was all her fault that we were locked in the stairwell to begin with, so she had to be the one to open the emergency door. But even though I was afraid to open the door, I was more afraid of making Jessie hate me. My heart was beating fast and hard. I could hear it thumping in my ears. "Fine," I said.

Haley and Jennifer backed away from the door. Instead

of a doorknob there was a long silver lever. I put my hand on it, took a deep breath, and pushed down. I heard the click of the lock turning, and the door swung open. "We're free!" Haley shouted. We ran outside and waited for the alarm to sound, but it didn't go off. I could see the sidewalk of our street a few feet away at the end of the alley.

"Let's get out of here," Jessie said, and we all started to run.

Six

Dad was sitting on the couch watching television. We walked in and Haley ran to him. "Oh, Daddy, I thought I would never see you again," she said. I turned to Jessie. She rolled her eyes again, and this time I couldn't blame her.

"Where's Mom?" I asked.

"I think she's lying down," Dad said. He turned to Haley. "So, let me see your loot."

"Wait, Dad," Haley said. "I have to tell you what happened to us." I knew I was about to get into trouble. I grabbed Jessie's arm and pulled her into my room. The farther away I was, the harder it would be to hear Dad yelling.

When we got to my room, Jessie said, "I guess I'll call my mom."

"You're not sleeping over?" I asked.

"I'm pretty worn out," she said.

Jessie didn't look that tired, and besides, it was a tradition for her to stay over on Halloween night. "But you always sleep over on Halloween—even when we have school the next day," I reminded her. But even as I said it, I knew things were different now. The old Jessie was almost completely gone. "Go ahead and use the phone," I said.

Jessie picked up the phone. I recognized her home number as she pressed the buttons; I had dialed it so many times, I knew the sound it made by heart. It sounded a little like the first verse of "Mary Had a Little Lamb."

After a few seconds I heard Jessie say, "Can you pick me up?" She paused and then said, "I'll tell you about it later." I wondered what Jessie would say about me. "Okay. Bye, Mom," she said, and turned to me. "My mom is going to meet me in the lobby in fifteen minutes," she said as she flopped down on Haley's bed. I looked at her from across the room and wondered what we could possibly find to talk about for the next fifteen minutes. Just then my dad walked in. I figured he would have plenty to say.

"What were you two thinking?" he said, his eyes moving back and forth between Jessie and me. Jessie and I had been friends for so long that my parents talked to her like she was their own daughter. If Dad was angry with me, he was going to be angry with Jessie, too. Somehow that made me feel better.

"We're sorry, Dad," I said.

"Did you think about what could have happened?"

The truth was, we hadn't thought about it, and thinking about it now was making me feel kind of sick. I didn't know what to say, which doesn't happen to me very often, so I just shrugged my shoulders. Dad shook his head. He looked tired. His shoulders slumped forward and his glasses had slipped to the edge of his nose. But Dad is never too tired to be angry with me. I braced myself for a long lecture about responsibility and setting a good example. "This was absolutely irresponsible and unacceptable behavior. I don't want to hear about anything like this ever happening again," he said.

I swallowed and nodded. "Okay," I told him.

"I mean it," Dad said.

"I promise," I told him.

"All right," Dad said. "Don't stay up too late tonight. We'll talk about this more in the morning." I watched him walk out the door, and I turned to Jessie.

"Your sister has such a big mouth and your father is so dramatic," she said.

I agreed with her about Haley, but I thought she was wrong about Dad. We definitely deserved to be yelled at, and

Dad hadn't even yelled that much. His voice had barely been raised above its normal tone. Usually my parents scream and threaten punishment when I do things wrong that involve Haley. They always tell me I need to be a good influence because she looks up to me and will follow whatever I do. Dad is especially protective of Haley, but this time he hadn't even yelled about going outside at night with Haley and no grown-ups. He hadn't told me it was terrible that Haley and Jennifer had been so scared, or even say that I am old enough to know better and that I have a special responsibility as an older sister. I knew Jessie and I shouldn't have taken the girls to the other building. I was sure Jessie knew it too, even though she was busy trying to be cool. For the third time that night I didn't know what to say, so I just nodded.

"I better get going," Jessie said.

"Hey, Jessie," I said, "do you remember Halloween last year? Remember that woman down the hall who gave out apples, and yours had a scratch on the side. Haley started crying when you ate it because she thought you were poisoned."

"Sophie, I really have to go," Jessie said. "My mom will be mad if I keep her waiting." It hadn't been fifteen minutes since Jessie had called her mother. It had barely even been five minutes, but I decided not to argue with her.

"Okay," I said.

"See you Monday," Jessie said. She walked out of the room.

I could hear her at the front door saying good-bye to Dad.

I sat back on the bed, but I wasn't sure what to do with myself. Even in my own room with everything I owned around me, it all seemed boring and pointless. I couldn't play any of the board games because I was alone, and there wasn't anything I wanted to read. Finally I stood up and walked over to my desk. As long as I had the room to myself, I could write to Katie. Even though she hadn't written me back yet, I had a lot to say, and it wasn't like there was anyone else to talk to. I pulled open my desk drawer for the box of stationery and a pen, and sat down to write.

Dear Katie,

Did you ever have one of those days when nothing goes the way it was supposed to? I've been having a lot of them in the past few weeks. The problem is mostly my best friend, Jessie. She's been kind of different lately. Tonight is Halloween, and we always spend Halloween together, but that is different now too. So now she's on her way home, and I'm alone in my room.

I just keep thinking about last Halloween, when everything was the way it was supposed to be. I remember it perfectly — it was only a year ago, after all, on a Friday night. Jessie

*and I pulled the sleeping bags down from the hall closet
and slept in the living room. We didn't want to sleep in my
room because Haley was there (I told you about her in my
last letter—she's my younger sister), and this way it didn't
matter how late we stayed up talking. I remember the year
before last Halloween too, when Halloween was on a school
night. My mom still didn't make a big deal out of it when we
ate our candy for dinner instead of the chicken my dad had
cooked and we stayed up late making up ghost stories. I know
we're too old for some of that now, but I don't understand why
Jessie thinks she's too grown-up or too cool or too something
to hang out with me at all.*

*I hope you don't mind that I'm telling you all this stuff. I
can't talk to Haley about it because she's too young, and
my parents would ask too many questions and not really
understand. Anyway, I guess if you don't want to hear about
it, you can always just stop reading my letter.*

Sincerely,

Sophie

Haley and Jennifer came into the room a while later. I
didn't have anything better to do, so I helped them set up the

sleeping bags on our bedroom floor. Jennifer used my sleeping bag because Haley wanted to sleep in hers even though her bed was in the room.

"We need flashlights," Haley said. "Can you get them from the closet? I can't reach."

"Why?" I asked. "You're still right next to the light switch."

"No," Haley insisted. "It's a campout. We don't use electricity."

The overhead light and both of our desk lights were on. "What do you think is lighting up the room now?" I asked her.

"So-o-phie," Haley said, turning my name into three syllables. She clasped her hands together and stepped toward me. "Please? Pretty please?"

Jennifer clasped her hands together too. "I'll be your best friend," she offered.

I had a feeling I didn't need to give in and get them flashlights for Jennifer to be my best friend. I looked down at her and Haley. I almost told them that they were being stupid. The words were on the tip of my tongue, but I closed my mouth. It wasn't their fault that Jessie had left, and at least they thought they needed me.

"We should probably pitch a tent, too," I said. "You know, to keep the bears out."

"Oh, yeah. The bears!" Haley said. I told Haley to get a

sheet, and Jennifer and I pulled the chairs in from the dining room table. We lined up the sleeping bags next to each other and then we set the chairs up at the corners of the sleeping bags. Haley helped me drape the sheet across them, and then she and Jennifer climbed underneath. "Get the candy," Haley called to me. "If we leave it outside, the bears will get it."

I slid their bags of candy under the legs of one of the chairs. "Aren't you coming in?" Jennifer asked.

"No," I said. "I'm going to watch a movie."

"Turn the light off on your way out," Haley said. I flicked the switch and could see the circles of light coming from the flashlights underneath the sheet. "Now we have to tell scary stories," I heard Haley say.

I walked into the bathroom across the hall from our room. There is an antique mirror above the sink that Mom once found at a flea market. It has a scratch in the top right corner, so she got a good deal on it. I don't mind the scratch; Haley and I are both too short for it to bother us when we look in the mirror.

I stood up against the sink and bent forward, staring closely at my reflection. It is the strangest thing about faces: Sometimes they look the way you expect them to, and sometimes they look like someone you've never seen before. My cheeks were looser than I remembered them being. I fingered the edges of my eyes, where my mother was starting to get wrinkles that she calls crow's-feet. Whenever she said that, I thought of gnarled feet and toes riddled with bunions. Old, shriveled feet—like the feet the Wicked Witch of the East had in *The Wizard of Oz*, right after Dorothy's house fell on top of her. I blinked to get the image out of my mind and then peered more closely at my own face. I didn't have any crow's-feet. Eleven was definitely too young for that, but my eyebrows were getting darker, even darker than the hair on my head, and I was growing a slight bump on the bridge of my nose. I wished I had freckles like Haley. She doesn't have a lot of them, just a small sprinkling across her nose. She gets a few more in the summer when we're outside all day long. But I never have any at all. My cheeks were chubby even though I was still skinny everywhere else. I thought kids were supposed to get rid of their baby fat as they got older, not the other way around. I sucked in my cheeks and pressed a finger down on my nose, and I looked better. *Is that what being popular is about?* I wondered.

I blew out my cheeks and shook my head, feeling stupid and embarrassed, even though no one had seen me, and I went into the living room. Dad wasn't in there anymore, but the light was still on. I looked through our shelf of movies, but there wasn't anything that I felt like watching so I just turned on the television and flipped through the channels. Saturday night is not a good night for television. Thursday is much better, but finally I found reruns of old shows playing on one of the cable stations. I pulled an afghan that my grandmother had made off the arm of the couch and curled up under it. Grandma used to knit a lot, but that was a long time ago. Now she has arthritis in her fingers. I hated the idea of getting old. My mother worried about the lines around her eyes and about Grandma living alone in Florida. The afghan on the couch is wearing thin. It has a brown stain in the center from when Haley spilled her Coke. Mom always tries to fold the afghan so you can't see that part.

After a couple of episodes I was starting to feel pretty tired. The television looked blurry and I couldn't concentrate on what the people were saying. I turned off the light and turned off the television. The screen faded to black and the room became dark. I wondered if Haley and Jennifer were still telling ghost stories. If they were, I couldn't hear them. The apartment was quiet except for the hum of the refrigerator in the next room.

Sometimes it's hard for me to fall asleep, especially nights when I have a lot to think about. I would lie awake listening to Haley breathing in the next bed and wish I could fall asleep so easily. Dad once said I should try counting backward from one hundred when I can't sleep. Sometimes that works, but usually it doesn't. A lot of times I start counting, but get too distracted thinking of other things. That night, even though I was really tired, I couldn't stop thinking about Jessie, and how maybe she'd gotten home and called up

Lindsay or Amy and gone over to one of their apartments instead.

I don't know how long I was awake, but I must have fallen asleep at some point because I woke up when I heard voices. For a second I couldn't remember where I was, but then I felt Grandma's afghan on top of me. As my eyes adjusted to the dark, I could make out the wall unit and the coffee table. In the dark it looked like everything in the room had changed colors. It was all in different shades of blue. I strained to hear who was talking.

I heard my mother's voice. "How can you do this, Jack?" she said.

"Oh, Andrea, don't act like this is a surprise," Dad said.

"We can't even afford a divorce," Mom said. "We'll have to take the girls out of private school. Do you really want to do that, Jack? Do you really want to do that to your own daughters?"

Dad said something I couldn't make out. Then I heard my mother again. "Dammit, Jack!" she said, and something fell to the floor.

"Keep your voice down," Dad said, but he sounded like he was yelling too.

I thought I must have still been dreaming. There was no way my parents were talking about getting a divorce. I once heard that if you pinched yourself in a dream it wouldn't hurt, so I pinched my arm. It didn't hurt too much. My heart was beating faster. I pinched myself again, harder. This time it hurt a lot. My eyes felt hot. I could feel the tears beginning to fall. I wished I could just fall back asleep. People fight all the time. My parents had fought before, and they had always made up. When I woke in the morning, they would have forgiven each other.

I heard their bedroom door open, and then the front door opened and closed. A few moments passed. I wondered if it was Mom or Dad who had left. Maybe it was just Dad taking the garbage to the compactor chute down the hall. Any second and he would be back. I took a deep breath and held it. If he came back before I needed to take another breath, then everything would be okay.

I held my hand to my mouth to try to hold my breath in longer. My chest tightened and the back of my throat burned. When my head started to feel light, I let the air out and started breathing normally again. In and out. In and out. The front door stayed closed. *Please come back,* I thought. *Please.* A few minutes later I heard footsteps moving toward the kitchen. The refrigerator door opened and closed, and the footsteps started again, moving closer and closer to me. I closed my eyes and pretended to be asleep. They stopped and I could feel someone watching me. It is hard to pretend to be sleeping when you are actually crying. Finally I opened my eyes.

"Mom," I said. In the darkness her skin looked like the

milky blue-white color of skim milk. It matched all the furniture.

"What are you doing in here?" Mom said. Her voice was soft and crackly.

"Haley and Jennifer are having a campout in the other room. I wanted privacy," I said.

"Where's Jessie?"

"She had to go home," I said.

Even in the darkness I could tell Mom was surprised, but she didn't say anything about it. She just said she was sorry for waking me up. I could tell she had been crying too. I had only seen my mother cry three times before. Once when she stepped on a tack that I had accidentally left on the floor. She had to get a tetanus shot and she was mad at me for a week. The other two times were when she fought with Grandma.

"Are you and Daddy really getting a divorce?" I asked.

My mother sighed. She motioned for me to move over. I moved my feet up, and Mom sat next to me and pulled my legs onto her lap.

"Oh, Sophie, I'm sorry you had to hear all that. We never would have been so loud if we'd known you were out here. It's nothing for you to worry about. Just forget that you heard it." But there was no way I was going to be able to forget what I had heard.

"It's all my fault," I said.

"Oh, no, that's ridiculous," Mom said. "It is never the

kids' fault when their parents have problems." But I knew my mother was wrong. Maybe I would be the first kid in the world to actually cause her parents' divorce.

"You don't understand," I told her. "It really *is* my fault."

"What are you talking about?" Mom asked.

"I'm the reason that Daddy was in a bad mood. I'm the reason he was angry. Jessie and I took Haley and Jennifer down the block to the big building. We got locked in the stairwell, and Haley told him. Now he's mad at me. He's just taking it out on you."

"It's been a rough night, hasn't it?" Mom said. She rubbed my legs through the afghan. "But Daddy isn't angry with you. We were fighting even before you came home from trick-or-treating." I turned away from Mom and took a deep breath. I know it didn't change the fact that Dad wanted a divorce, but at least no one could blame me.

"Will we really have to change schools?" I said. Mom leaned forward and gathered me in her arms. She pulled the afghan around both of us. Even though it's old and worn out and has a brown stain on it, it's still the best blanket in the house.

"We were fighting, sweetheart," Mom said. "Sometimes you say things you don't mean when you fight. You know, like sometimes you tell Haley that you hate her. I say things like that to Daddy when I'm mad at him. It doesn't mean that it's true."

"But you could get divorced, right?"

"I don't know," she said. "But I promise that you and Haley will stay at Victor no matter what. It will be okay, Sophie. I promise you."

"I'm scared," I said.

"Don't be scared," Mom said. "Maybe nothing will even happen. Daddy and I have a lot to figure out, that's all."

When I was younger and my mother told me everything would be okay, I believed her. The thing about getting older is you start to realize that even your parents don't always know how things will turn out. I had thought that as I got older, I would be able to understand things better, but I just felt more confused and alone. I couldn't stop being scared no matter what my mother said.

"You shouldn't tell me not to be scared," I said. "That's a really dumb thing to say."

"You're right," Mom said. "I just don't want you to worry."

Mom looked so sad and sorry, and I felt bad about what I'd said. Sometimes I don't know whether to feel sorry for people or to be upset with them. "Are you going to go back to bed?" I asked.

"Maybe I'll sleep out here with you," Mom said. "Is that okay?"

You know that feeling when you really want to stay wherever you are but you know that you can't—like when you wake up in the middle of the night and your bed feels wonderful and warm but you really have to pee? I wanted to stay sitting exactly as we were, wrapped in Grandma's afghan with Mom's arms around me, but my nose was all stuffed up and I felt uncomfortable, too.

"Can you do me a favor first?" I asked Mom.

"Anything," she said.

"Can you bring me a tissue?"

My mother laughed and hugged me tighter. Then she got up to get a box of tissues from the hall closet. She came back. I blew my nose and then lay down in her lap to go to sleep. Sometime during the night I heard the front door open and Dad's footsteps move from the front hall to his bedroom. But I didn't call to him or even open my eyes. Mom didn't move either, so I don't even know if she was awake and heard him come in.

Seven

The next week at school Ms. Brisbin took everything off the back bulletin board and put up a giant map of the United States. She said we should write the names of our pen pals on the states where they lived. Some people didn't know exactly where to put their pen pals' names, but luckily mine was easy. Everyone knows where California is, and I knew that Redwood City was in northern California. I had looked it up on the Internet. So when it was my turn, I wrote "Katie Franklin" on the map very neatly, and then I drew a little picture of a redwood tree next to her name. They're a special kind of tree that grows in California—I knew that from the letter I'd gotten from Katie and from the research Ms. Brisbin made us do.

Ms. Brisbin made us look up all kinds of stuff about the states our pen pals were from. She gave us a list of questions to consider, such as what kind of climate the state had and what important landmarks there were. She said the questions were just starting points and we should feel free to use our imaginations and research the things that we thought were interesting, and then write reports about what we had learned. I didn't spend much time on it. I took the questions Ms. Brisbin gave us and went to Mom's computer to download information about California. There was a Web site of California facts. I learned that the state bird is a quail, the state flower is a poppy, and the capital is Sacramento. I wrote a few short sentences about California. My handwriting looked messy and I knew I wasn't going to get a good grade, but I didn't really care.

Ms. Brisbin had also made room on the board to display the letters we got from our pen pals. The board was filling up quickly but I kept forgetting to bring in Katie's letter. It had come on Monday. The only mail I ever get is on holidays and my birthday, and even then it is usually just a card from Grandma. She sends a check too, but my parents always make me put it in the bank to save for when I'm older.

Katie's letter was on pink stationery. I don't think it was custom made like mine was, because it didn't have her name on it. It looked like the kind you can buy in a card store. She had put confetti in the envelope, and because I wasn't expecting it, I accidentally spilled it on the floor in the front hall.

Mom was standing next to me as the confetti drifted to the floor. The light from the window hit it and it sparkled on the way down, as though the individual flakes were diamonds. "Oh, Sophie," Mom said. I knew she didn't care that it looked pretty.

"It's not my fault," I said. "How was I supposed to know that was in there?"

"Just clean it up," she said, and she walked into her office and closed the door. Of course she was allowed to close the door whenever she wanted.

I would have cleaned it up even if Mom hadn't told me to, but first I wanted to read Katie's letter. Haley was still at ballet, so I had my room all to myself. Usually the first thing I do when I get home is take off my uniform skirt and put on a pair of jeans, but I sat on my bed and read the letter twice before I thought about changing.

Dear Sophie,

Sorry I haven't written yet, but thanks for your letter.

Things here are great. My class just won field day at school. For the final game we had to climb this rock wall to get a red

flag, and then drop the flag down to our partner, who would run to the finish line. I was partners with my best friend, Jake. We split it up so I did the first part and he did the second part because I'm a better climber and he's a faster runner. Actually Jake is the fastest runner in the whole sixth grade, just so you know. Of course he was the first person to the finish line so my class won. I was so excited that I lost my balance on the rock wall and fell to the ground. My teacher ran over and totally thought I had broken my leg. I just said, "Do we still win?" She said we did, and my leg was fine anyway.

I'm supposed to tell you some stuff about California. Well, I live in a city called Redwood City. It's named after redwood trees. There are a lot of them in California. In fact, there's a forest full of them called the redwood forest. Sometimes my dad takes my sister Julie and me to a part called Big Basin and we have campouts. But there are all different kinds of trees in Redwood City, not just redwood trees, so I'm not really sure why they named the whole city after them.

I visited New York a couple years ago. I would really love to go again, but if we want to go to a city we can go into San Francisco, which is also really cool, and it's only about a half hour away from our house. There are a lot of things in San Francisco that you've probably heard of, like cable cars and *the Golden Gate Bridge. If you are ever in San Francisco, you should let me know because I could probably meet you there.*

Well, I hope you are having fun in New York and I hope you write back to me soon.

Sincerely,

Katie

P.S. I'm sending you my school picture from last year. I would send you one from this year, but they didn't take them yet and I look the same anyway. Please send me a picture in your next letter.

I hadn't seen a picture when I'd opened the envelope, but maybe it was still in the envelope, or maybe it had fallen onto the floor with all the confetti. "Sophie," Mom called from the front hall. "I thought I told you to clean this up."

"I forgot," I said.

"Well, do it now," she said. I opened the envelope wider and saw Katie's picture was still inside. I knew I didn't have time to look at it carefully, but I pulled it out to look at it quickly and could see that she had blond hair pulled back into a ponytail and straight teeth that probably didn't need braces. Then I put the letter and the picture back into the envelope and into my desk drawer for safekeeping, and I went to clean up the confetti. When I got there, Mom was sitting on her knees picking it up off the floor.

"I said I would do it," I said. I hoped she wouldn't punish me just because I'd forgotten. Lately it seemed like I was forgetting a lot of things. It was hard to concentrate on anything that I had to do. At school I was worried about Jessie, and at home I was worried about my parents. I watched everyone so carefully that sometimes it seemed they were doing everything in slow motion. Every movement seemed to mean something, but I didn't know what it was. When I had time to myself, I tried to figure it out. If Jessie passed me a note during class, did that mean she was still my best friend? If Dad touched Mom's shoulder, did that mean they had decided not to get a divorce? When he went out for some fresh air, did he really leave because he hated her? It was so exhausting to try to make sense of everything and still try to act normal.

I got down on my hands and knees and helped Mom pick up the rest of the confetti. They were just little squares of silver and gold, but I decided to save them. Mom gave me all the confetti she'd picked up, and I put it all in an envelope. I would keep it in my desk drawer along with Katie's letter. "But I'm warning you, Sophie," Mom said. "I really don't want to see that all over the floor again!"

• • •

By the end of the week most kids had gotten a letter from their pen pal. Lindsay claimed she had received a second one, but there was only one letter from her pen pal on the back bulletin board. I wondered what Lindsay wrote to her pen pal about New York. She probably wrote about all the clothing she bought at Bloomingdale's.

Ms. Brisbin said during our free periods we could get up and read the letters on the bulletin board to see what other kids' pen pals had written and learn about the places their pen pals came from. During the week I read all the letters on the bulletin board over and over again. I practically memorized some of them. It was strange to imagine all these other kids in other schools—their stuff was up on the bulletin board at Victor, but I would never meet them.

On Thursday afternoon I went to the meeting for the school paper. The other sixth grader on the paper, Claire Watson, started talking about the pen pal project Mr. Warren had signed us all up for, and she said maybe she would write an article about her pen pal. "What do you think, Sophie?" Claire asked.

"That'd be cool," I said.

But really I started to feel nervous. My letters to Katie were different from all the letters on Ms. Brisbin's bulletin board. I didn't write much about where I lived. Instead I wrote about really personal things, like Haley and Jessie.

And my letters could be on display somewhere in California, in Katie's classroom. . . . Or worse—Katie could be writing an article about my letters for her school paper. I didn't want anyone besides Katie reading what I had to say. What if someone at her school just happened to know someone in New York, and that person just happened to be at Victor, and then Jessie found out all about it? She was already starting to not be my best friend anymore. That would drive her completely away for sure. I decided the next time I wrote to Katie, I would tell her not to show my letters to anyone. Mail is private, after all.

At lunch the next day I met up with Jessie in the line to get apple juice. "I'll meet you at the table," I told her.

"I don't think I'm going to sit there today," Jessie said.

"Where are you going to sit?"

"I don't know," Jessie said. "Some other table. We don't have to sit next to each other every day. Melissa says I spend too much time with you anyway." I didn't know what to say back to her. There were too many people around us and I was afraid that if I opened my mouth, I would start to cry. So I just picked up my tray and walked away.

A few girls from Mr. Warren's class were sitting at a table next to the one that used to be Jessie's and mine. I noticed that there was an empty chair at their table. Two of the girls, Marachel and Lily, had been in my class the year before and we had been pretty friendly then, so I walked over to them. "Is this seat taken?" I asked, feeling stupid because everyone knew I always sat with Jessie. Marachel was sitting next to the empty chair and she shook her head. She swallowed the food in her mouth and smiled. "Sit," she said. I put my tray down, but before I sat down I looked over my shoulder to see where Jessie was sitting. She, Lindsay, Amy, and Melissa were at the back of the room with a couple of other girls from our class. They were laughing about something, and I wondered if Jessie had told them what she'd said to me.

That afternoon Ms. Brisbin asked all the kids who hadn't received a letter yet to raise their hands. Three girls' hands shot up. "Okay, Alyssa, Jillian, and Samantha," Ms. Brisbin said. She made a mark in her grade book. "Let me know if you don't get anything over the weekend, and don't feel bad about not receiving anything yet. The mail can sometimes be unpredictable." Ms. Brisbin bent back down to her book. "Sophie," she said. "I don't have you checked off as getting a letter either. Did you bring one in?"

"Oh, I didn't get one yet either," I mumbled.

"Why didn't you raise your hand, then?" Ms. Brisbin asked.

I shrugged. I knew I had to remember to bring Katie's letter in on Monday, or else Ms. Brisbin might report her and Katie could get into trouble. Then again we could pretend it had gotten lost in the mail and neither one of us would get into trouble. Even Ms. Brisbin had said the mail was unpredictable.

I looked across the table at Jessie, but she was looking down toward the desk and I couldn't catch her eye. I didn't think she had noticed that I had been wearing glitter on my eyelids for the whole week. Amy, Melissa, and Lindsay were still not my friends, and Jessie still had more to say to them than to me. No matter how hard I tried, I was still standing on the outside of their group looking in. There's a line in a Tori Amos song about feeling far away from someone even when you're right next to them. That's how it felt to be with Jessie. There she was, right across the table from me just like she had been since the beginning of the school year. I could reach my feet out and touch her legs. I could slip a note to her so fast that Ms. Brisbin probably wouldn't even notice. But I didn't even know if Jessie would take it from me. Would she even want to know what I had to say?

At the end of the day Ms. Brisbin gave us back our state reports. I didn't do as badly as I thought I would, but I still didn't want anyone to see my grade. I usually get really good grades on papers. I folded it up and stuffed it into my backpack. Even though it was Friday, I couldn't walk Haley home because all the sixth graders had to meet about the school dance, which was exactly two weeks and one day away. We were broken up into two groups. Half of us were assigned to the setup committee, which meant that we had to be at school an hour before the dance. The other half of us were on the break-down committee and had to stay after the dance for an hour, or as long as it took to clean everything up. Lindsay, Jessie, and I were on the setup committee. Amy and Melissa were on the break-down committee.

"Does anyone have any questions?" Mr. Pomeroy asked. He's the Head of School, which is another way of saying he's the principal. He was helping with the dance. Lindsay raised her hand. "Yes, Lindsay?" Mr. Pomeroy said. He knows the name of every single girl at Victor.

"I'd like to be switched to the break-down committee," Lindsay said.

"Do you have a conflict?"

"Not exactly," Lindsay said. "I just need to be switched."

Mr. Pomeroy shook his head. "I'm sorry, but unless a student has a conflict, I expect them to show up for their assigned committee."

"Can we trade committees?" Lindsay asked.

"No," Mr. Pomeroy said. "No trading. If anyone has a conflict, please leave a note in my office by the end of next week and I'll reassign you. Any other questions?"

No one had any other questions. Mr. Pomeroy started talking about the rules for the dance. Basically, we were not allowed to trash the school, and if we saw anyone from another school doing anything to damage Victor property, we were to report to him immediately. I heard Lindsay whisper to Jessie, "I'm going to get my mom to write me a note so I can switch committees. I can't show up before the dance and work for an hour. I want my hair to look fresh. You should have your mom write you a note too." I didn't hear what Jessie said back. She had a much softer whisper than Lindsay. So I turned back to Mr. Pomeroy.

He looked at us sternly. "I don't have to tell you that this is your school too, and it is your responsibility to act respectfully and keep it clean." If he didn't have to tell us, then why did he bother to say all that? "And that's it," Mr. Pomeroy said, and he cracked a smile. "Have a good weekend, girls."

I watched Jessie race out of the building with Lindsay, Amy, and Melissa. I knew they were going to see if the Dorr boys were waiting for them. Sure enough, when I got to the corner a few minutes later, I saw them all hanging out together. Madden Preston was standing with his hands shading his eyes, and he turned toward me as I passed him. I couldn't be sure, but it looked like he winked at me. I just kept walking toward home. I didn't stop by the deli even though I had brought money for a black-and-white cookie.

Mom and Dad ordered pizza for dinner. Usually the four of us split a mushroom and extra cheese pizza, but that night Haley said she wanted a hot dog pizza.

"I'm afraid a hot dog pizza is not on the menu," Mom told her.

"Whoever heard of a hot dog pizza?" I asked.

"It's a kind of pizza," Haley insisted. "Instead of mush-rooms there are little pieces of hot dog on the pizza."

"That's gross," I said. "Where did you ever eat that?"

"I didn't eat it yet. I just know it will be delicious," Haley said.

"Gross," I said again.

"What's gross about it?" Haley wondered. "I love hot dogs and I love pizza."

"Well, Haley," Dad said, "how about if I make you a hot dog and when the pizza comes we can cut it up and put it on top of the pizza?"

"Oh, goodie!" Haley said.

The pizza came. Haley picked all the mushrooms off one of the slices and then put pieces of hot dog on top of the holes where the mushrooms had been. She held out a handful of mushrooms toward me. "Do you want them?"

"Not after your fingers have been all over them," I told her.

I watched Haley eat her hot dog pizza. I wanted to taste it, but I knew my parents would give me a hard time if I asked, since I had just told Haley how gross it was. So I just ate my mushroom slice, the same as always. I imagined Jessie was hanging out with Lindsay, Amy, and Melissa. They were probably at a restaurant, talking about the school dance and Madden Preston. Even though I knew I would feel strange hanging out with them, it felt worse to be home and not invited.

I was so busy thinking about the hot dog pizza and wor-rying about Jessie and her new friends that I didn't even pay attention to my parents and Haley that night. I should have paid more attention so that there was more to remember about it, because it was the last meal like that we ever had. The next day Dad told Haley and me that there was some-thing important he and Mom had to tell us. We followed him into the living room. My chest felt tight and strange. I stared out the window the whole time, as Dad explained that even though he and Mom loved us very much, they were having problems with each other and would be separating. I could see people in the apartments across the street. I wanted to be somewhere else, in someone else's family. I wanted to be in one of those other apartments, where it seemed like nothing bad was happening.

Eight

It all happened very quickly. That afternoon Dad packed
a bag and left our apartment. He said he was going to check
into a hotel and invited Haley and me to meet him the next
day for lunch and order room service. After he left, I went
into my room to lie down. It wasn't that I was tired. I just
didn't know what else to do. I hadn't made my bed that
morning, so I just slipped back in and pulled up the covers.
I wished I had had a television in my room, but my parents
had never let me get one, so I turned my head toward the wall
and looked at the wallpaper instead. There were pale pink
flowers against a cream-colored background, and in between
the flowers were lines Haley had drawn a few years before
with a red crayon, connecting the roses to one another like

those connect-the-dots coloring books we used to have. Mom always said one of these days we would get new wallpaper, now that Haley was old enough to know better than to color all over the walls. I traced with my index finger the lines Haley had drawn. I remembered hearing Mom yelling at Dad that we didn't have enough money for a divorce, and I had a feeling it would be a long time before we got new wallpaper now.

I heard Haley's footsteps a few minutes later and I turned around. "How did you know I was here?" she asked.

"You're a loud walker," I told her.

Mom came in behind Haley. "Why don't we give Sophie some space today," Mom said.

Now that Mom was finally telling Haley to give me some space in my own room, I didn't even feel like having privacy. "No, you guys can stay," I said. Haley jumped up onto my bed and settled herself against my legs. "When is Daddy coming to get the rest of his stuff?" I asked.

Mom sat across from us on Haley's bed. "He's going to take some time off work this week when you girls are in school," she said.

I thought about Dad coming back into our apartment when we weren't there and packing up all of his stuff. Maybe it was because we lived on the thirteenth floor. Maybe that's why everything was so unlucky. "This really stinks," I said.

"Oh, Sophie," Mom said. "You'll see. Having a house with no fighting is going to be better. I promise you."

"Sophie and I fight," Haley reminded her.

"Yes," Mom said, "you're right about that. But Daddy and I won't fight so much anymore."

"Is Daddy going to live in a hotel?" Haley asked.

"For a little while," Mom said, "until he gets a new apartment."

"Do I have to pack my things too?"

"No, Haley," Mom said. "You're going to stay here with Sophie and me."

"How long?" Haley asked.

"How long what?" Mom said.

"How long before Dad comes back."

"Sweetheart," Mom said, "Daddy isn't going to come back to live here. He's going to have his own apartment."

"I don't understand," Haley said.

"Come here, Haley," Mom said. Haley slipped off my bed and went to sit on Mom's lap. Mom petted her hair. "You know Rachel," Mom said.

"Rachel in my class?"

"Yes," Mom said. "You know how Rachel's dad doesn't live with Rachel and her mom?"

"They're divorced," Haley said.

"That's right," Mom said.

"But Daddy said 'separate'," Haley said. "He didn't say 'divorce'."

"It's the thing that comes before divorce," I told her.

Haley sat up and cocked her head. I could tell she was thinking about it, trying to figure it all out. She had a look on her face that Dad calls a "pensive face." But usually he says that about me, not Haley.

"But why would Daddy want to divorce us?" Haley asked.

"Oh, honey," Mom said. "It's a grown-up thing, but it has nothing to do with you and Sophie. Daddy and I love you as much as ever." I don't know why parents always say divorce has nothing to do with the kids. We lived there too, and he'd moved away from us, too. Now he was separated from all of us, not just Mom. But I didn't say that out loud because of Haley.

"Rachel's dad lives far away," Haley said. "Is Daddy going to move far away?"

"No," Mom said. "Daddy is going to stay here in Manhattan so he can see you girls whenever you want to see him."

"That's good," Haley said. "I think it's better that way." She smiled and leaned back against Mom. "Will I have two sets of toys?"

"I'm sure Daddy will have toys for you at his place," Mom said.

"That's good," Haley said again. "Can we order in for dinner again?"

It's so much easier to be someone like Haley. It's so easy for her to be happy. Maybe it has to do with being pliant. She's willing to go with the flow and do whatever Mom and

Dad say, but I just wished we could go back to the way it was before. There were certain things Dad always did—like build things and carry the heavy bags and make pancakes for breakfast. Who would do all of that if he wasn't around? Mom was acting like everything was going to be fine, but what if it wasn't? Didn't she say we didn't have enough money? Would we have to leave Victor? Would we have to move? If we moved into a smaller apartment and Mom didn't have room for an office, then maybe she wouldn't be able to work and we would get even poorer, and it would all be Dad's fault.

Dad called the next morning. I was sitting next to Mom on the couch in the living room when she answered the phone. She glanced at the caller ID on the back of the phone. "It's your father," Mom said, holding the phone out to me. It was still ringing but I shook my head. Mom clicked the button to answer. "Hello," she said. Usually when she answers the phone she says the word "hello" like a question, but this time her voice was low, like she was disappointed. "He wants to talk to you," Mom said, and she held out the phone again.

I felt so bad for Mom. "I don't want to talk to him," I said.

Mom looked like she was going to say something else to me, but she changed her mind and stood up. "Haley," she called, "Daddy's on the phone for you."

Haley came racing into the living room and grabbed the phone from Mom. "Daddy!" she said, almost shouting.

I listened to Haley's end of the conversation and could tell they were making plans for Dad to pick Haley up and bring her back to the hotel for lunch. "Okay. I'll tell Sophie," Haley said. Dad must have said something back because Haley paused. Then she said, "Bye, Daddy," and turned to me.

"Dad says we can have room service for lunch—whatever we want," Haley said. "He says they even have pancakes and grilled cheese sandwiches and we can get both."

"I don't want to go," I said.

Haley looked shocked. "Sophie, this is a *hotel*. They have *room service*." She spoke very slowly, as if I were the younger sister and she had to explain things to me.

I looked over at Mom. "You can do whatever you want," she told me.

"I don't want to go," I said again.

But that was a lie. I really did want to go to Dad's hotel. I love hotels and I especially love room service. Last year when we went to Florida, we stayed in a hotel instead of Grandma's condo because she was having it painted, and we got to have room service almost every day. But this was completely different. I didn't want to go to Dad's hotel and let him think that I was okay about him leaving. I didn't want him to think it was okay at all or that there was anything fun about it, and I especially didn't want to leave Mom home alone. What would she do if Haley and I both left? It would probably make her feel even lonelier if she had to be alone all day.

Haley left to get dressed and then came back into the living room. "Please come, Sophie," she said. "Pretty, pretty please." She clasped her hands together and knelt down in front of me, but it didn't work this time. The doorman buzzed from downstairs.

"Do you want to go downstairs and say hello to your father?" Mom asked me. I noticed that she kept calling him my "father." I shook my head. Mom told Haley she could take the elevator downstairs by herself and to call from the lobby when she got there.

After Haley left, I told Mom I had some work to do and I went into my room to write to Katie. I had to make sure she wasn't going to post my letters on the bulletin board in her school. I couldn't write a whole letter about that, but I wasn't sure what else to say to her. Even though all the letters on the bulletin board at school were about the different places the kids lived and things going on at their schools, it seemed stupid to write about New York or Victor. There was so much happening in my house that was more important. Still, I wasn't ready to tell Katie about my parents. I wasn't even ready to write the words down at all. I decided to just write a quick note to thank her for her letter, and slip in the part about not showing my letters to anyone else. I wrote the words really big so it took up more space on the page.

Dear Katie,

Thank you so much for your letter. I would love to visit you in California one day. There is nothing much going on in New York right now. I hope you are having a good weekend in Redwood City. Please write me back soon.

Sincerely,

Sophie

P.S. Please don't show anyone else my letters.

I folded it up and put it in the envelope that matched my stationery. After I sealed the envelope and put a stamp on it, I realized I had forgotten to send Katie a picture. I hoped she wouldn't be mad. I would just send Katie a picture with the next letter.

Haley came home full of information about Dad's hotel. When Dad had checked in, they'd been all out of single rooms so they'd given him a suite. There was a bedroom, a living room, and *two* bathrooms.

"You should have seen it, Sophie," Haley said. "The bed was so big. Dad even let me jump on it!" I glanced at Mom to see if Mom was going to be angry. She never lets us jump on our beds at home. But Mom didn't say anything this time, and Haley continued. "There's a Jacuzzi in the bathroom and we ordered a ton of room service. And they have all the Harry Potter movies on pay-per-view, but we didn't have time to watch them all."

"Did you watch any of them?" I asked.

"We watched the one where they play chess on that giant board and they get to be the pieces," she said. "Daddy said he is leaving the hotel soon. I wish he could live there forever. There were so many movies I didn't get to see."

"I'm sure Daddy will let you rent movies when he is in his new apartment," Mom said.

"Oh, I forgot something," Haley said. She went to the closet and pulled an envelope from her jacket pocket. "Dad said to give this to you." I took the envelope and saw my name in Dad's handwriting written across the front. He had used all capital letters. For some reason Dad never writes in lowercase letters. Haley and I had given up trying to correct him.

"Open it," Haley said.

"Later," I said. I folded the envelope up as small as I could and held it between my hands. Maybe I would read it, or maybe I would throw it away.

"Daddy didn't write *me* a letter," Haley complained.

"You got to *see* Daddy," Mom reminded her.

Later that evening when Haley was taking a bath, I went into my room to read Dad's letter. I unfolded the envelope and ran my fingers across my name: SOPHIE. Then I tore open the envelope and pulled out the letter. It was written on hotel stationery. The paper was pretty small, and Dad had used up the entire page. It was covered in his slanted capital letters. My heart started to beat faster as I began to read, and I felt stupid for being nervous. He was still my father, after all.

DEAR SOPHIE,

I MISSED YOU VERY MUCH TODAY. I KNOW YOU ARE CONFUSED RIGHT NOW. IT IS HARD FOR A PARENT TO EXPLAIN TO HIS CHILD WHY HE NEEDED TO LEAVE. LET ME ASSURE YOU IT HAD NOTHING TO DO WITH YOU OR HALEY. IT IS NOT YOUR MOM'S FAULT THAT I LEFT EITHER. WE GREW APART FROM EACH OTHER, WHICH IS SOMETHING NEITHER ONE OF US COULD HELP. ONE DAY, WHEN YOU ARE GROWN, MAYBE YOU WILL UNDERSTAND.

I WILL BE GETTING A NEW APARTMENT SOON, AND THERE WILL BE A ROOM FOR YOU AND HALEY. I THINK THE APARTMENT WILL BE ON THE WEST SIDE AND I HOPE THAT YOU WILL DECIDE TO COME AND VISIT SOON.

I'M SURE THE NEXT FEW WEEKS AND MONTHS WILL BE DIFFICULT FOR YOU. I UNDERSTAND YOUR RETICENCE (CAUTION). BUT NO MATTER WHERE I AM, YOU WILL ALWAYS BE MY DAUGHTER, MY FIRSTBORN. YOU AND HALEY ARE THE MOST ESSENTIAL (IMPORTANT) PARTS OF MY LIFE. I WILL BE THERE FOR YOU WHENEVER YOU NEED ME.

LOVE,

DADDY

It was just like Dad to try to turn the end of his letter into a vocabulary lesson. Well, I already knew what the word "essential" meant; if we were so essential, then why had he left? And I didn't care at all what the word "reticence" meant. I folded the letter back up and put it in my desk drawer, beside the letter from Katie. I wasn't sure if I would write him back.

nine

The next day I asked Mom if I could stay home from school. I thought I should be able to stay home the Monday after the weekend that Dad moved out, but Mom said I still had to go. "Please," I said. "I really don't think I can sit there all day."

"You can't miss school because of this," Mom said. "I know it's hard. But the sooner you go, the easier it will be." I was pretty sure she just wanted me to go to school so she could have the apartment to herself. I should have just told her my stomach hurt. She wouldn't have made me go if she'd thought I was sick. It wouldn't exactly have been a lie, since I had felt like throwing up since Saturday. But I went into my room and put on my uniform, just like it was any other day. It had been only two days since Dad had left, but I felt like a different person. It was strange to go through the exact same motions as I had the week before, as though I were exactly the same person with exactly the same life. Something so big and important had happened, but other things hadn't changed at all. I still had to get out of bed and put on my gray skirt and go to school. I would still get into trouble with Ms. Brisbin if I didn't wear my uniform.

At lunch I didn't even try to sit with Jessie. Instead I went straight to Marachel's table.

"Hey, Sophie," Marachel said when she saw me coming. "Sit here." I knew I was lucky to have other people to sit with. There used to be a girl in our class named Libby who had no friends at all, and she ate alone unless one of the teachers happened to see her and sit with her. She moved away after fifth grade. I wondered how Libby was doing in her new school. Nobody there had to know that she had no friends in New York. She could be a completely new person; maybe she was even popular.

"How was your weekend?" Marachel asked me.

I decided then that I wasn't going to tell anyone about my parents. It wasn't because I thought everyone would feel sorry for me and make a big deal out of it. After all, Marachel's parents were divorced too. And it wasn't like I was pretending that it hadn't happened and that Dad would be coming home after work tonight. I knew he would be going back to his hotel, and eventually would be moving into his new apartment. Mom said he wasn't going to take any of the furniture from our apartment, just his clothes and papers. I pictured him picking out new furniture for his own place. He didn't like antiques the way Mom did, so I was pretty sure all his stuff would be modern. It would look so different from our home. I hated thinking about it, and I blinked quickly to get the image out of my head. It was just that I really didn't want to talk about it. I didn't want anyone asking how it had happened and where Dad was going to live now—especially since I didn't know all the answers. I turned to Marachel. "The weekend was fine," I said. "What about yours?"

"Pretty good," she said. "I went to my dad's house."

Marachel's dad lives in Connecticut, which is the state right next to New York. Still, his house has to be at least an hour away from the city. I wondered if my dad would ever move away like that. Mom liked living in Manhattan, but Dad had always wanted a house. Maybe once he got used to not seeing us every day, he would change his mind about living near us and leave the city. I wondered how long it had been after Marachel's parents divorced before her father moved away. Actually, there were a lot of things I wanted to ask Marachel, like whether she had seen it coming or had been as surprised as I was when her dad left, and whether she was really angry about it, and when all the bad feelings went away. But I didn't ask her about any of it. If I acted too curious about other kids' divorced parents, they might figure out that my parents were getting divorced too. Instead I just said, "What did you guys do?"

"Nothing much," Marachel said. "We just hung out." She seemed so casual and easygoing about visiting her dad. I wondered if I would ever feel that way about my parents, if it would ever seem normal to have to leave my home to see my dad, and have his home be somewhere completely different. At that moment it seemed all wrong.

"How's Abe?" Lily asked her.

"Oh, he's so cute," Marachel said. "He can almost walk now."

"Who's Abe?" I asked.

"My brother," Marachel said. "Actually, he's my half brother. He's almost one." If Marachel had a half brother, that meant she had a stepmother, too. I didn't know that Marachel's dad had remarried. I would hate it if my dad got remarried and had new kids. If he liked his new wife better, would he like his new kids better too? One thing I was sure of was, even if I had new brothers and sisters, Haley would always be my favorite. It would be up to me to protect her.

We finished eating and sat around until the five-minute bell rang. I picked up my tray and walked toward the conveyor belt. From behind me I heard someone calling my name.

"Sophie, wait up!" I knew it was Jessie. For a split second

I thought maybe she had changed her mind about me, and then I thought she probably just wanted me to tell her about last night's reading. I turned around.

"Hey," I said.

Jessie looked uncomfortable. We had barely spoken to each other in the last week. I waited for her to say something and shifted my weight from one foot to the other.

"I just wanted to say I'm really sorry about your parents," Jessie said.

I was so surprised that she knew that for a moment I didn't know what she was talking about. She was watching me and I knew I had to say something. "How did you know?" I asked.

"Your mom told my mom," she said. Our mothers were pretty good friends, so that made sense. Still, it didn't seem fair. I thought it should have been up to me to decide when people at school found out about my parents. But if Jessie knew, I was sure that Lindsay, Amy, and Melissa knew as well—maybe they had even told more people about it. I guess it wasn't a secret after all.

When I got home from school that afternoon, all of Dad's stuff was already gone. Mom said he had taken the day off of work so he could pack everything up while Haley and I weren't home. I was glad because I didn't want to see him anyway. Mom also said that Dad already had an apartment to move into.

"How did he get an apartment so fast?" I asked Mom.

"He must have looked over the weekend," Mom said, but she didn't sound convinced herself. I knew it wasn't that easy to find a new apartment. Jessie and Liz had moved last year, and Liz had looked at different places for a whole month before she'd found something she liked. I realized Dad must have been planning to leave for a while. Maybe he had even been looking for apartments the day we went to the pumpkin farm, and that was the real reason why he hadn't come with us. After all, he didn't bring his briefcase with him that day, and he always had his briefcase when he was going to the office. It was just like Dad to pretend everything was normal when really everything was completely messed up. I hated that he thought he could fool me.

"Do you know where the apartment is?" I asked Mom.

"Somewhere on the West Side," she said. That was the same side of the city that Lindsay lived on. Maybe they would see each other on the street. I imagined Dad bumping into Lindsay as he waited for the crosstown bus so he could come to the East Side and pick up Haley and me. I wasn't sure Dad knew who Lindsay was. The last time Lindsay had been at our apartment was for my birthday party in the second grade. Still, if they did see each other at the bus stop and started talking, I was sure it would be about me—after all, what else did they have in common? I would hate that. Luckily, I realized, Lindsay's parents had so much money that she probably always took cabs instead of the bus.

Haley went to see Dad's new apartment at the end of the week. It had two bedrooms—one for dad, and one for Haley and me to share, just like at our real home. Dad still didn't have a couch or a table, but he had a card table and folding chairs in the living room so he had a place to sit down and eat, and there were beds in the bedrooms. Dad had even picked out bedding for Haley and me. Haley said we each had a pink comforter and sheets with flowers on them.

"He shouldn't have picked them out without us," I complained. "He doesn't even know what we like anymore."

"No, it's pretty," Haley said. "Really."

Haley also gave me another letter from Dad. This time I didn't wait so long to open the envelope. I finished talking to Haley and then I went to my room to open it. His letter mostly just described his new apartment, but I already knew about it from Haley. At the end he wrote about how much he missed me and wanted to see me. "I don't want to pressure you," he wrote, "but I also want you to know how much I miss you. Whenever you are ready, I am here." I read that part a couple of times. Then I put the letter back into the envelope and put it into my desk drawer with the other letters from Katie and Dad. For someone who didn't usually get any mail, I was getting quite a collection.

• • •

Over the weekend Mom announced that we were going to clean the whole apartment and organize everything. Things looked kind of messy since Dad had come in and taken all his stuff, but I hated cleaning. It was just one more awful side effect of Dad's leaving.

Mom had taken all the leftover books and papers from the shelves in the living room and put everything in the center of the floor. "Come on, girls," Mom said. "I need your help with this pile."

Haley went over to Mom but I stayed on the couch. Mom looked over at me. "I really need your help with this," she said. Ordinarily I would have given her a hard time about making me clean, but I didn't want to disappoint her. I got up off the couch, and Mom patted the floor next to her. "We need to decide what to keep and what to give away," Mom explained. "So any books that you two no longer want, just pile in that corner."

Haley and I went through the stack of books together. Most of my old books we decided to keep, since Haley wanted to read them.

"What about this one?" Haley said. She held up a book I didn't remember seeing before. "Is this a good book?"

I took it from her and read the title, *The Best Names for Your Baby*. "This isn't a book you read," I told Haley. "It's a book of names for when you're having a baby." I didn't say it out loud, but I thought that was definitely a book we should get rid of. If Mom got remarried, I didn't want her to find it and decide to have another baby. "We don't need it," I told Haley. "Put it in the give away pile."

"Hold on a sec," Mom said. "Let me see that. I haven't seen it in years!" She took it and flipped through the pages, smiling. It was the first time she had smiled all day. "Daddy bought this for me when we found out I was pregnant with you," she told me.

"Can I see it?" I asked.

"Of course," Mom said. All the names were listed alphabetically and defined, just like in a dictionary. I flipped through the pages to get to the *S*'s and looked up my name. "Sophie," I read. "Meaning: wise."

Haley clamored for the book. "I want to see my name too!"

"Hold on," I told her. "I'll look it up." Haley bent over my shoulder and I turned the pages to the *H* section. "There it is," I said, and I pointed.

Haley read it out loud. "Meaning: hero. Oh, cool!"

"Why did you name me Sophie?" I asked Mom.

"You know this story," Mom said. "Daddy's mother was named Sophie, and she had just passed away, so Daddy really wanted to name you after her."

"What if I was a boy?"

"I don't know. Maybe we would have picked out a boy's name that started with an *S*. We really didn't talk about it. I just knew you were going to be a girl."

"How did you know?"

"Mother's instinct," she said.

"Did Dad know I was going to be a girl?"

"I guess he did," Mom said. "He knew he was going to have a girl to name after his mother."

I thought about the pictures of my grandma Sophie. She looked so old. Sophie sounded like a good name for an old lady. Maybe that's why it meant wise — it was a good name for someone who was very old and had a lot to remember and think about. But being wise seemed like a really big responsibility for someone who was just eleven. I wished my parents had picked a different name; maybe then everything about me would have been different. "Sometimes I don't like my name," I said.

"Nobody ever likes their name," Mom said. "But I love your name. It was the first thing we picked out for you, your first present." Mom took the book from my hands. "Let's not throw this one away," she said.

"Okay," Haley said. "Are we done cleaning now?"

"No," Mom said, "but we can take a break for a little while."

"Can I call Jennifer and see if she can come over for dinner?" Haley asked, and Mom nodded. Haley skipped into Mom's office to get the phone. I knew I had at least a few minutes of privacy, so I went into my room to write to Katie.

Dear Katie,

My mom is making Haley and me help her clean the house — I guess it's like "spring cleaning" even though it's fall. We just finished cleaning the bookshelves. Haley and I found this book of names. You know, the kind of book you get when you're having a baby. It lists all the names and defines them all, like in a dictionary. My mom got it when she was pregnant with me. My name means "wise." I'm not really sure that it fits me. I'm named after my grandmother, so maybe she was wise. Haley's name means "hero." I'm not sure if Haley is a hero. She's only seven, and I think that is still too young to know. But her name definitely has a better meaning than mine does.

I made some new friends the other day — at least I think I did. There are these girls in the other sixth-grade class who I've been eating lunch with. They're really nice, but I still miss Jessie. Even though she's being mean, I miss her. I guess that's pretty stupid, but I can't help it. Does that make any sense?

Anyway, I hope you are having a good weekend. Write me soon, if you can.

Sincerely,

Sophie

I reread my letter before folding it up and putting it in an envelope. I still didn't write anything about my parents. I wasn't ready to tell Katie about them yet. But at least I could send her a picture. I went to the drawer in Mom's office where she keeps the extra photos of Haley and me. But when I looked through them, I couldn't find any of just me that I liked enough to send. My hair looked so flat in all of them and you could see the bump on my nose. I hoped Katie would just forget that she had ever asked me for one.

Jen

✳   ✳   ✳

I didn't even want to go to the dance. I was supposed to be at Victor by six o'clock because I was on the setup committee. But when Mom came into my room, I was still in the same jeans and sweatshirt that I had been wearing the whole day.

"Sophie, you have to be at school in half an hour!" she said.

"So?"

"So, you're not even dressed!"

"I'm dressed," I said. "What do you think these things are on my body?"

"Very funny," she said. "I mean dressed for the dance."

"Oh," I said. "I don't want to go."

"You don't want to go?" she asked.

Wasn't that what I had just said? "No, I don't want to go," I repeated.

"Why not?"

"I'm just not into dances," I told her.

"Why not?" she asked again.

"Because I'm just not into them!"

"But, Sophie," Mom said, "this is your first school dance."

"It's not a big deal," I told her.

"Yes, it is," Mom said. "It's very special. In a couple years you'll be in high school and you'll have these things all the time. But this is the first one and you're going to regret not being there."

"No, I'm not," I said. High school seemed so far away. I doubted I would even remember the sixth-grade dance by the time I got there. There were already so many other important things to remember about sixth grade.

"Please, Sophie," Mom said. "I really want you to do this. Go for me." I looked up at her. Things were so hard for her already. At night sometimes when I couldn't sleep I would walk by her room and hear her crying. By the time Haley and I woke up in the mornings, Mom acted like everything was fine. She got us ready for school and did her work, just the same as before, but I knew the truth. Even though I was sure that I wasn't going to have a good time at the dance, I didn't want to let Mom down.

"Fine," I said to her. "I'll go. But at least can I wear your blue earrings?"

"Not Grandma's earrings," Mom said.

"Why not?" I said, even though I wasn't sure why I was pushing her. I didn't care about the dance to begin with.

"Because they're expensive," Mom said. That seemed like a dumb answer. I wasn't like Haley. I never lost anything or ruined anything. I was eleven, after all.

"How come you don't trust me?" I asked.

"Listen, Sophie," Mom said, "those are special earrings and I'll let you borrow them for a special occasion, but not for tonight."

"I thought you were the one who thought tonight was so special. If it's not special, then why do I have to go?" The words were out of my mouth before I could stop them. I knew I sounded mean and angry. Sometimes even when I'm trying to be nice and helpful to Mom, it still comes out the wrong way.

Mom sighed. "You don't *have* to go," she said. "I just think you should."

Then I sighed. "I said I would go," I told her.

"And change your shirt at least," Mom said.

"How come?"

"Oh, Sophie, come on. You can't wear a sweatshirt."

I knew she was right about that. Even though I didn't want to go, I didn't want to look dumb when I got there. I opened my shirt drawer and pulled out a black shirt with silver designs on it that looked like starbursts. It was the fanciest shirt I had that went well with jeans. Then I went into the bathroom and pulled my hair up into a half ponytail. Mom says I look more mature when my hair is off my face. I put on a little of Mom's blush. I definitely thought I looked older.

When I came back out, Mom's face looked pensive. She stared at me as though she didn't quite recognize me, and then she smiled. "You look so grown-up and so beautiful," she said. "You're going to have a wonderful time."

But when I got over to Victor, all the other girls were dressed up and in makeup too. Some of them were even wearing eye shadow and dark lipstick. I didn't think anyone would even notice the blush on my cheeks, and I felt plain and young-looking all over again. Jessie and Lindsay weren't there yet—they must have gotten switched over to the break-down committee after all. It was amazing how Lindsay always got her way, and Jessie was becoming just like her. But Marachel and Lily were both there, and I went over to them to help with the crepe paper. We twisted red and blue crepe paper together and then strung it around the gym—red and blue are Victor's school colors. Then Mr. Pomeroy made us help set up the tables and chairs so there would be a place for people to sit down if they wanted to. There were big bowls of chips and sodas on the tables. I had never had soda in school before. Usually the lunchroom only had juice, water, and milk, but I guess they relaxed the rules for a weekend dance.

People started to arrive even before it was seven o'clock. Besides the Dorr boys, we had invited kids from two other schools. I knew everyone from Victor, and I recognized some of the boys from Dorr, but most of the other kids I didn't know at all. There was music playing, but nobody was dancing. People were just standing in small groups and talking. I saw Jessie with Lindsay, Amy, and Melissa. They were all facing outward, looking over at Madden Preston, who was standing with three other boys, but they didn't go over to talk to them. I stood against the back wall with Marachel and Lily.

"What do you think?" Marachel asked. She was sort of yelling because the music was pretty loud.

It wasn't at all what I had expected. I shrugged my shoulders.

"Look," Lily said. "All the boys are on one side of the room, and all the girls are on this side." I hadn't noticed it before, maybe because I'm used to being around all girls since that's all there is at Victor. But I looked up to see, and she was right.

"This is kind of dumb," Marachel said. "I wonder if anyone is going to dance."

"I'm not," Lily said.

"Me neither," I said.

But after a while a few kids did start to dance. Even though most of the girls stayed on one side of the room and most of the boys stayed on the other, there were a few kids in the center of the room. I looked to see if Jessie was dancing with Madden Preston, but she wasn't. Lindsay was dancing with a boy I didn't recognize, and Jessie was standing by the soda with Amy and Melissa, still watching Madden Preston. Madden and his friends were over by the bleachers. Madden had a handful of pretzels and was tossing them, one by one, into another boy's mouth. Even from the distance, I could tell he was mostly missing his target. I was glad Lindsay and Jessie were on the break-down committee—they would have to clean up all the pretzels Madden dropped, and everyone else's messes too. Madden turned and saw me watching him. I couldn't be sure, but it looked like he winked at me.

Then, all of a sudden, he was walking toward us. He got closer and closer. I was afraid he was angry with me for looking at him and he was coming to tell me it was rude to stare. I turned toward Marachel. "Hey," I heard Madden Preston call. "If it isn't Sophie Turner." I knew it would be even ruder to ignore him so I turned around.

"Hi," I said.

"What're you doing?" he asked. I wasn't sure if he was asking me that because I had been staring at him or if he was just coming over to say hello.

"Nothing," I said.

"You wanna dance?" he asked.

"I don't know."

"Ah, come on," Madden said. He took my hand and pulled me away from the wall. "Don't you love this song?"

"It's all right," I said. Actually, I had never heard it before, but I followed him to the center of the room. Madden seemed to be looking me up and down. I hoped I hadn't spilled anything on myself. I thought Marachel or Lily probably would have said something to me if I had.

"I think I should call you 'Sophie the Shrimp.' I bet you're the shortest one in this whole room." I looked around to see if there was anyone shorter, but I didn't see anyone. I knew he was right. I was almost a whole head shorter than Madden, and I was sure I looked stupid standing next to him. "Relax," Madden told me.

I didn't know what to say to him and I was relieved the music was so loud. It made it easier to not talk and just dance. I had never danced with a boy before, and I didn't think I would be very good at it, but I shouldn't have worried because Madden was terrible. "You keep stepping on my feet," I complained after a few minutes.

"Well, they keep getting in my way," he said. He stepped on me again, but that time I think it was on purpose. I started to laugh. I knew it was wrong because Jessie liked him, so I shouldn't have been having a good time with him.

I turned my head to see where she was and saw her coming toward us.

"Hi, guys," Jessie said. She was smiling, but I could tell it was a fake smile. After all, we had been best friends for five and a half years. I knew when her smile was really a smirk. "Do you mind if I cut in?" she asked.

"Jess," Madden said, "we're right in the middle of a song. Besides, I don't think Sophie wants to stop dancing yet, do you, Soph?"

Madden was right—I was having fun and I wanted to keep dancing. For a second I thought about telling Jessie that she would have to wait her turn, but she was standing there smirking at me and I couldn't do it. I knew Jessie thought I was a terrible person for dancing with Madden in the first place. If I told her I wasn't ready to stop dancing, she would never be my friend again. Jessie narrowed her eyes into little slits, the way she does whenever she's really mad at someone. I took a deep breath and turned to Madden. "It's okay," I told him. "You guys can dance now." I walked over to the back of the room where Marachel and Lily were standing.

"Sophie, that was awesome," Lily said.

"Yeah, and you said you weren't going to dance at all," Marachel added.

I watched Jessie dancing with Madden and I started to feel mad at her even though that didn't make any sense. I had never cared about Madden before, and I had known all along that she liked him. "Jessie's going to kill me," I told Marachel and Lily. "She really likes Madden Preston. I wish he hadn't danced with me. He doesn't even like me."

"Of course he likes you," Marachel said. "After all, he danced with you."

"No, trust me," I said. "He doesn't. He told me I was the shortest person in the whole room and he called me a shrimp."

"See, he does like you," Marachel insisted. "Boys always tease you when they like you."

"Are you sure?" I asked.

"Definitely," she said.

"Yeah," Lily added. "She's totally right."

I looked back over at Madden and Jessie. Jessie had hooked her arms around Madden's neck. But when the song ended, Madden walked back over to where I was standing with Marachel and Lily. He stopped in front of me and then leaned forward, resting his hand against the wall behind me. Our faces were really close and for a second I was afraid he would kiss me. I didn't know whether to be excited or scared. "See you around, Shrimpy," Madden said into my ear, and he went back over to his friends by the bleachers.

"See you," I said. I saw Jessie glaring at me from across the room. Even from that distance I could tell her eyes were still narrowed into little slits.

"What did he say?" Marachel asked.

"He said he'd see me around."

"You see, you see!" she said, jumping up and down. Luckily the music was still loud, so I didn't think Madden could hear her. I didn't know what to say. It didn't seem like that big of a deal, but Marachel certainly thought that it was.

"You look great tonight. You're way prettier than Jessie, by the way," she said.

I knew she was just saying that to be nice. "No, I'm not," I said.

"Are you kidding?" Marachel said. "Jessie's hair is all frizzy and she never smiles. You're definitely prettier than she is."

Was that true? Did people think I was pretty? I didn't care about being prettier than Jessie, I was just happy to be pretty at all. Sometimes I thought I was, but I could never be sure.

Mom picked me up at nine o'clock. I couldn't wait to get home because I wanted to write down everything that had happened so I could remember it better. I decided to write a letter to Katie about it. Since my last letter to her had been so short, I felt like I owed her one. "Dear Katie," I wrote, "I just got back from our school dance. It was really great, and the best part was that I didn't expect it to be good at all." I told her all about dancing with Madden Preston—although I left out the part about Jessie. When I finished, I went into

Mom's office and made a copy of my letter on her Xerox machine. I wanted to keep a copy of it for myself. Then I pulled open her drawer of pictures and found one of Haley and me. I looked better in pictures that weren't of just me, and I decided to send it to Katie. That way she could see what we both looked like.

Eleven

After the dance everything went back to normal. Not normal like the way it should be, but a new kind of normal, where Dad lived somewhere else, Jessie wasn't my friend, and I felt lonely most of the time. I got into the habit of counting backward. Each day when I woke up and looked at the calendar above my desk, I would think, *This time last year I was in fifth grade, Dad was here, and Jessie was probably sleeping over.* Everything was different now, but I didn't really cry about it. I just thought it was strange how quickly and completely things had changed. None of it seemed real.

Mom and Dad had made an official agreement that Haley and I would have dinner with Dad every Tuesday night, because that was the day neither of us had any after-school activities, and then we would stay with him every other weekend. Except I wasn't seeing Dad at all. I didn't get on the phone when he called, and I didn't answer the phone unless I was sure it wasn't Dad calling. Dad still wrote me letters. He sent one home with Haley each time she went to see him. I saved them all in my desk drawer, but I never wrote back.

The next weekend Haley and I were scheduled to go to Dad's apartment. Haley pulled her duffel bag out from under her bed. "Are you coming this time?" she asked me.

"No," I told her.

"Why not?" she asked.

I couldn't tell Haley what I really felt—that I was too angry, that I was afraid of hurting Mom, that I wasn't sure if he still loved us as much, or if I even loved him, and that I really wanted to punish him. Instead I just said, "Because I need some time away from you." Sometimes it was just easier to be mean to Haley than to figure out how to explain things to her. Still, I knew it was wrong and that I could get into trouble for it, so before she could run to Mom and tell on me, I offered to help her pack for the weekend.

Haley went to the closet and stood on her tiptoes, pulling at different skirts. She still wore a skirt over her jeans on the days it was too cold to wear just a skirt alone. "I need to find the skirts that go best with pants," she told me. "How about these ones?"

Haley brought four different skirts over to my bed. "You don't need so many," I told her. "You're only going for two days."

"But I like to have choices," she said.

"I don't know if there's going to be room in your bag. We haven't packed your shirts and underwear yet."

"It will fit," Haley said. "I'll just sit on top of the bag and you can zip it up." Haley loved that trick. Mom always over-packed when we went to Florida, so when it was time to zip up her suitcase, she'd make us sit on either end of the bag so she could zip it up.

"I don't know if that works with a duffel bag," I told Haley. She looked disappointed. "Well, figure out what shirts you want. Maybe it will all fit."

Haley went to the dresser and pulled out a few shirts, some socks, and underwear. We stuffed everything into the bag.

"Now let's close it," Haley said.

"What about sleep shirts?"

"I'll just wear one of Daddy's," Haley said.

"It'll be too big for you," I told her.

"I don't care."

"Well, you still need to add your brush and toothbrush," I told her.

"I don't need to," she said. "Daddy bought us all kinds of bathroom stuff to keep at his apartment."

"Oh," I said. "Then I guess we can zip this up." I held the sides of the bag together and Haley ran the zipper up the middle.

"I told you it would all fit," she said.

Dad called on his way to pick up Haley. I could always tell when he was on the phone because Mom would look tired and annoyed every time she spoke to him. I remembered how Dad used to act extra cheerful around Haley and me whenever he was mad at Mom. I bet he had stopped pretending to be cheerful now that he lived alone. "I'll send her downstairs," Mom said. She paused and turned to me. "Sophie, your father wants to speak to you."

"I don't want to talk to him," I said.

Mom covered the mouthpiece with her hand. "Come on, Sophie," she said softly. "He's your father."

"No," I said. I didn't care if Dad wanted to talk to me. No one could make me talk to him if I didn't want to.

She uncovered the mouthpiece. "She doesn't want to talk to you, Jack." I guess my dad said something back to her, because then Mom said, "What do you want me to do? I can't make her talk to you." She hung up and turned to me. "How long are you going to keep this up?" she asked. I knew I could wait a long time. I'm not as pliant as Haley. I shrugged my shoulders and Mom reached out and rubbed my cheek with the back of her hand. "Oh, Soph, it's all going to be okay," she said.

• • •

On Saturday morning I woke up and looked over at Haley's empty bed. I hated to admit it, but I kind of missed her. I wondered what Mom and I would do all weekend without Haley around. I kicked back the covers and walked into Mom's room. She was sitting up in bed doing the crossword puzzle. I got in beside her, settling into the side of the bed that used to be Dad's.

"You slept late," she said.

"Uh-huh."

"Tough week at school?"

"It was all right."

"That's good." I could tell Mom wasn't paying attention to my answers. She hadn't moved her eyes from the cross-word puzzle. "Aha," she said all of a sudden. "Finished!" She put the paper down and turned to me. "Jessie likes Chinese food, right?"

"Why?"

"Because she and Liz are coming for dinner tonight."

I sat up and glared at her. "How could you invite them without asking me first?"

"I don't understand," Mom said. "What's the problem here?"

"The problem is that Jessie and I aren't friends anymore!"

"Since when?" Mom asked.

"Since practically the beginning of school," I said.

"But you girls were so close."

"Not anymore," I said. "Don't you remember? She didn't sleep over on Halloween. She hasn't even been here since."

"I'm sorry, honey," Mom said. "I won't do it again."

"But you're still going to let them come tonight, aren't you?" I said, even though I already knew the answer. I wished Mom hadn't been so distracted lately. If she had been paying any attention at all, she would have known not to invite Jessie over.

I didn't even feel better when I checked the mail and there was a letter from Katie, but I opened it anyway. I forgot all about the confetti, but luckily Mom was in the other room, and I cleaned it up before she even saw it was there.

Dear Sophie,

Boy, has it been busy around here lately! I haven't had time to write at all. In fact, the only reason I am writing now is because our teacher, Mrs. Katz, found out that a bunch of us haven't written to our pen pals all month, so for the next ten minutes we all have to write letters. Not that I didn't want to write to you anyway, but like I said, it's been so busy.

Mostly I've been practicing for the middle school talent show, which is on Thursday. Jake and I are performing together.

At first he didn't want to, but then he decided we could pretend to be Abbott and Costello. They were comedians from a long time ago and they have a whole act about baseball. Jake likes anything that has to do with sports, so that's what we're doing. We've been working hard to memorize our lines and get the timing just right. I think it's going to be awesome. All the parents are coming Thursday night to watch. Well, my mom's not coming because she has to help my sister, Julie, study for some test the next week. I don't really mind because my dad and my aunt are coming to watch me, but Julie's really upset about it. She wanted to perform with her friends. They're all OBSESSED with clothing, and they planned this whole fake fashion show for the talent show. The whole thing was actually Julie's idea, but my mom says she needs to study.

Uh-oh—I see Mrs. Katz is standing up now. That means she's about to call time. I guess I should wrap this up. I hope everything in New York is good. Write me back soon.

Sincerely,

Katie

Twelve

Liz and Jessie came over around seven thirty, even though they were supposed to be there at seven o'clock. I was sitting on the couch in the living room when they walked in. Liz came over to me, bent down and hugged me. "Hey, sport," she said. Liz always called me sport—short for "good sport." Sometimes Mom would point out to Liz that I didn't always act like one. I hated when she did that. I wanted Liz to think I was always a good sport. But Mom didn't say anything like that this time, and Liz stood up and ruffled my hair. "I'm sorry you're going through a rough time," she said. I knew that she meant it even if Jessie didn't care about me at all. Jessie was still standing by the door. She looked over at me, and our eyes met, but she didn't say hello. Mom put her arm around Jessie's shoulder. "Come on in, honey."

"I'm sorry we're late," Liz said to her.

"Don't worry about it," Mom said. "I knew you would be. I just called to order the Chinese food."

"What, you're not cooking?" Liz asked, and then she and Mom started laughing as though Liz had just said the funniest thing in the world. Everyone knew that Mom hated cooking. We had been eating a lot of delivery since Dad had moved out.

"Red or white?" Mom said in Liz's direction.

"Either. . . . No, red," Liz said. Mom went into the kitchen to get the wine and Liz followed her. "Why don't you girls go to Sophie's room and catch up?" Liz said over her shoulder. I knew she was just trying to get rid of us so she could talk to Mom privately. I looked at Mom, waiting for her to say we could stay. After all, she knew that Jessie and I weren't friends anymore. But Mom didn't say anything. I stood up from the couch and walked toward my room. Jessie followed behind me.

Jessie hadn't been in my room since Halloween. I remembered walking in the door that night and seeing Dad sitting in the living room watching television. It seemed like a long time ago. Now I felt even more uncomfortable being alone with Jessie. I could tell she would rather have been anywhere else, and I realized Liz must have made these plans without consulting her, either.

"What do you want to do?" I asked Jessie.

"I don't care," she said. She sat on Haley's bed and began pulling at the stitches of one of the throw pillows. It was a good pillow—not the kind you sleep on, but one meant just for decoration. It had flowers embroidered on one side and Haley said they kind of looked like the flowers on the bedding that Dad had picked out for us. I hoped Jessie wouldn't ruin it, because we probably wouldn't have enough money to replace it now. Everything Jessie did seemed wrong. She had a piece of gum in her mouth and she was chewing it with her mouth open.

Chewing gum reminded me of something I had seen on television about the way cows eat. They chew their food and swallow, then spit it back up, and then chew it again. I could never chew gum for that reason. I hated the sound Jessie made as she smacked it from side to side, like you could hear her saliva. It made me think of Jessie's favorite card game. It was a game called Spit. Usually I didn't like playing with her because she gloated when she won, which was most of the time, but I couldn't think of anything else that she would want to do. I wanted to distract her from ruining Haley's pillow, and besides, I knew she was mad at me because of the dance and Madden Preston. Even though I didn't do anything wrong, I wanted to make it up to her so we could be friends again. Playing that stupid game seemed like the least I could do. "Do you want to play Spit?" I offered.

"You hate that game," Jessie said.

"I don't mind playing if you want to," I told her.

"You don't have to act like we're friends," Jessie said. "No one's in here except us."

"You don't have to act like we're enemies," I said.

"Well, what do you think we are?" Jessie asked.

It was one of those times when someone says something so awful that for a second everything seems to stop. The same thing had happened when Dad had told Haley and me that he was leaving. All of a sudden I knew exactly where I stood with Jessie. There was nothing to be confused about anymore. I looked at her and felt my face get hot. My heart was beating so hard I was sure she could hear it. I knew my cheeks were turning red and that I must look really stupid. I sat back on the bed and said, "I didn't know you hated me." My voice caught because I was trying hard not to cry.

Jessie rolled her eyes. "Oh, come off it, Sophie. You think just because your parents are divorcing that people will feel sorry for you and you can do whatever you want. Well, I can see right through you."

"I don't know what you're talking about," I said.

"You're a wannabe. You were so jealous because I had new friends and you couldn't be with me every second of every day anymore, so you went after Madden."

"I didn't!" I said, and I knew I was talking too loudly. "He came up to me."

Jessie snorted. "Yeah, right," she said. "Like he would really want to dance with you."

It was the first time I had had a fight like that—when I wasn't the one doing any of the fighting. With Haley and me, it was usually the other way around. I put my hand over my mouth because I was afraid otherwise I would start to sob. If I was so horrible, then why had Jessie been my friend for so long? It was like everything before didn't count for anything. Even though I was pressing my palm hard against my mouth, I couldn't hold it all in. Finally all the tears I had been holding in came pouring out. I started to cry out loud.

Mom was calling us from the other room. Her voice sounded strange because I was crying and the room looked blurry through my tears. Jessie walked out but I stayed in my room. Nobody could make me come out. I got up to close the door. I wanted to slam it shut and lock it. I really didn't care if I got into trouble, but Mom was in the doorway when I got there, so I didn't get to do any of it. "Honey," she said when she saw me, "what happened?"

I just shook my head and fell into her.

Suddenly Liz was in the room and she was calling for Jessie. I heard her asking Jessie what had happened, but Jessie didn't answer. "Don't you have something to say to Sophie?" Liz asked. She paused, I guess waiting for Jessie to say something, but Jessie was silent. "I'm sorry about this, Andy," Liz said to Mom. "Maybe we'll get going."

"Please," Mom said, "take some food home." But Liz said no, we should keep it for when Haley got home. They were having this whole stupid discussion about whether Haley would eat the moo shu chicken, and I just stood there, crying into Mom's shirt, while Jessie stood impatiently in the doorway.

"We'll show ourselves out," Liz said. "Let's go, Jessica Anne." I could tell Liz was really angry by the way she said Jessie's name, and I was glad. I hoped Jessie would be in a lot of trouble.

I heard the front door open and close, and I lifted my head from Mom's chest. There was a dark blue circle in the middle of Mom's favorite light blue shirt, wet from my tears. I hoped it wouldn't stay that way. I worried that she would be angry with me about the shirt and for ruining her dinner with Liz, but Mom just pulled me back to her, and rocked and rocked me. I felt like a baby. But I had been so upset for so long and there wasn't any way that I could hold it in anymore.

"I hate that Daddy left," I finally said.

"I know," Mom said.

"I hate Jessie."

"I know," she said again.

"I wish I was Haley," I said. I thought Mom would tell me that I shouldn't say such a thing, but she just kept saying, "I know, I know." Sometimes it's good to feel understood, even if it doesn't change anything.

I don't remember when we moved from the doorway over to the bed. But that is where we ended up. Mom sat on the edge of the bed, and I lay my head in her lap. I thought about trying to be more like Haley, to just accept everything that happens and be happy with the way things are. But I didn't think I had it in me. I kept thinking that maybe this whole thing was Dad's fault. Maybe the reason I let Madden dance with me in the first place was because I was too distracted about the separation. I squeezed my eyes shut and wished I could go back in time to change everything, but of course that didn't work. When I opened my eyes again, I was still facedown in Mom's lap.

Mom smoothed my hair back from my face. "I'm so sorry," she said.

"Jessie hates me," I told her.

"She doesn't hate you."

I turned toward Mom. "You don't know what she said," I told her. "She hates me for sure. I don't think we'll ever be friends again. Maybe I'll never speak to Jessie ever again. Dad either!"

"You know what I remember?" Mom said.

"What?"

"Years ago, when you were around two or three, we were by the pool at Grandma's club in Florida. You know the club where all the old women go to have lunch and wade in the pool?"

"Uh-huh," I said.

"Well, one of those women walked up to you. You were just standing by the edge in your water wings. You were so tiny—those things practically took up your whole body. I was sitting on the steps, and I guess the woman didn't know you were with me. She bent down to you and said, 'Whose little girl are you?' And you put your hands on your hips the best you could, because those water wings got in the way, and you said loudly, 'Mine!' I was so proud of you then because you were your own person—independent and self-assured."

"I don't feel that way anymore," I said.

"Things are hard right now," Mom said, twisting a strand of my hair between her fingers, "but don't lose who you are. Daddy and I love you so much for just being Sophie."

I thought about what Mom said for the rest of the weekend. During the next week at school Ms. Brisbin surprised us after lunch by saying that she needed a grading period, so we could have a free period to get started on our homework. I knew she meant for us to do our math assignment, or read that night's chapter in *To Kill a Mockingbird*, but I didn't feel like doing either. I ripped a sheet of paper out of my notebook. I thought I would write back to Katie. After all, the pen pal thing had started as a homework assignment. If Ms. Brisbin asked, I could just say I thought writing to our pen pals was ongoing homework. I wrote the word "Dear" at the top left-hand side of the page, and then, instead of writing "Katie," I wrote "Dad." I sat back and looked at the words, "Dear Dad." And then I started to write some more.

Dear Dad,

I'm in school right now. Ms. Brisbin is at her desk grading papers and we are supposed to be starting our homework. I know I should probably do my math sheet, but first I wanted to write to you.

I've been thinking a lot about things since you left. I want you to know that even though I am writing you now, I am still mad that you left. I know you said it is not my fault, but that doesn't make it any better! Sometimes you do a lot of things that I hate—like when you always take Haley's side without finding out my side first, or when you call me Thumbelina. Why do you do that? You know I hate that name. Why can't you just call me Sophie, like everyone else does? You picked that name, after all!

I don't know when I will be ready to see you. I hope you're not mad at me just because it was easier for Haley. I do miss seeing you. I think maybe I will call you soon.

I didn't know what else to write, so I decided to end it there. I was going to sign "Love, Sophie," but I wasn't ready to say that. So I wrote "Sincerely, Sophie," just like I did when I wrote to Katie, and then I folded the letter up. I knew Haley was going to see Dad during the week, but I wasn't going to give it to Haley to bring to him. I didn't want anyone to know about it but me. I would just pretend I was mailing something to Katie and would ask Mom for a stamp. I didn't know Dad's new address, but I did know his office address and he got mail there, too.

When I got home, I asked Mom for an envelope and a stamp. She didn't even ask me what it was for. I printed Dad's work address neatly on the outside of the envelope, stuck the stamp in the upper right corner, and put it in my backpack. I would mail it on my way to school the next morning.

Thirteen

The next week Mom announced that Grandma was sending us money to go to Florida for New Year's. We had never gone to Florida for New Year's before. Usually Dad cooked a big dinner just like on Thanksgiving—with turkey and all the usual holiday foods that go with it—and Liz came over with Jessie. There was always too much for just six people to eat, so we'd have leftovers for days. I liked the leftovers even better than the dinner itself, because Mom sometimes made us grilled cheese sandwiches with turkey in the middle. It was really the only meal she was good at making. But now, since Dad was gone and Jessie and I weren't speaking, things were different. I knew I couldn't count on much of our old routines. And even though Dad was the one who had caused a lot of the changes, he wasn't too happy with our new plans. I knew because I heard Mom arguing with him over the phone later that night.

It was past the time when I was supposed to be in bed, but I couldn't fall asleep. Haley was asleep and breathing loudly in the bed next to mine, and that made it even harder. I put a pillow over my head, but then I couldn't breathe, so I got up and went to see if Mom was still awake. Her door was closed, but she was talking so loudly that I could hear her anyway. She cursed and I was glad Haley wasn't there. Then she said, "What do you mean, I can't just go and decide things? It seems like you've done an awful lot of deciding yourself lately, Jack."

There was a pause, and then Mom's voice again. "I don't know what you expected—that the girls would be with you? Sophie still won't even meet you for dinner!" Mom paused again and I wondered what Dad was saying back to her. Even though she was right about me not seeing Dad, I wished she hadn't mentioned me. I didn't want to be the reason they were fighting. "I'm not staying alone in New York for New Year's," Mom said.

Another pause. I moved even closer toward the door. "Don't you dare," Mom said, her voice catching. Then she was quiet again, this time much longer. I pressed my ear to the door in case she was just speaking more softly, but I couldn't hear anything. She had probably hung up the phone, so I turned the knob and opened the door.

"Sophie," Mom said. "I didn't hear you knock."

"I didn't knock," I told her. Mom wiped her eyes quickly, but I saw it anyway. I had seen Mom cry more times since Dad had left than I had before in all the eleven and three quarter years of my life. "I thought you said there wouldn't be any fighting after he left," I said.

"Oh, Sophie," Mom said.

"Just forget it," I said. I knew she had been making it up. If they were going to fight anyway, then I'd rather have both my parents in the same house, but of course I didn't have a choice. Mom couldn't always be counted on to tell the truth.

"Why don't you try to get some sleep?" Mom said. "You have school tomorrow." I knew she was trying to get rid of me.

"What did Dad say he was going to do?" I asked.

"What?"

"When you said 'Don't you dare,' what had Dad just said?"

"You shouldn't have been listening to that," Mom said. "It was a grown-up conversation." I thought about telling her that sometimes I acted like more of a grown-up than she did, but I didn't say anything. I just walked out of the room. Mom called "Good night" after me, but I didn't answer. My heart was beating fast again, and I tried to figure out what I was scared of. Dad had already moved out, so what else was left to happen?

A few minutes later Mom came into my room. I was turned toward the wall, counting backward from one hundred to try to fall asleep, and even though I was still awake, I didn't know she had come in. "Sophie," Mom whispered, and I jumped.

"I didn't mean to scare you," she said. "I just wanted to check on you."

"I'm fine," I said.

Mom sat down at the edge of my bed. "There's always going to be a little fighting, Soph. We're still working this all out. But really, it's nothing for you to worry about. Nothing."

"Are we still going to Florida?"

"Do you want to go?"

I thought about it before I answered. I didn't really want to be in New York for New Year's. It would just remind me of how sad it was that Dad and Jessie weren't there. A few days by the pool at Grandma's club without having to think about either of them sounded much better. "Yes, I want to go," I told her.

"Okay," Mom said. "Then we'll still go."

"What about Dad?"

"Don't worry about him," Mom said. "He just misses you, that's all."

Mom kissed me good night and went back to her room. I looked at the clock and saw it was already almost midnight. I had to be awake in seven hours, which wasn't very long at all. I thought about what Mom said—I hadn't worried about Dad in a while, at least not about how he *felt*. Even though I wanted to go to Florida, I was sorry he would be alone during the holiday. Isn't it funny that he was the one who had left Mom and now he was the one who was alone? A week earlier, Haley had given me another letter from him. "My Sophie," he wrote, "I called you Thumbelina because you were small and full of love, just like in the song. I'm sorry you didn't like the nickname, but that is always how I will see you. However, since you say you despise (hate) it, I won't do it again."

I rolled over in my bed and starting counting backward from one hundred again, but I don't think I ever got to the number one. Somewhere in the middle I fell asleep.

Fourteen

✴ ✴ ✴

Haley and I sat on the edge of Mom's bed and watched Mom pack for Florida. With Mom, packing is more of an event than a chore, and she takes a very long time doing it. I don't know why she thinks it is so hard — she always ends up taking everything she owns anyway, so it's not like she has to decide anything. When she had finally finished, Haley and I sat on the ends of her suitcase so she could zip it up.

Haley and I packed for ourselves without Mom. It goes much faster that way. Right before we zipped up our bags, we called to Mom so she could check that we had enough for the long weekend. Of course we did; I'm a very good packer.

"It looks perfect," Mom said.

"I'm very efficient," I told her, using a word Dad had taught me when I was Haley's age.

"You certainly didn't get that from me," Mom said.

We left for Florida on a Wednesday. The night before, Haley had gone to have dinner with Dad. I didn't go with them, but I did give Haley a card to give to Dad from me. I thought maybe he should have something from me so he wouldn't feel so alone on New Year's. "This is for *Dad*?" Haley said, sounding shocked.

"Just give it to him," I said. "And don't make a big deal out of it."

"But, Sophie," Haley started. Then she stopped. Sometimes even Haley knows when to hold back.

The next day the plane was really crowded with families going away for the holiday. We had gotten our tickets on the late side so we had seats at the back of the plane. I hated it because it meant we were seated right by the bathroom and it smelled awful every time someone opened the bathroom door. The flight seemed to last twice as long as usual, and when we finally landed, it took forever to get off the plane. But the minute we stepped off the airplane, I felt better. The air was a lot warmer. Florida is warm all year long, even during the winter. I was wearing jeans and a sweater, and carrying my jacket, because it had been freezing when we'd left New York, and I couldn't wait to change into shorts and a T-shirt.

Grandma was waiting for us at baggage claim. "I was getting worried because you took so long coming out," she said.

"We were at the back of the plane, Ma," Mom said.

"Yeah, and it stunk," Haley said. She pinched her nose with her fingers. "Pee yew!"

"Oh, you poor girls. I worry about you so much," Grandma said.

"You don't have to," Mom said. Mom always tells Grandma not to worry. Meanwhile *she* worries about Grandma all the time.

In the car to Grandma's house, Grandma kept asking Haley and me how we were doing.

"We're doing okay," I told her. But Grandma wasn't really listening to my answer. She just shook her head and made a clicking sound with her tongue.

"I'm doing great," Haley piped up. "I made a reindeer piñata at school. Right now it's hanging in my class, but next week when we go back to school, Mrs. Warshall is going to take all the Christmas decorations down so I get to take it home. Then Sophie and I are going to smash it open and eat all the candy."

"Oh, no. You'll ruin your teeth," Grandma said.

"Ma, you worry about everything," Mom said.

The next day was New Year's Eve. Since Mom is a terrible cook, and Grandma doesn't move around as easily as she used to, we went to Grandma's club for dinner. The club is right across the street from Grandma's house. You can see it from the front porch. Grandma said we had to be there no later than five o'clock, which seemed like a very early time to eat dinner, especially on New Year's Eve. I wanted to stay up at least until midnight to see the ball drop back in New York, and I knew I would get hungry again. But Mom said people eat earlier in Florida.

I was ready to leave for dinner by four thirty, and I sat by the window watching people walking over. Grandma lives in a development called Highland Park. Really it is just one big street called Highland Park Road that winds and winds around. There is a guard at the entrance, so only the people who live there and their guests can come on the street. The club is in the center of the development and it is called the Highland Park Room. I guess whoever named things in the development wasn't that creative. Mostly older people live there, and practically everyone was going to the club for the holiday dinner. Mom was right about people going there early; even at four thirty I could see people were already arriving at the Highland Park Room.

Haley came over and sat down next to me. "Only seven hours until it's a new year," she said.

"It's more than that," I said.

"Well, when we get to dinner, it will be only seven hours until the new year," she said. "Guess what I told Dad the other night?"

"What?"

"I said, 'See you next year.' Get it?"

"I get it," I said.

"Aren't I funny?" she asked.

"A riot," I told her. Haley grinned even though I was being sarcastic.

Twenty minutes later Mom was also ready to go. "Ma," Mom called. But Grandma didn't answer her. "Haley," Mom said, "go tell Grandma we're all ready."

Haley skipped away toward Grandma's room. She was in her favorite purple skirt with no jeans underneath, since it was so warm in Florida. I was wearing a skirt too, but at least it was a jean skirt. I hoped Grandma wouldn't mind, because she likes us to get dressed up when we go to the club.

Haley came back over to us without Grandma. "Grandma can't find her keys," she said. "She thought they were in her purse but they're not there."

"Ma," Mom called again.

Grandma walked out of her room wringing her hands. "I'm so stupid," she said.

"It's all right, Ma," Mom said. "We'll find them."

"Oh, I'm so stupid," Grandma said again.

"Mom, why does Grandma keep saying that?" Haley said.

"It's hard to live alone," Mom told her. She got up and put her arm around Grandma's shoulder. "Let's worry about it later, Ma. Where are the spare keys?" Even though Mom was the daughter and Grandma was her mother, Mom acted like she was the grown-up. I wondered if Mom would be like Grandma when she got older. She would be alone too, since Dad was gone and Haley and I would grow up and move out. Maybe that's why lately I had felt like I had to take care of Mom.

The spare keys were in a dish by the front door, and Grandma's keys were right next to them. "You see," Mom told her. "I knew we'd find them."

"But I never put my keys there," Grandma said.

"Well, this time you did," Mom said. "Come on. You don't want to be late for dinner."

We walked across the street to the club. Grandma didn't say anything about my jean skirt, maybe because losing her keys had distracted her. Haley skipped up the sidewalk in front of the club. "Give our name to the host," Mom told her.

"Table for Vivian Woods," Haley said in her most grown-up voice. Vivian Woods is Grandma's name—we have to use her name to go anywhere in Highland Park.

"Right this way," the host said.

I had never seen the club so crowded. The host seated us at a table at the far side of the room. There was a big buffet set up in the middle. Grandma said not to take too much food, because we could go back as often as we wanted and there was no reason to waste. Haley and I stood to get food, but before we had a chance to leave the table, two other women walked up to our table. "Oh, Vivi, your girls!" one of them said. She pinched Haley's cheek hard. "I just love your freckles." Haley rubbed her cheek, which was turning red.

"Haley, say thank you," Grandma told her.

"Thanks," Haley muttered, and then walked over to Mom and hid behind her. I used to do that when I was little, but Haley is not the kind of kid to be shy and hide behind Mom. I think she just wanted to make sure she didn't get pinched anymore. I had never been so happy to not have freckles.

We finally got our food, but eating it was interrupted a bunch of times. Grandma was so happy to have us there. She forgot all about losing her keys and she kept seeing other people she wanted to introduce us to. It was kind of annoying, because it meant that we had to keep getting up in the middle of dinner and follow Grandma across the room to yet another old couple she wanted us to meet. But Mom said we had to do it for Grandma.

"This has been my best New Year's," Grandma said when we got back to our table after meeting another one of her friends.

"How come?" Haley said.

"Because my family is here," Grandma said. "Come here and give me a hug."

Fifteen

Dear Katie,

Happy New Year! We're in Florida now. We've been here
since Wednesday and now it's Saturday. It's really nice to be
away from all the stuff in New York—you know, the stuff
with Jessie—even if it's just for a few days. In Florida I
can pretend that everything is the same as before. My only
problem here is that my grandmother thinks it's too cold
for Haley and me to go to the pool. There's a pool at the
development where my grandmother lives, and I keep telling
her there are other kids there and their grandmothers are
letting them swim. But Grandma doesn't care. She said, "If
other grandmothers were letting their grandchildren jump

*off the Brooklyn Bridge, I wouldn't let you." I think that
is a pretty dumb thing to say. It's not like I'm asking to do
anything crazy like that! Besides, it's so warm out that I'm
practically sweating every time we walk outside. But my
grandmother says that there's a chill in the air and I should
wear a sweater.*

*Anyway, we're leaving tomorrow so I'll write you again when
I'm back in freezing New York.*

Sincerely,

Sophie

It wasn't until Sunday, our last day in Florida, that
Grandma finally agreed it was warm enough to go in the
pool. We went down to the club for Sunday brunch, and the
big thermometer outside said it was eighty degrees. "Haley,"
I called. "Haley, look!"

"Does that mean it's warm enough?" Haley asked. I
looked over at Mom to make sure she wasn't going to say no.

"What do you say, Ma?" Mom said to Grandma. "I think
it's warm enough, don't you?"

"If it's still eighty after we eat," Grandma said.

"All *right*," I said.

Haley ran ahead into the club and gave Grandma's name to the host. "Right this way, Mrs. Woods," the host said, which Haley thought was hysterical.

"He doesn't really think Haley's name is Mrs. Woods," I whispered to Mom.

"I know," Mom whispered back.

We sat at a table by the window. I didn't even need to look at the menu—after eating at the club for four days in a row, I knew exactly what I wanted: a grilled cheese sandwich with extra crispy french fries. So while Haley, Mom, and Grandma decided what they were going to eat, I looked around to see if anyone we knew was also at the club. I really wanted to make sure that none of Grandma's cheek-pinching friends were there. Even though they had stuck to Haley's cheeks on New Year's Eve, I knew they might attack me, too, if they saw us. I looked to the left and saw we were all clear, and then I turned to the right.

"Mom," I said. "Look! Jackie and Vicki are here!" Jackie and Vicki were girls we always saw when we were in Florida for spring break, but I hadn't known that they came to Florida for New Year's, too. Jackie was one year younger than me, and Vicki was one year older. Vicki's real name was Victoria, and secretly I called her Tori, for Tori Amos, since Tori can be a nickname for Victoria too. But out loud I called her Vicki, like everyone else did.

Jackie and Vicki's grandparents also lived in Highland

Park, but the girls lived in Illinois, so we never saw them during the year. Every time we were in Florida, we saw one another every day. It was fun to be friends with people who didn't really know anything about our real life. They had met Jessie because she had sometimes come to Florida with us, but they knew me better, and they didn't know anything bad about me. I could pretend that I was the most popular girl in school.

"Where are they?" Haley asked.

"There," I pointed. They were wearing bathing suits, which is something Grandma never let Haley and me do in the club. She thought we always should be dressed for lunch. Jackie and Vicki had pulled their hair back into ponytails. The tips of their ponytails were wet from the pool. I told Mom what I wanted to order, and then I ran over to them. We made plans to meet at the pool after lunch. I could hardly wait for everyone to finish eating. Mom and Grandma took so long to eat their sandwiches, but finally everyone was done. Grandma signed for our meal and Haley and I ran home and quickly changed into our bathing suits.

"Come on," I called to Mom. "We're ready to go." I'm a pretty good swimmer and I don't really need Mom to watch me, but there's a rule at the Highland Park pool that kids under sixteen are not allowed to be there alone.

"I'm almost ready," Mom said.

Haley and I went to wait on the porch. I looked across

the street toward the club. I couldn't see the pool, though, because the clubhouse itself was right in front of it. I was sure Jackie and Vicki were already in the pool, and each second that I waited for Mom seemed to last even longer than usual. Finally Mom came out onto the porch. Grandma stood by the screen door. "Don't forget to wear sunblock, girls," she said.

"They know, Ma," Mom said.

"I mean you too, Andrea," Grandma said. "The last thing you need is skin cancer."

"You're going to get cancer?" Haley said.

"No, of course not," Mom said. She turned to Grandma. "I can take care of myself," she said. "We'll be back in a couple hours."

We got to the pool and dumped all our stuff on one of the lounge chairs. Mom never swam with us and she spread a towel out so she could lie down and get tan. She said she didn't like swimming because she didn't like to get her hair wet, but Dad once told me that Mom was afraid of the water because she fell off a boat when she was young. If that had happened to me, I know Mom would have told me to get back into the water. But she never made herself do things she didn't want to. She turned her chair toward the pool so she could watch us.

"Are you sure you won't come in?" Haley asked her.

"Maybe I'll come in later," Mom said. I knew that meant no, but Haley thought that meant Mom might really come into the pool. I shaded my eyes with my hand and spotted Jackie and Vicki over by the deep end. "Jackie! Vicki!" I yelled. They looked up and waved.

"Wait, Sophie," Mom said. "Put some sunblock on first."

"Yeah, you don't want to get cancer," Haley said.

"Don't you start too," Mom told her. "You're too young to worry like Grandma."

I took the bottle of sunblock from Mom and squeezed some onto my hands. I rubbed it into my legs and arms. "Can I go now?" I asked Mom, and she nodded. I ran over to Jackie.

"Don't run, missy," someone called. I turned and saw the woman who had pinched Haley's cheeks on New Year's Eve. She was sitting under a big umbrella that blocked all the sun. "You may fall," she told me. Old people worry about everything. But I stopped running and just walked quickly the rest of the way.

"Good, you're here," Jackie said. "Now we can start the races."

"Hold on," Vicki said. "We have to wait for Haley." Even though Vicki was closer to my age, she liked Haley best. I think she thought Jackie and I were too babyish, but it didn't bother her that Haley was even younger. Whenever we played games in teams, Vicki always picked Haley. It wasn't that I minded being on Jackie's team. I just wished Vicki would want to be on my team too.

Haley came over after Mom finished rubbing her down with sunblock. She hadn't rubbed the lotion into her face all the way and there was a little white glob by the side of her nose. Even though I knew it was just sunblock, it looked gross and I didn't want to touch it. I rubbed the side of my nose to signal to Haley, but she didn't notice. "What are we playing?" she asked.

"We're having swimming races," Vicki told her.

"Can I race too?" Haley asked.

"Of course," Vicki said.

Vicki said she and Haley could race each other first. They jumped into the pool. Jackie and I were the judges, so we sat on the edge with our legs dangling in the water. "On your marks, get set, go!" Jackie shouted.

Haley kicked off from the back wall and swam as fast as she could to the other side. Vicki was a really fast swimmer. I watched her move underwater and I knew that if I were racing her, she would definitely beat me. She came up for air just before she reached us and turned around to see where Haley was. Then she waited until Haley had nearly touched the wall before she swam the last couple strokes. I knew she did it just to let Haley win. It wasn't fair, but I didn't say anything. I didn't want Vicki to think I was a baby.

"I won! I won!" Haley shouted. I noticed that the glob of lotion on Haley's face had rubbed off in the water, so it no longer looked like there was snot by her nose.

"You were really fast," Vicki told her.

Since Haley had won, she was in the next race against me. I jumped in and held on to the side of the pool. "On your marks, get set, go!" Jackie shouted. I kicked off the back wall and swam as fast as I could. I didn't let Haley win. "Wow, Sophie," Haley said after we had finished, "you're even faster than me." She looked so proud of me that I sort of felt bad for not letting her win.

We held a few more races, and then Vicki suggested that we have a diving competition. Dad had taught Haley and me to dive the last time we were in Florida. Haley had a tendency toward belly flops. She would stand at the edge of the pool with her arms up and knees bent, in the perfect diver's stance. Then she would lean forward and fall straight into the pool so that her body hit the water at the same time that her hands and arms did. I was pretty good at making sure my hands hit the water first. The hardest part for me was remembering to straighten my legs after I jumped.

Jackie called her dad over so he could be the judge. Vicki went first because she was oldest. When it was my turn, I walked to the edge of the pool, letting my toes go a little bit over the edge. Then I swung my arms up, took a deep breath, and dove in. I tried to remember to straighten my

legs. I was concentrating so hard on my legs that I accidentally swallowed some water and I tried not to cough too hard
when I came up to the surface.

"Impeccable," Jackie's dad said. I swallowed to try
to make the choking feeling go away. I wasn't sure what
"impeccable" meant, but I didn't want to ask. I wanted Vicki
to think I was smart. Besides, Jackie's dad was smiling when
he said it and I was pretty sure it was something good.

I'll check what it means with Dad, I thought. That was when I
realized that maybe I would see him when we got home. The
thought of it made me so scared, and I wasn't sure I could
do it. *It was like going back into the water after you fall off a boat.*
I smiled even though there was still water up my nose, and
climbed out of the pool to watch Jackie take her turn diving.

Sixteen

We got home late on Sunday night. Mom gave Haley the key to check the mail before we went upstairs. I hoped there would be a letter from Katie. After all, it had been more than a month since her last letter. According to Ms. Brisbin, we were supposed to write each other at least once a month, so Katie really owed me a letter. But maybe she was too busy to write me. Or maybe Katie had decided not to write to me because I wrote her too much. Maybe she didn't like me at all, just like Jessie.

"Sophie, you got something," Haley said. She waved an envelope back and forth in front of my face. I recognized my name written in Katie's handwriting.

"All right. Gimme that," I said, and I grabbed it from Haley.

"Can I read it too?" she asked.

"No," I said. "Mail is private."

"But it's not fair," she whined. "I never get anything in the mail. Please?"

"No," I said. I held the envelope above my head so Haley couldn't reach it.

"Mom!" Haley called.

"Girls. That's enough," Mom said. "Let's get upstairs and go to bed."

We rode up in the elevator. Mom told us we were over-tired and needed to go to bed right away because we had school the next day. I don't know why she thought she knew how I felt. Maybe Haley was whiny and overtired, but I wasn't at all. When Mom wasn't looking, I got the flashlight from the hall closet. Of course if I'd had my own room I wouldn't have needed the flashlight. Luckily, Haley really was tired and she fell asleep quickly. As soon as I heard Haley's breathing deepen in the next bed, I opened Katie's letter, careful not to spill any of the confetti I knew would be in the envelope.

Dear Sophie,

Thanks for all your letters. I'm sorry I haven't written in a while. I've been really busy finishing up everything for school

before vacation. The talent show was awesome, by the way. Everyone laughed at all the right parts and they told Jake and me that we could take our show on the road.

How are you? I hope you're having a good vacation and that you made up with your friend Jessie. Everything here in California is good. Julie and I are planning a New Year's party. My parents are going out. Julie thinks she is babysitting me, but really she is only two years older than me, so I think we're pretty equal. Anyway, Julie and I each get to invite a friend over. We're going to decorate the house and make a cake so it will seem like a party even if it's just four people. I think it will be a lot of fun as long as Julie cheers up. She has been in a really bad mood lately because she hates school, but she's getting happier now because it's vacation.

So I bet it's really cold now in New York, right? It's still pretty warm here. I wish it would be cold enough to snow at least one day out of the winter! I haven't even seen snow in three years. But that will change because my dad is going to take Julie and me skiing in Lake Tahoe next week. We've never gone before, but my dad used to ski when he was in college and he's going to teach us. Julie's afraid, but I'm not. Dad said we'll start out on the easiest trail, but I bet I'll be able to go down a really hard trail by the end of our trip! That's my goal, at least.

I hope you have a good vacation and I hope you write me back soon.

Sincerely,

Katie

Katie was lucky—my parents would never let me stay home alone until midnight, even if I did have an older sister there with me. But I thought I would be too afraid to be home alone anyway. Katie definitely seemed to be a braver kind of person. I folded the letter up and slipped it back into the envelope. Then I got out of bed as quietly as I could and put the letter into my desk drawer. Haley never woke up.

Seventeen

✳ ✳ ✳

The next morning we had to go back to school. It was as if vacation had never happened. Haley had ballet after school so I walked home by myself. I made up my mind that I was going to finally call Dad, and when I got upstairs, I called him at his office before I could change my mind. My heart was beating fast as the phone rang. I hoped he wasn't mad at me about New Year's. After two rings Dad answered the phone in his work voice. "Jack Turner," he said.

I took a deep breath. "It's me, Dad," I said. "It's Sophie."

"Oh, Soph," Dad said, and I knew he wasn't mad at all. Even though it was a Monday, Dad said he would come to take me to dinner that night if I wanted, just the two of us. Haley wasn't even invited.

"I have to check with Mom," I told him. "I'll call you back." I went into Mom's office. She was reading résumés at her desk, and I sat in one of the chairs that her clients sit in.

"I called Dad," I told her.

Mom put down the papers she was holding. "Do you feel okay about it?" she asked.

I nodded. "He said he wants to take me to dinner tonight," I said.

"Do you want to go?"

"Am I allowed to go?" I asked. "I know it's not a Tuesday."

"Honey," Mom said, "of course you're allowed."

"Are you mad?" I asked.

"Why would I be mad?" I didn't know what to say so I shrugged my shoulders.

"Sophie," Mom said, "you don't have to stay away from Dad for me. You know that, don't you?" I sort of knew it, but I was still afraid of hurting Mom's feelings. I just shrugged my shoulders again.

"So that's what this was about," Mom said softly.

"Sometimes I hear you crying," I told her.

"Oh, Sophie," Mom said. She got up from her desk and came over to hug me. "Why don't you call Dad and tell him to pick you up after work," she said.

Later that night the intercom buzzed and I knew that Dad was waiting in the lobby for me. I got my jacket from the hall

closet and went to the elevator. Dad was talking to the doorman when I got downstairs. But when he saw me walking
toward him, he turned to me and opened his arms. I started
running. Dad bent down and lifted me up. I was glad no one
was around to see.

Dad said we could go anywhere I wanted to eat. There
are a lot of restaurants near where we live, but my favorite
place to eat is a pizza place downtown. They fire the pizza
in a brick oven and the crust gets really thin and crisp. It's
Dad's favorite pizza place too, so I knew he wouldn't be upset
that I picked somewhere kind of far away. We walked to the
subway together. After all those weeks of not seeing Dad, it
was like nothing had changed when I did see him. Dad put
his arm around me while we waited on the subway platform.
There's always a rush of air when the train pulls up, and I hate
it because my hair flies all over the place and the dust sometimes gets in my eyes. I pressed my face into Dad's shoulder.

When we got to the restaurant, we ordered a mushroom
and extra cheese pizza, just like we always did. Dad told
me that he didn't get to take any time off of work during
New Year's because Ed Simon had gone away and forgotten
papers in the office. He called Dad on New Year's Day and
made him go into the office. "There I was," Dad said. "I was
already missing my girls, and then I had to be all alone at the
office on a national holiday. I thought I would defenestrate
my desk chair."

"What does 'defenestrate' mean?" I asked.

"It means to throw something out a window," he said. "Now you use it in a sentence."

"If the pizza doesn't come soon, I'm going to defenestrate myself," I said. And just at that moment the waiter came over with our pizza. It was still so hot from the oven that the cheese was bubbling.

Dad laughed. "Perfect timing," he told the waiter. "You just saved my daughter's life."

I remembered how Marachel had talked about visiting her father, like it was so normal, like nothing was wrong. *So this is how it is when your parents are divorced*, I thought. *It still feels okay to be with them.*

Dad walked me home after dinner. The doorman opened the door for me when he saw me. But before I walked in, I wrapped my arms around Dad's middle. "See you tomorrow for dinner," I said.

"I can't wait," Dad said.

I turned to go inside. I knew Dad was going to stand and watch until I got into the elevator and the doors closed. I turned back around. "Hey, Dad," I called. "What does 'impeccable' mean?"

"It means perfect," Dad said. "Just like you." I smiled and headed for the elevator. When I got upstairs, I pulled a piece of stationery out of my desk drawer to write back to Katie. "Dear Katie," I wrote, "I didn't tell you this before but my parents are getting divorced. It was really hard at first but it's getting better." I told her about going to dinner with Dad after not seeing him for so long. I wondered if she would think I was brave. "I hope you had fun skiing with your dad and Julie. Write me back and tell me all about it." I signed my letter, "Sincerely, Sophie" just like always, but this letter seemed more important than all my other letters.

Eighteen

A couple of weeks later Ms. Brisbin announced that she was going to break us up into pairs so we could write reports on the chapters in *To Kill a Mockingbird*. We had finally finished reading it. "The only fair way to do this," Ms. Brisbin said, "is for me to assign you randomly." She had all our names on scraps of paper in a bowl, and she picked two at a time to determine the pairs. I sat with my hands folded in my lap and I could feel my palms starting to sweat. There were a lot of people in my class that I did not want to work with. Ms. Brisbin reached into the bowl. "Alyssa and Samantha," she said. She made a note in her grade book and then reached back into the bowl. "Lindsay and Jillian."

I let out a breath. *Thank goodness I'm not with Lindsay,* I thought.

Ms. Brisbin reached back into the bowl. "Jessie and Sophie," she said. I squeezed my hands together tighter. They were sticky from my sweat. Jessie let out a low groan, but she was so quiet about it that I didn't think anyone heard but me. I kept my eyes on Ms. Brisbin because I was afraid to look at Jessie. I knew she was watching me with her eyes narrowed into little slits, even though I hadn't done anything wrong. Ms. Brisbin finished making up the pairs. "Any questions?" she asked.

Lindsay's hand shot up and Ms. Brisbin nodded toward her. "Can we trade partners?" Lindsay asked.

"No," Ms. Brisbin said. "Absolutely no trading. You can work alone on this if you have a good reason, but remember I'm assigning work meant for two people, and it will be a lot to tackle by yourself." Lindsay sat back and crossed her arms. I was too nervous about being paired with Jessie to be happy that Lindsay was upset about her partner too.

That afternoon I had to walk home with Haley. She was late getting out because she couldn't find her mittens. By the time we got outside, Jessie was on the corner with Lindsay, Amy, Melissa, and a bunch of the Dorr boys. I took Haley's hand, lowered my head, and walked past them, hoping they wouldn't see me. But then someone called out. "Hey, Sophie!"

It was a boy's voice, of course. I knew Jessie and the other girls would never call me, and I wanted to pretend that I hadn't heard, but Haley said, "Someone's calling you." I shook my head and pulled her hand harder, hoping she would understand.

"Hey," the voice said again. "Sophie! Sophie the Shrimp!" I turned and looked up, and there was Madden. Jessie was next to him, glaring at me.

Haley saw her too. "Hey, Jessie!" she called.

"Hi, Haley," Jessie said. She smiled a little bit, but she still didn't say hello to me.

"Come on, Haley," I said. "We have to go."

I got home and went into my room. I decided to work on my article for the school paper. I was supposed to write about the student art exhibit in the lobby at Victor. It was better than doing my homework—especially the *To Kill a Mockingbird* project. Every time I thought of *To Kill a Mockingbird* I felt like I was getting sick. I really did like the book, and I hated how everything with Jessie was ruining it for me. Maybe there was a way for Mom to write me a note so I could get out of working with Jessie. Ms. Brisbin had said we needed to have a good reason to work alone. Was the fact that Jessie hated me a good enough reason? I wouldn't care if I didn't have a partner at all and I had to do it all by myself. I pulled a piece of paper out of my desk and tried to work on my article. I had to think of a word to describe the colors of the paintings in the lobby besides the word "colorful." Haley wandered in with a paper heart that she'd made at school and hung it on our bedroom door.

"Do you like it?" Haley asked. I was lying on my bed trying to concentrate and I didn't really care about Haley's artwork.

"It's fine," I said without looking up.

"Valentine's Day is next month," she said. "Do you know what that means?"

Haley didn't seem to notice that I wasn't paying attention to her, and she continued. "It means it's my birthday soon . . . and your birthday soon." I noticed that Haley listed her birthday before mine, even though mine was actually two weeks before hers. "I haven't even made my present list yet," she said. She climbed onto my bed with a pad of paper and a pen. "You can tell me your list too," she said. "I'll be the secretary and write everything down."

But I didn't think I was going to ask for any birthday presents. I remembered hearing Mom and Dad fighting and Mom saying we wouldn't have enough money if Dad moved out. Well, now Dad had moved out. They had already just spent money on our Christmas presents. If we made them buy us too much, maybe we would have to leave Victor and go to a school that wasn't so expensive. I had been at Victor

since kindergarten. Even if I wasn't friends with Jessie anymore, I didn't want to think about having to go to school
anywhere else. I shoved Haley and she tumbled off the bed.
"Do that on your own bed," I told Haley. "I'm working. And
I'm not making a list this year."

Haley went over to her bed, but she kept talking. "How
are Mom and Dad going to know what to get you if you
don't make a list?" she asked. I ignored her and she continued. "I know what I'm going to ask for." She bent toward the
paper and said out loud as she wrote, "Daddy back home."

"That's a dumb thing to put on your list," I said from
behind my paper. "You know you're not going to get it."

"It's not dumb," Haley said. "Dad said he would give me
whatever I wanted!"

"That's not what he meant," I said.

From behind the paper I heard Haley start to sniffle. I
figured she was just pretending to cry to get my attention.
"But it's the most important thing on my list," she said. "It's
not fair. You got to live with Dad until you were eleven, but
I'm only seven. I should get four more years!"

I had never thought about it that way, but Haley was
right. I lowered my paper and looked over at her. She wiped
her face with the back of her hand. Her eyes were glossy
and her cheeks were flushed. She really was crying after all.
Maybe it was harder to be Haley than I'd always thought.

"Come here," I said to Haley.

Haley slid of her bed and came over to me. She snuggled up against me and I petted her head as though she were a dog. "Don't cry," I told her.

"I can't help it," she said. "I just want it to be like it was before."

I knew exactly how she felt. It had taken me months to get used to Dad living somewhere else. "At least you get two sets of toys," I reminded her.

Haley was quiet for a few seconds. She wrapped her arm around my waist and I hugged her back. Finally she pulled away and lifted her head. "Do you think I could ask for two Samantha dolls—one for Dad's house and one for Mom's?" she asked.

I didn't know what to say. Two dolls cost a lot of money, but I wanted her to stop crying. "I guess you could put that on your list," I said.

Haley got up to get the pad and pen. "Here," she said. "You write it down."

I sat up and balanced the pad in my lap. I wrote "Haley's Birthday List" across the top of the page and then wrote "Two Samantha dolls" on the first line.

"Anything else?" I asked.

"Some new music," she said.

"New music," I said as I wrote it down. "Check."

Haley smiled. "Leg warmers," she said.

"Leg warmers?"

"Yeah, to wear with my skirts instead of having to wear jeans."

"Okay," I said, and I added them to the list. "Leg warmers, check."

"Some new clothes and books. Oh, and some clothes for Samantha, too."

I wrote down everything that Haley said, even though her list got kind of long. She had stopped crying completely, so I thought it was okay to tell her she was asking for too much. "You're not going to be able to get everything," I told her.

"How come?"

"Because it costs too much," I said.

"How do you know how much it costs?"

"I can just tell," I said. "And anyway, we really have to save money for important things."

"All right, I won't ask for anything else," Haley said. "Now it's time to make your list."

"I told you," I said, "I'm not making a list."

"Well, I want to show Mom mine," Haley said. "Come on." She pulled my arm.

Mom was in the living room. Haley ran up to her. "I made my list, Mom," she said. "Give it to her, Sophie."

I handed Haley's list to Mom and she looked it over. "That's some list," Mom told her.

"Sophie said that I can't have everything."

"Why not?"

"Because we don't have enough money," Haley said.

"Sophie," Mom said, and I knew I had made her mad. "You have to let me be the mom."

"But what if we run out of money?" I said.

"Honestly, Sophie," Mom said. "You need to stop worrying so much. Have I ever let anything bad happen to you?" I didn't know what to say. After all, she had let Dad leave. I knew she couldn't have done anything to stop it, but still . . . What if the same thing happened with money?

"Sophie still needs to make her list," Haley said.

"No, she doesn't," Mom said. I wondered if that was my punishment.

"How come?" Haley asked.

"Because I already know what she's getting," Mom said.

"What?" I asked.

"You'll see," Mom said.

I went back to my room to do my work, but it was hard to concentrate. I wasn't sure Mom could take care of everything on her own, and I didn't want to pressure her about money at all. But there were definitely things I wanted for my birthday. It wasn't really fair for Haley to get things and not me. Besides, if Mom was going to get me something anyway, maybe I should tell her what I really wanted.

The phone rang and I knew it had to be Dad. He always called around the same time at night when he got home from work. Ever since we'd gotten back from Florida, I had been getting on the phone to say hello. Usually I even went with Haley to see him too.

"Sophie, it's for you," Mom called.

I was right. I thought maybe I would ask Dad about the money stuff, and I picked up the phone. "Daddy," I said, purposely trying to sound like a baby. I was hoping I could trick him into thinking I was Haley.

"Sophie?" a voice said—a girl's voice. I felt my face flush.

"Jessie?" I asked.

"Yeah, it's me," she said. I could hardly believe it was her. I guess Liz wouldn't write her a note to get out of working with me.

"What do you want?" I asked.

"I didn't want to call," she said. "But we have to work on this stupid project. You know we're supposed to have an outline of our report by Friday."

"Did you even read the book?" I asked.

"Part of it," Jessie said. I wondered if that was even true. I had always filled Jessie in on the books we were reading in school because she hated reading. I didn't mind helping her back then. But now we weren't even friends anymore and I didn't want to do all the work.

"Did you at least read the chapter we're supposed to do?"

"I didn't get that far," Jessie said. I didn't know what to say. I could hear Jessie breathing loudly and impatiently on the other end of the phone. "Look," she said finally. "I was really mad at you. You shouldn't have danced with Madden Preston. You knew I liked him."

"But it wasn't like that," I said. "I don't even want a boyfriend. I didn't even see him again until today on the street."

"I know," Jessie said.

"How do you know?" I asked.

"Madden asked me about you the other day. He said he hadn't seen you around in a while."

Even though I didn't want him to be my boyfriend, it sort of made me feel better to hear that he had asked about me. But I knew better than to say that to Jessie. "Did you tell him we're not friends anymore?" I asked her.

"No," Jessie said. "It's none of his business."

"Yeah, I guess," I said.

Jessie was quiet for a few seconds. Then she said, "You know you're still the only one I ever showed my photo album to."

I wondered if that meant we still were friends after all. I didn't want to ask in case I was wrong, so I didn't say anything at all.

"Sophie," Jessie said, "are you still there?"

"Yeah," I said.

"So," she said, "will you do the outline?"

"The whole thing?" I asked.

"I told you I didn't read that far in the book," she said.

"Besides, you know you're better at these things. You're the one who writes for the Victor paper."

"So you're not going to help at all?" I asked.

"No," Jessie said. "I just told you that."

"We're not friends anymore, are we?" I asked. But I knew I didn't even have to ask her. Jessie had only mentioned the photo album to try to get her way. If we really had been friends, she would have come over so we could work on the outline together. Even if she hadn't read the chapter, she would have offered to get my favorite black-and-white cookies from the deli and keep me company while I wrote it. I didn't even wait for Jessie to answer me. "You have to do half of it at least," I said. "Or else I'll just ask Ms. Brisbin if I can work alone."

"Sophie, please," Jessie said. Something about the way Jessie said "please" made it sound like she needed me. The funny thing was that I didn't feel like I needed her anymore. I remembered being at the dance a few months before. I was so afraid of losing Jessie that had I walked away from Madden and let her get her way. If she had asked me to write the outline back then, I would have said yes right away. I would have written it, and put both our names on it, and hoped it would make her want to be my friend. I was different now. I wasn't so afraid anymore.

"No," I said. "I mean it."

"You know, this is exactly why we're not friends anymore,"

Jessie said hotly. "You only care about yourself."

I pictured Jessie with a smirk on her face and her eyes narrowed. I knew she was wrong about me. I knew none of it was my fault. But she wouldn't believe me if I told her. And I guess it didn't really matter anyway. The only thing that mattered was that we weren't friends anymore. I would miss her, but I was relieved, too. At least now it was over.

All of a sudden I didn't even want to be on the phone with Jessie anymore. I decided that after we hung up I would call Marachel. It seemed funny and I started to smile a little to myself—the whole reason I'd started hanging out with Marachel to begin with was because Jessie hadn't wanted to be with me. Now I wanted to hang up with Jessie so I could talk to Marachel. It wasn't the same as a best friend, but it was a lot better than someone who doesn't like you anymore. Maybe she'd want to make plans to see a movie over the weekend. Maybe Lily would want to come too. Maybe one day I'd feel as close to them as I used to feel to Jessie.

"I gotta go," I told Jessie. "Tell me tomorrow what you want to do." I heard her take a breath like she was going to say something back, but I hung up before she had a chance.

nineteen

Two weeks later Mom and Dad gave me my birthday present—my very own room. They hired someone to come in and build a wall where the dining room used to be. Mom pushed the dining room table against the wall in the living room. She said we could pull it out from the wall whenever we had company over for dinner.

It was ready four days before my actual birthday. I walked into my new room. My bed was in there, but there weren't any sheets on it yet. There was a small dresser that looked like an antique, and matching end tables on either side of the bed. I ran my finger along the top of one of the end tables. Everything was so clean and bare. Mom came in behind me. "What do you think?" she asked.

I turned around and around. It was about half the size of the room I shared with Haley. I had to climb over the bed to get to the dresser. There was no carpeting on the floor. It was perfect.

"It must have cost so much money," I said.

"Not so much," Mom said.

I shook my head, knowing she was lying. "Mom," I said, "they built a whole new wall. It had to be expensive."

"You're right that we have to be careful with money," Mom said. "But it's okay to spend on things that are important. Dad and I think you are old enough now that your privacy is important."

"I love it," I said. "I really love it."

"I picked out the tables and the dresser at an antiques dealer upstate. They said if you didn't like them, we could bring them back."

"Oh, no," I said. "They look great."

"I'm so glad," Mom said. I wondered if Haley would get a dog now that I had my own room. But maybe Haley didn't even remember that she had wanted one. It hadn't even been on her birthday list.

"Hey, Mom," Haley called from the other room. "Can we order dinner now?"

Mom kissed my cheek. "I'll come in later and help you make the bed," she said.

I stood in the center of the room and turned around and

around until I was dizzy, and then I flopped onto the bed. I watched the room still spinning. Everything I saw was all mine—the walls, the floor, the bed, the end tables, the dresser.

Even though Mom had said she would help me make the bed, I wanted to fix my room up as soon as possible, so I didn't wait for her. I stood up and went to the hall closet to get fresh sheets. I stretched them out across the bed, folded the sides, tucked them under, and pulled my comforter onto the bed and arranged the pillows. Then I ran back down the hall to my old room to get some of my stuff. I lined up my books on top of the dresser and put my important papers in one of the end tables, like my letters from Dad and Katie. I tacked my *To Kill a Mockingbird* book report up on the bulletin board above my dresser. Ms. Brisbin had written "Outstanding Work A+" across the top in big red letters. Mom had called Ms. Brisbin to talk to her about the changes in our family and had told her I'd be more comfortable working alone. I couldn't believe I had gotten an A+ even though I'd done the report all by myself. It looked perfect pinned up on the bulletin board. Just then, I heard Mom calling me. "Sophie, dinner!" she said.

I knew I had to thank Dad for my new room too, so when we finished dinner, I took the cordless phone into my new room to call him. He answered after the first ring.

"Guess where I am?" I said.

"South America," Dad said.

"Dad," I said, "be serious. Guess."

"I know where you are," he said. "What do you think?"

"It's the greatest. It's the absolute most impeccable present I've ever gotten," I said.

"You're welcome," Dad said.

"Thank you. I was just about to say thank you."

"I have one more surprise for you, if you want it."

"What?"

"Well, since you and I missed out on so much time together, I thought you might want to come with me on my next business trip. I have to go to San Francisco for a deposition, but it should take only half a day. You can hang out in the hotel while I'm there and we can stay over the weekend."

"Just you and me?"

"Just you and me," he said. "If you want to come."

"I think I do," I said. "I really think I do."

"Good," Dad said. "I'll get the tickets in the morning."

I looked around my new room. Things change and you get used to them. I was getting used to my new room already.

The next day I left school a little late, and when I walked by the corner, Madden Preston and his friends were already there, talking to Jessie and Lindsay. I didn't slow down to talk to them, but I didn't put my head down and start to walk faster to get away from them either. "Hey, Sophie!" Madden called. I looked up. Jessie wouldn't meet my eyes, but Madden was smiling right at me.

"Hey," I said.

"How are you?" he asked.

"I'm great," I told him, and then I started laughing because I realized it was true.

"Cool," Madden said. "So I'll see you around, right?"

"See you around," I said.

When I got home, I realized I had been so busy with my new room I'd forgotten to write to Katie to tell her I was going to California. I pulled a piece of stationery out of my desk. I didn't have much time to write because I had to change and meet Marachel and Lily in Central Park to go skating, but I wrote her a quick letter.

Dear Katie,

My birthday is next week and I'm going to be twelve. I already got two presents, even though I'm still eleven years old right now. The first one is a new room that I don't have to share with Haley. And the second one is the one I really have to tell you about. . . . My dad is taking me to San Francisco

in May, *so I will get to meet you in person! I really can't
wait to see you!*

*Well, I've got to go now because I'm going skating tonight
in Central Park. I'll get you a souvenir from the rink so you
can have something from New York.*

Sincerely,

Sophie

✱ ✱ ✱

Sincerely,
Katie

✱ ✱ ✱

For Lindsay Aaronson & Amy Bressler,
my very first readers

One

* * *

The whole reason I had the idea was because I was writing a letter to Sophie. Last fall, my social studies teacher, Mrs. Katz, signed our class up for something called Pen Pals Across America. All of our names were entered into a big database, and we were each matched up with a pen pal who lived in another state. I was matched up with Sophie Turner from New York City. I went there once with my parents and Julie, my sister, and it was great. There are about a million stores and restaurants crammed into the city and there are always things to do. We stayed in a hotel on Fifth Avenue, which is a pretty famous street, and everything we needed was right there when we walked out the door. It's the same for Sophie. All she has to do is cross two streets and she's at

school. I think the people who live in New York City probably don't ever have to leave, unless they want to visit someone who lives somewhere else.

My family lives all the way across the country in Redwood
City, California, which as far as I can tell is nothing like New
York. For one thing, most people in New York live in apartments, not houses. Also, in Redwood City we need to drive
most places. School is only half a mile away. Sometimes Dad
drives us, but Julie and I walk most days. Still, it's a much
longer walk than the walk Sophie has to her school. And
if we need to go to the supermarket or library or even to
my best friend Jake's house, we need to drive there. There
also aren't any skyscrapers in Redwood City like there are
in New York. Even in downtown Redwood City, most of the
buildings are only about two or three stories high.

Sophie and her dad are coming to California soon. I bet
I'm the only one in my class who's actually going to meet
her pen pal. Plus, I plan to visit Sophie in New York some-
day. Julie really wants to go back to New York too. In fact,
ever since we came back from New York, Julie has said that
she wants to live there permanently. She really likes fashion and movie stars, and they have a lot of both of those in
New York. But I would miss California too much, especially
our house at the top of the hill. When I was younger, Dad
would take me for walks in the woods behind our house and
I thought we were hiking through a jungle. Now I'm almost

twelve years old, and the trees that used to seem as tall as the New York skyscrapers just look like regular trees to me. Still, I love the smell of them in the backyard, and I don't think I could ever get used to sleeping in New York City with all the noise outside going all night long.

Mrs. Katz told us we should write to our pen pals once a month. At first I didn't always write as much as I was supposed to, even though Sophie did. Sometimes she wrote me about really private things. I got to know her really well even though we've never met in person, and now I write to her whenever anything important happens. She knows a lot about me, too. I don't know if anyone else in Mrs. Katz's class still writes to their pen pal, but I wrote to Sophie today during our free writing period because something important had happened.

Each Monday, Mrs. Katz picks two students to do reports on important current events. If you're picked you have to read the newspaper all week and then get up in front of the class on Friday and talk about the most important story you read.

Three weeks ago Mrs. Katz picked me to give one of the reports. I started looking through the paper that Monday night. My parents get two newspapers at home every day — the local Redwood City paper called the *Redwood City Daily News*, and also the *San Francisco Chronicle*. We live about a half hour away from San Francisco. It's one of the closest "big cities" to our house. In fact, whenever anyone in

Redwood City says they're going to "the city," they mean San Francisco. So it's a pretty important newspaper to get.

Anyway, I looked through both newspapers on Monday night. There were a lot of articles about things like the budget in Washington and some speech the president was making, but there wasn't anything at all that I wanted to report on. The problem was that usually the current events reports were really boring, and I wanted to do something interesting. Especially because Mrs. Katz had recently figured out that the other kids in the class didn't really listen to the current events reports, so she'd started giving us quizzes on them. I figured if I had a really cool report, people wouldn't mind listening to it, and then they'd thank me when they all got good grades. But it didn't look like that was going to happen.

"There's nothing good in these papers," I complained out loud to no one in particular. Mom was at the counter chopping carrots for a salad, and Julie was eating them off the counter instead of putting them into the salad bowl.

"Don't be ridiculous," Mom said. "There's plenty of important stuff in the paper every day."

"Nothing that kids in school want to hear about," I said.

"There are some really important debates going on about the health care system. You should report on that," Mom said.

"Mom," I said, "no offense, but no one wants to hear about that."

"Well, maybe they *should* hear about it. . . . No offense,"

Mom said. I should have known Mom wouldn't understand. I went up to my room and hoped there would be something better in the paper the next day.

And then something awful happened. There was a horrible earthquake in Mexico.

I happen to know a lot about earthquakes because we live in California. Earthquakes happen along fault lines in the earth's surface. There are a lot of fault lines in California. So far I've been in three earthquakes. Mom and Dad told Julie and me that we should go stand in a doorway whenever there's an earthquake. It's a good place to stand because it's very secure and can protect you if other things fall down around you. At school if there's an earthquake we're supposed to go under our desks for the same reason. If we're outside, we're supposed to crouch down onto the ground and hold our hands over our heads to protect our heads from things that might land on top of us. I've never been very scared of earthquakes because the ones I've been in haven't been too big. The worst thing that happened was the kitchen cabinets flew open and a bunch of dishes fell out and smashed on the floor. Then Mooner, our dog, walked into the kitchen and cut her paw on the glass before we were able to get it all cleaned up, and she needed four stitches. She cried when the vet sewed her up, and I thought that was pretty bad. But the earthquake in Mexico was completely different from anything I had ever been in. Thousands of people died.

I watched the news that night with my parents and Julie. They showed pictures of buildings burning. I saw people crying and holding up pictures of their family members who were caught in the rubble. Julie even started to cry.

Dad looked over and seemed surprised to see Julie and me sitting there. I think he had been paying so much attention to what was on television that he had forgotten we were even there. "Maybe you two shouldn't be watching this," he said.

"But, Dad," I said.

"No, really, Katie," Dad said. "This is grown-up stuff." Sometimes Dad forgets that Julie and I aren't kids anymore. I'm in sixth grade after all. And Julie's practically old enough to be in high school! She's a grade behind what she should be in school because of her dyslexia, which makes it hard for her to read. When she sees words and numbers on the page, they get all mixed up and backward. She needs extra help in school because of it and she had to repeat the third grade. Still, she's thirteen years old, and just because something on television was sad and scary didn't mean we should have to leave the room. Luckily, Mom agreed with me.

"Let them stay, Peter," Mom said. "It's important to watch." She turned to Julie and me. "But only if you want to."

I said I wanted to keep watching, and Julie said she did too, even though she was crying. Dad folded his arms across his chest and turned back to the television. I think sometimes he feels ganged-up on because he's the only boy in our house. Even Mooner is a girl. I try to do things that Dad likes so he doesn't feel left out. Even so, I wasn't going to leave the room just to make him feel better.

We watched the news reports about the earthquake until it was time to go to bed. During breakfast the next morning Dad brought the papers to the kitchen table to read. The earthquake was on the front page of both newspapers, and I knew what my report would be about. Mom had said it was important to watch. I thought it was important to talk about too.

I picked the article that was on the front page of the *San Francisco Chronicle* because the headline took up the entire top of the page. Mrs. Katz said it's called a banner headline. The whole class seemed to be paying close attention while I gave my report. This girl named Tesa gave the other report, and she talked about the earthquake too. Mrs. Katz was so sure that we all knew about it that she even skipped the usual current events quiz.

But then the weekend came. Dad drove Jake and me to this place called Sawyer Camp Trail so we could ride our bikes. It's this road along the reservoir where no cars are allowed, so people go there with bikes or skates, or even just to walk. Jake and I brought all sorts of food in our backpacks. We picnicked along the side of the road overlooking the water. There's a small island in the center of the reservoir that you can see from Sawyer Camp Trail. You can tell no one lives there—it's just filled up with trees. Jake and I had this idea to start a company called the Dynamic Duo. We're not sure yet what our company will do, but the island in the middle of the reservoir seemed like the perfect place for the Dynamic Duo headquarters. I told Jake about my plan, but he said it would never work. He said there are laws to protect the drinking water so we wouldn't be able to build an office on the island. Maybe he's right, but sometimes I think he just makes stuff like that up. Anyway, I sort of forgot all about the earthquake that weekend. The days continued to pass. Every so often I would see pictures of it on the news again, but it was nothing like those first few days with all the fires and the rubble. So it slipped to the back of my mind . . . until today, that is.

As usual Mrs. Katz had picked two people to give current events reports. A kid named Morgan went first. I hang out with him sometimes because he's on the track team with Jake. He reported on an election that was being held in another country. It was kind of boring because I had never heard of the candidates. Still, I tried to pay attention because it could be on a quiz. I pulled out a sheet of paper to take notes, but mostly I just doodled in the margins.

Morgan finished his report and a girl named Doriane stood up to give her report. I don't really know her. She's really quiet and shy, so I don't think anyone knows her so well. I'm not that quiet at all, but I get along with almost everyone. I might not be the most popular girl in my grade, like Julie is, but most people like me. I think it's because at school I'm sort of like a cheerleader. Not an actual cheer-leader—I'm not on the squad or anything, but I'm friendly and energetic, and I want everyone to be happy. Doriane walked past my desk to get to the front of the room and I moved my arm over the paper on my desk so she couldn't see my doodles. I didn't want her to think I wasn't going to pay attention to what she had to say.

She got to the front and cleared her throat. "My report is on a girl named Emily who was in the earthquake," she said softly.

"Try to speak up," Mrs. Katz said from the back of the room. "It's hard to hear you back here."

"Okay," Doriane said more loudly. "Anyway, Emily is from California and she went to Mexico with her parents and sister, Julie, and they were there when the earthquake hit." I noticed Doriane's voice had gone back to its usual soft tone. I leaned forward to hear her better in case we were quizzed on what she said. Doriane wrapped a strand of her hair around her index finger and tugged at it as she contin-ued talking. "Emily's in a hospital now in Mexico. Her medi-cal treatment so far has cost ten thousand dollars, but they think she'll make a full recovery. They don't know where any of her family is. They don't know if they're just buried in the rubble or if they died."

I was watching Doriane so at first I didn't notice that Jake had dropped a note into my lap. He sits next to me in social studies, and we're pretty good at passing notes without Mrs. Katz noticing. But now she was in the back of the room so we couldn't see her. I leaned forward on my desk and cupped Jake's note in my hand. Doriane continued her report. She said they were having a tough time in the region where the earthquake hit because all the resources were getting used up and there was so much damage. I didn't take any notes on what she said because I was concentrating too hard on trying to hear her, but that was okay because I knew I would remember it.

The thing is, usually you read things in the news and the next day they're onto the next story—but hearing Doriane's report made me realize the story of the earthquake was still going on and probably wouldn't end anytime soon. I was sure Emily wasn't the only kid missing her family.

Doriane finished and Mrs. Katz walked back to the front of the room and started writing on the board. I unfolded Jake's note in my lap. "What do you think of Doriane?" he'd written. I looked at him and shrugged. He bent down and started writing again. I crumbled his note and stashed it in my bag while Mrs. Katz wasn't looking. Jake handed me another note. "She's so sensitive, don't you think?" he had written. I wrote, "What do you mean?" and passed the note back to Jake. But then we had to stop writing because Mrs. Katz had turned to face us again.

• • •

After class I went to my locker to get my books for English, my last class of the day. Jake came up behind me. "So," he said, "what do you think?"

"About what?" I asked.

"Doriane," he said. "Isn't that what we were talking about?"

"Oh," I said. "She's okay, kind of quiet."

"She's just so sensitive," Jake said. "You know, it's kind of nice."

"What do you mean?"

"Well, she could have reported on anything, but she picked the earthquake," he said.

"I reported on the earthquake too," I reminded him.

"Oh, yeah," Jake said.

The bell rang signaling it was time for our next class. "I better go," I said.

I was still thinking about Doriane's report when I walked into English class. Our teacher, Mrs. Herman, told us to take our seats and pull out our notebooks. Every so often she makes us do a Free Write, when we write whatever we want for ten minutes straight. She doesn't collect what we write; it's just an exercise to get our minds working. The only rule is that we're not allowed to stop writing for the whole ten minutes. It's a lot harder than it sounds because you can't think before you write. You just have to start writing as soon as she says go, and you can't lift your pen from the page until she calls time. She's really strict about that. If you so much as look up to see how much someone else has written, she'll yell at you to look at your own paper, even though it's not like you were trying to cheat or anything like that. I pulled out a piece of paper and waited for Mrs. Herman to say go. This time I knew exactly what I would write about, and since it was important, I decided to write about it to Sophie.

"Go," Mrs. Herman called.

Dear Sophie,

Today this girl Doriane in my social studies class gave a report about a girl from California who was in the earthquake and now her family is missing. You know, the big earthquake that was in Mexico a few weeks ago? Anyway, the girl in Doriane's report had parents and a sister, just like me. Her sister was even named Julie, just like my sister. But I don't know if her sister is older or younger than she is. Still, I keep thinking about all the vacations I've gone on with Mom, Dad, and Julie. I don't know what I would do if anything ever happened to them. Sometimes they really drive me crazy, but still . . . I don't think I'd want to come home without them. How could I be in my house if they weren't there? I feel so bad for this girl. Jake said he thought Doriane was really sensitive for reporting on the earthquake, but I think I'm sensitive too. I keep thinking about the girl in the earthquake. Her name is Emily. I wonder what she looks like. I don't even know her last name or what city in California she lives in, but I really wish there was something I could do to help her. I wish there was something I could do to help all the kids who maybe got hurt in the earthquake, or who lost people from their families. I just don't think there is anything I could do from here, but someone has to do something to help.

I snuck a look at the clock at the front of the room, which technically we're not allowed to do during Free Write. But I saw that it was almost time to stop so I finished up my letter to Sophie and signed my name, "Sincerely, Katie," just as Mrs. Herman was calling time. I read over my letter quickly while Mrs. Herman handed out a grammar work sheet. I realized that I hadn't used any paragraphs, but Mrs. Herman says grammar and punctuation don't count during Free Write. I continued to read over my letter. One line in particular stuck out at me: "Someone has to do something to help." That was when I decided I was going to figure out something to do to help.

Two

The worst thing about my school, Hillside Middle School, is that it's at the bottom of a huge hill. To get home Julie and I have to walk all the way back up it. But Julie went to her friend Val's house after school. I walked part of the way with Tesa and another girl named Sara. Tesa lives only halfway up the hill and Sara was going to Tesa's house, so I walked the rest of the way by myself. I was almost home when I decided to stop at Aunt Jean's house. She's my dad's sister, and she's a good person to go to if you need someone to just sit and listen to you, or if you want someone to help you figure things out. Luckily, Aunt Jean lives just a few streets away from us. I made a left turn onto her street and skipped down the block to her house.

It's true about what I wrote to Sophie—sometimes my family drives me crazy, especially my mom. I know it's not a nice thing to say, but there are times when I wish Aunt Jean were my mother. Sometimes when I go over there, I even pretend that I'm her daughter instead of her niece. It's not that I don't love Mom. I really do. But there's something so much easier about Aunt Jean. It's just that she always understands me. If I do something wrong, she doesn't stand there with her hands on her hips telling me I should've known better. She gets what it's like to be young. And it would be nice to be an only child instead of a younger sister.

Mom says our family is like a team, and we all need to be team players. But things get hard at my house sometimes because of Julie's dyslexia, and my cheerleading personality doesn't always work at home. The problem is that Mom and Dad didn't know what was wrong with Julie for a long time. She's really smart, but she was doing badly in school and had to be held back, so now instead of being two grades apart in school like we should be, we're only one grade apart. Mom is obsessed with Julie's schoolwork and says I have to be sensitive to Julie. It's not always easy, especially since Mom almost always takes Julie's side. She acts like our family team should be called Team Julie. Her favorite thing to tell Julie is that she can do anything she puts her mind to. Maybe I wouldn't care as much if Julie were my cousin instead of my sister and we didn't have to live in the same house.

I feel guilty about thinking those things, especially when I think about not having Mom or Julie around at all—like Emily, who may have lost her whole family in Mexico. Sometimes it's like I'm two different people. At school everyone thinks I'm friendly and nice, but at home I sometimes worry I'm not a good enough person.

It's not that I want Mom and Julie to disappear completely. Even when I'm mad at them I still like knowing they're around. I just think it might be easier living down the road with Aunt Jean instead of in the same house. I think it would be good for Aunt Jean, too. Right now she's all alone. Aunt Jean used to be married but her husband died. I was a baby so I don't even remember ever having an uncle. They didn't have any kids so I don't have any cousins on my dad's side.

Even though she doesn't have any kids and lives alone, she has a much bigger house than we do. That's because her husband left her a lot of money when he died. Dad tells Aunt Jean she should travel more with all that money. She used to go to Europe all the time with her husband, but she always tells Dad it's no fun to travel by yourself. I think Dad should leave Aunt Jean alone. Older siblings think they know everything. Julie's a know-it-all too. She says stupid things, like Jake and I won't be best friends for much longer because he's a boy and there are certain things we won't be able to tell each other as we get older. But she doesn't understand Jake and me. Anyway, Aunt Jean says she likes it better right here in Redwood City. She volunteers at the library in the mornings and she's usually home in the afternoons.

I took the steps two at a time up the walkway to the front door and I rang the bell three times. I started doing that when I was little so Aunt Jean would know it was me at the door.

"Just a second, Katie," Aunt Jean called.

I slipped my backpack off my back because it was getting heavy. After a few seconds I heard Aunt Jean's footsteps and the door opened.

"I had a feeling I would see you today," Aunt Jean said. "I made cookies." Aunt Jean loves to feed people.

"Oh, awesome," I said.

"Come on into the kitchen," Aunt Jean said. "They're still cooling off."

We walked down the hall to the kitchen. I think it's probably the best room in the house, which is funny since I don't like to cook at all. At home Mom always makes me do the dishes after dinner since Julie helps her cook, and I hate that, too. But Aunt Jean's kitchen is different. For one thing, I don't have to do any chores when I'm in there. And for another, there's a big skylight in the ceiling so the room is flooded with light as soon as the sun is out. When it's raining you can tilt your head back and see the raindrops coming down straight from above. Today the sky was mostly blue with some clouds swirling slowly across so there were shadows moving along the table. Aunt Jean brought a plate of cookies over and sat down across from me. I reached over and took one. It was still warm from the oven and I could tell the chocolate would be gooey inside.

"So," Aunt Jean said, "tell me everything about your day."

Usually when my parents ask me about my day, or about school, I just say it was fine. But I don't mind giving Aunt Jean more details. First of all, I like the way Aunt Jean asks the question, like she really wants to know. And she doesn't make things complicated like my mom does. The problem is that Mom gets jealous sometimes, because Aunt Jean ends up knowing more about me. I don't see what the big deal is, since Mom is usually so busy worrying about Julie anyway. I swallowed the bite of cookie that was in my mouth. "Mostly it was the same as usual," I told her. "Except this girl Doriane gave a report on a kid who was hurt in the earthquake. You know the one in Mexico?"

Aunt Jean nodded. She picked up a cookie, blew on it to cool it off, and took a bite. I filled her in Doriane's report. Aunt Jean shook her head. Maybe she sort of understood what it was like for Emily since she had lost her husband. "You know," I said, "when the earthquake first happened, I thought it was the worst thing I'd ever heard. But then everything just went back to the way it was before and I stopped thinking about it."

"I think that's natural," Aunt Jean said.

"Yeah, but the thing is, nothing in Mexico went back to the way it was before. Things might never go back to normal for them."

"It's awful," Aunt Jean said.

"I know," I said. "When Doriane finished her report, Jake went on and on about how sensitive Doriane was for caring about the earthquake. But I think I'm sensitive too. I haven't stopped thinking about Emily since Doriane gave her report. I mean, the same thing could have happened to me. It could have happened right here in California."

"Chances are that it won't," Aunt Jean said.

"But we have fault lines here," I said.

"I know," Aunt Jean said. "But the really big earthquakes don't happen that often. It's a random event, and it happened in Mexico. I don't want you to be too worried about it."

"I'm not worried, exactly," I said. "I just want to do something to help."

Aunt Jean smiled. "We should find out what hospital Emily's in. Maybe there's a way to get a letter to her or some sort of care package."

"Actually, I thought I could do something more than a care package," I said.

"More?" Aunt Jean asked.

"Yeah," I said. "Like raising money to help somehow."

"That's a great idea," Aunt Jean said. "You could have a

bake sale, or even a lemonade stand. Your father and I used to have lemonade stands when we were little."

It's hard for me to think of Dad and Aunt Jean as little kids. I tried to picture them outside Grandma and Grandpa's house, sitting behind a little table set up to sell lemonade, but they still looked like grown-ups in my head. "How much did you make?" I asked.

"I remember once we got twenty-five dollars and we thought we were rich," Aunt Jean said, laughing.

"That's not very much," I said.

"Well, it was a long time ago," she said. "Twenty-five dollars went further back then."

"But even if we made twice as much, it still wouldn't be enough. Doriane's article said that Emily's hospital bills are already ten thousand dollars. Even if her family can pay that, I bet she isn't the only kid who is hurt or missing her family. There were a lot of Mexican kids in the earthquake too. Some of them must have lost everything—their families and their houses and all their money, too."

"I'm sure you're right," Aunt Jean said.

"And Doriane talked about how the resources in Mexico were getting all used up," I continued. "They don't have enough money or equipment to help everyone and rebuild things. So we have to do something bigger than a lemonade stand. The thing is, I know I want to help and I know it has to be big, but I can't think of what it should be."

Aunt Jean folded her arms across the table. "Something big," she said. "Well, we need to brainstorm, then. Why don't you grab some paper and a pen?"

I got the pad of paper and pen that Aunt Jean keeps by the phone in case she needs to write anything down. We have a pad next to the phone in our kitchen too, which Mom calls the message pad. But Aunt Jean lives alone, so she doesn't have anyone to take messages for.

I brought the paper over to the table. "It needs to be something that would raise a lot of money, obviously," I said.

"You could start researching on the Internet and I could get some books about fund-raising from the library," Aunt Jean offered. "We need to make a list of our other resources too."

"Our resources?"

"Yes," Aunt Jean said. "You know, things we already have here that could help us."

"You mean like people I can ask for money?"

"Sort of," Aunt Jean said. "Like asking some of the local businesses to be sponsors of a fund-raiser."

"That's a great idea," I said.

"Thanks," Aunt Jean said. "Write it down."

"Okay," I said, picking up the pen and making a note on the page. "What else?"

"Well," she said, "we could write a letter to the people we know asking for their help."

"I could ask the teachers at school," I suggested.

"Absolutely," Aunt Jean said. "You should go to the principal, too. Maybe the school could host something."

"Like have a fund-raising event at school?" I asked.

"Mmm-hmm," Aunt Jean said. "Something you and your friends could work on together, and get the whole school involved."

I sat back and tried to think about what the kids in my school would like. One of the great things about California is that it's warm and sunny outside most of the time, so we spend a lot of time out on the fields behind the school and on the track. That's why Jake is such a fast runner. He's actually on the track team. There are mostly seventh and eighth graders on the team. Jake and Morgan are the only sixth graders, and Jake is practically the fastest kid on the team.

Suddenly it hit me: If we had some sort of race and could get people to sponsor us for running laps around the track, Jake could raise a ton of money. It was perfect—Jake and I could plan it together. "Maybe we could have a race at Hillside," I said. "Kids could get their parents and friends to sponsor them to run around the track, and the more laps they run, the more money they get."

"Like a jog-a-thon," Aunt Jean said. "Now you're talking."

"Yeah, but it has to be different from an ordinary jog-a-thon," I said. "It has to be something that a lot of people will really want to come and watch. That way we can get more than just the students involved—it could be people from the local businesses, too, like you said."

"You mean like some kind of entertainment?" Aunt Jean asked.

"Yeah," I said. "Like they have when there's sports on TV."

"A halftime show," Aunt Jean said.

"Exactly," I said. "Maybe we could get the cheerleaders to do some cheers. And different clubs could be different entertainment. You know, like the band and the chorus."

"You're on a roll," Aunt Jean said. "Make sure you write it all down."

I went back to my list and wrote: "Hillside jog-a-thon. Sponsorships to run around track. Bigger sponsorships from companies. Halftime show with school clubs perform-ing. Cheerleaders. Band. Chorus." I showed it to Aunt Jean. "Did I forget anything?" I asked.

"I think you got it all," she said.

"Now I have to figure out how to convince Mr. Gallagher to get the school involved," I said. Mr. Gallagher is the prin-cipal of Hillside Middle School. He and I didn't exactly get along.

"You should see if you can meet with him on Monday," Aunt Jean said.

"What if I write him a note about it?" I asked.

"You can write him a note asking for a meeting," Aunt

Jean said. "But I think this is the kind of thing you need to talk about in person."

I knew Aunt Jean was right, but I hated having to go to the principal's office. It's not because I'm shy. Actually, I'm not shy at all. Some kids, like Doriane for example, get really nervous before they have to talk in front of the class. But things like that don't scare me at all. I see all those kids every day anyway. But going to Mr. Gallagher's office was something completely different. I was afraid he would say no just because he didn't like me.

It all started the first week of sixth grade. During lunch we're supposed to stay either in the cafeteria or outside near the track. But Jake had dared me to go back into school and get the chocolate from our homeroom teacher's desk. Mrs. Brenneke kept it in there to give to us in the afternoons. It was really nice of her, but we each got a small piece and Jake said he wanted more. I wanted to show him I was brave—braver even than he was. I told him I wasn't scared because all the teachers were at lunch too and not in their classrooms. But my heart was pounding as I went into the room. I walked as quietly and as quickly as I could over to the desk and I pulled open the bottom drawer. There was a bag full of miniature chocolate bars. "There it is," I said to myself, and I reached in. I didn't even hear Mrs. Brenneke come in behind me. She sent me up to Mr. Gallagher's office. He gave me detention for two weeks and he hasn't liked me ever since.

When my parents found out, they punished me too. My mom was really upset because Mr. Gallagher has been so nice to Julie. When her dyslexia was finally diagnosed, one of the teachers told Mom and Dad that Julie needed to be in special ed. But Mr. Gallagher didn't think so. He set up a special program with Julie. She meets with him every week to go over her work and make a study plan, and he always makes sure she has extra time to take her tests. I didn't know what the big deal was—it wasn't like Mr. Gallagher was going to stop being nice to Julie because I did something wrong, but Mom said I couldn't watch television or go on the Internet for two weeks—the entire length of detention—and Dad agreed with her.

I really didn't want to go speak to Mr. Gallagher in person. For a second I thought about forgetting the whole thing, even though the idea was so perfect. "What if Mr. Gallagher says no?" I asked.

"Then we'll come up with a plan B," Aunt Jean said.

"I really hope he says yes," I said.

"I have a good feeling about this," Aunt Jean said.

"Are you sure?"

"Of course I'm sure," Aunt Jean said. She pushed the plate of cookies toward me. "Here, eat another one. It will make you feel better." I already felt a little better because she seemed so confident, and Aunt Jean was usually right about things. But I took another cookie anyway and looked up, out of the skylight. It was starting to drizzle a little, and I knew I had to get home to let Mooner in since she's afraid of the rain.

"I better get going," I told Aunt Jean as I finished my cookie. I folded the list we'd made and put it into my backpack. Aunt Jean walked me to the door.

"Keep me posted," she said.

"I will," I promised. I walked out the door. Even though I was scared to talk to Mr. Gallagher, I was also excited because we had a plan.

Three

Julie spent most of the weekend at Val's, which meant they spent the whole time shopping at the mall. Julie babysits just so she can have money to shop, plus she spends her entire allowance on clothes and jewelry.

On Sunday evening I came in from walking Mooner. (By the way, I know Mooner is kind of a dumb name for a dog. When we first got her, she was scared of all of us. She used to hide in the corner of the den with just her butt sticking out, like she was mooning us. So Mooner it was.) As soon as we got inside, Mooner ran into the kitchen to get a drink of water. She always drinks right after getting back from a walk, as though she's getting ready to have to go back out again. Mom was sitting at the table working on the crossword puzzle from the morning's paper. She looked up when she saw me. "Hey, kiddo, how was the walk?"

"Fine," I said. I looked at the newspaper on the table and remembered the article about Emily. I thought maybe I would tell Mom about my idea for a jog-a-thon, but just then I heard Julie's key in the door.

Mom got up and walked into the foyer. Julie's arms were filled with shopping bags. "It's getting dark," Mom said. "You should have been home hours ago."

"I said after lunch and we had a late lunch," Julie said.

"Well, it's practically dinnertime now," Mom said.

"It's not so late," Julie told her. "It just seems later because it still gets dark early."

"Julie, it's April," Mom said. "Not February. You can't use the sun setting early as an excuse!" Julie tried to squeeze past Mom to go upstairs, but she was carrying a bunch of shopping bags and Mom stayed planted in front of her. "You know the deal," Mom told her.

"Yeah, yeah, I know the deal," Julie said. "I'll do it now, okay?"

The deal is that Julie is supposed to spend one day each weekend on her schoolwork. The other day she can shop, or go over to a friend's house or babysit. I don't have a deal like that with Mom since I do my homework on my own and I usually get good grades. But sometimes I wish Mom would obsess a little bit about my homework. I'm not sure what's worse: being the one Mom doesn't pay much attention to, or being the one she pays too much attention to. Somewhere in between would be the perfect mother. I have a feeling that's what Aunt Jean would be like if she had kids.

Julie tried to move past Mom again, and this time Mom turned and let her pass. "Hey, Katie, wanna see what I got?" Julie asked me.

"Julianne," Mom said in her warning voice.

"I'm just going to show her my clothes. I'll start working in five minutes," Julie said.

"Five minutes. That's it," Mom said. Julie rolled her eyes and I followed her up the stairs.

Julie and I sort of look alike—we both have greenish brown eyes and long blond hair. Our hairlines come to a point on our foreheads—widow's peaks, which Julie told me is supposed to mean you're pretty. I once asked Jake if he thought Julie was pretty, and he said yeah, but she was too much like his older sister. She used to boss him around too. The thing is, Julie's kind of the prettier version of me. Her eyes are bigger, her hair is thicker and shinier, and her widow's peak is just a little bit pointier. I try not to let it bother me. Anyway, you can still totally tell we're sisters. That is, until you get to our rooms, which are completely different. Julie's room has clothing hanging everywhere—clothing on hangers on every doorknob, shirts draped over her desk chair, and a pile of sweaters at the edge of her bed. Somehow she manages to sleep on her bed without cleaning her clothes off. She also has pictures of fashion models taped onto the wall behind her bed, which she uses as inspiration when she gets dressed in the morning. My room is much more ordinary-looking. I have a bulletin board above my desk and a bunch of bookcases against the walls. There's a Berkeley pendant on the wall, because that's where Dad went to college. Sometimes he takes Jake and me there to watch football games. Next to that I have a collage that Aunt Jean made of pictures she took of Jake and me, and I have a picture that Sophie sent me of her and her sister. Aunt Jean says it's nice to have photos around, and I agree, but Julie thinks I should get some new posters and make my room more exciting. She always offers to help me decorate, but so far I've told her no. I think it's funny how the same two parents can have two kids with completely different personalities.

I sat on Julie's bed and she told me to close my eyes. "Do I have to?" I asked her.

"Yes, this is the Sunday Night Fashion Show," Julie said. "It will be better if you see the whole outfit at once and don't watch me get dressed."

"Why don't you get dressed in the closet," I suggested. "Then you can make a grand entrance."

Julie seemed to consider my idea for a second but shook

her head. "It's too dark in there," she said. "Come on, close your eyes."

I decided to just do what she said. I sat on her bed and held a pillow up to my eyes. "You better hurry up," I said.

Julie put on some music, I guess to keep up with her fashion show theme. All I knew was it took longer for her to get ready because she had to pick the right Madonna song, and I was starting to get annoyed. Julie says Madonna is a fashion icon, and she's also one of Julie's favorite singers. She wants to meet Madonna more than anyone else. I think secretly she'd like to *be* Madonna. But she never says that out loud.

"All right. You can open your eyes," Julie said, just as Madonna began to sing "Vogue." I opened my eyes and saw Julie all dressed up like she was going to a nightclub. Her skirt was black and very short. I knew Dad would hate it. Her shirt looked like it was made out of some kind of metal. I noticed that her chest looked bigger than I remembered it being. Julie started wearing a bra when she was eleven, like I am now, even though she was still flat-chested and she hasn't grown that much since. It's one of the things we have in common, being flat-chested. I never wear a bra, but Julie does every day. I had a feeling she had stuffed it to look bigger. She walked up the length of her room like a supermodel, and turned sharply on her toes. Her dangly earrings bounced up and down when she turned like that. She looked like she could be on TV.

"So, what do you think?" Julie asked.

"It's nice," I said.

"I got a bandana belt too," Julie continued. "It just doesn't match this outfit. But I can try it on with my white skirt if you want to see it. That's what I bought it to go with."

"That's okay," I said. I was already bored by Julie's fashion show.

"You're so lucky I shop, because you can have all this stuff when I'm done with it," Julie said. "I'll give you my old black skirt now. It would look good on you."

I shook my head. I had a few of Julie's hand-me-downs in my closet even though I didn't want any of them. She'd put them there without asking me first. She says she's just trying to help me, but I don't think she should go into my closet without my permission, and I hate that she wants to change me.

"Come on, Katie. You should take my advice. I could help you dress better. I've got a lot of old stuff that would probably fit you, and I could show you how to wear your hair so it would look good too." Julie reached out toward my hair, but I ducked my head. "Boys will like you better that way."

"Don't do that. I'm friends with the boys with my hair just like this."

"That's not what I meant," Julie said. She smiled and

looked down at me like I was just a little kid. I hate when she does that.

"I don't want your stinky old clothes anyway," I said.

Julie rolled her eyes and went to turn off the music. I knew I had upset her because I didn't want to be her project. "Get out of here if you're going to act so ungrateful," she told me.

"Fine," I said. "I didn't want to come in here in the first place." I moved toward the door and heard Mom shout from the hallway to Julie to get started on her homework.

Julie pushed my shoulder as I walked past her. "You heard Mom. Hurry up and get out," she said. "I have homework to do."

"I'm going," I said. But when I got to her door I turned and faced her. "Let me know if you need me to help you with your homework," I said hotly. Julie lunged forward, and I turned and walked out fast before she could slam the door in my face. Sometimes it's easier to be mean to Julie than to try to get her to like me.

Mom met me in the hall on my way to my room. "You shouldn't distract Julie when she needs to do her homework," she told me.

"Julie was the one who wanted to show me her clothes. You were there," I reminded her.

"I need you to be cooperative, Katie," Mom said. She

looked down at me — but not as far down as she used to. I'm just a few inches shorter than her now. I remembered something one of my teachers had written on my report card in fifth grade: "Katie is attentive and enthusiastic. It is a pleasure to have her in class." Sometimes I wished Mom could see me the way I am at school. Then maybe she would say I'm a team player and use those words to describe me too. It made me wonder if there were kids in school who were completely unpopular who went home to perfect families where no one ever fought.

"You only care about Julie," I told Mom. I went into my room, which is right next to Julie's room, and closed my door. I flopped onto my bed, thinking about my fight with Julie. I knew it was stupid to fight about clothing, and I shouldn't have said what I had about Julie's homework. She gets upset when she thinks I'm smarter than she is, and she would never ask me for help. Besides, I really don't know anything about seventh-grade work anyway. I really only said it to get back at her for thinking there is something wrong with my clothes and my hair. I knew the fight was mostly my fault. I'm just not very good at apologizing. Anyway Mom would have gotten mad at me if I'd gone back into Julie's room.

I decided to concentrate on my jog-a-thon idea instead. I was sure Jake would think it was a great project for the Dynamic Duo to organize. I just hoped Mr. Gallagher would agree. I tried to imagine how my meeting with Mr. Gallagher would go, but when I thought of going into his office, I remembered the way his face had looked when I'd been sent there by Mrs. Brenneke. I decided to call Jake. I reached for the phone and dialed. After a couple rings Jake's mother answered.

"Hey, Mrs. O," I said. Jake's last name is Oxman, but I always call his parents Mr. and Mrs. O.

"Hi, Katie," Mrs. O said. She knew it was me because I'm the only one who calls her Mrs. O, and also because she knows my voice since I call their house a lot. "I'll get Jake for you." I heard her calling for him and he picked up. The phone clicked as Mrs. O hung up.

"What's up?" Jake asked.

"I have a great idea," I said.

"What is it?"

"You have to promise not to tell anyone," I said. I wasn't going to tell anyone else from school just yet. I didn't want anyone to know about it, besides Aunt Jean and Jake, before I spoke to Mr. Gallagher about it.

"Okay," Jake said.

"You promise?" I asked. "I'm only telling you because you're my best friend. I didn't even tell my parents yet."

"You never tell your parents things," Jake said.

"Come on, do you promise?"

"Yeah, of course I promise," Jake said. "Tell me what it is."

"All right," I said. "I want to do a fund-raiser at Hillside. A jog-a-thon. The students can get people to sponsor them for how many times they run around the track, and the more times they run around, the more money they'll get."

"What's the money for?" Jake asked.

"For the people who were in the earthquake in Mexico," I said. "Remember, I reported on it a few weeks ago and then Doriane reported about it."

"Of course I remember," Jake said.

"Well, Doriane said they were running out of resources and needed money to rebuild things and help everyone, and that's when I had the idea to do something at Hillside," I said. "What do you think?"

"It'd be pretty cool," Jake said.

"And it's going to be bigger than an ordinary jog-a-thon," I said. "I want there to be a halftime show, with maybe the band and the cheerleaders doing cheers. And I want to get local businesses to give sponsorships so we can raise even more money."

"I'll help you with it if you want."

That's exactly what I'd hoped he would say. "Definitely," I said. "The first thing I have to do is talk to Mr. Gallagher. I spoke to my aunt and she said I should write Mr. Gallagher a letter to see if he'll meet with me. Aunt Jean is going to get books about fund-raising from the library, and I'm going to go over there after school tomorrow so I can read up on everything too. You could come to the meeting with me if Mr. Gallagher says yes."

"You should ask Doriane to help you too," Jake said. "After all, she's the reason you had the idea." Why did Jake have to keep bringing up Doriane? She may have done the report, but it was my idea to have the jog-a-thon.

"I know, I know," I told him. "She's very sensitive."

"What, are you jealous?" Jake asked. He laughed to himself, and I felt stupid.

"Of course I'm not jealous," I told him. "Anyway, I better go. I have to write to Mr. Gallagher."

"Okay," Jake said. "I'll see you tomorrow."

I was still thinking about Jake's new obsession with Doriane when we hung up. I told myself that he would get over it soon enough. I just couldn't imagine that Jake and Doriane would have anything in common. She was too quiet, and I don't think she cared about track at all. She probably wouldn't even want to run in the jog-a-thon anyway. I pulled open my desk drawer to get a piece of paper to write to Mr. Gallagher. I knew I had to concentrate, because the letter had to be exactly right. That way Mr. Gallagher wouldn't just think of me as the girl who'd tried to steal Mrs. Brenneke's chocolate. I picked up a pen. *Here goes nothing,* I thought, and I began to write.

Dear Mr. Gallagher,

I'm writing to you because I hope I can meet with you about an idea I had for our school that has to do with the earthquake in Mexico. I have Mrs. Katz for social studies, and we talked about the earthquake in class when we did our current events reports. One thing we learned was that there aren't enough resources in Mexico to fix everything that was damaged and help all the people who were hurt.

I know a lot of kids at Hillside are really sad about what happened in Mexico. The idea I have is about how our school can help the people who were hurt in the earthquake. I thought we could have a school fund-raiser and send the money we raise to Mexico.

I really hope I can meet with you about this because I have a lot of ideas for the fund-raiser that I'd like to talk to you about in person. My locker is number 917, if you want to leave me a note.

Sincerely,

Katie Lyn Franklin

P.S. Thank you for reading this letter.

I added the part saying thank you because I wanted him to think I was polite. I looked over my letter to make sure my handwriting was neat and nothing was spelled wrong. It looked pretty good, so I folded it up and put it in an envelope. I printed "Mr. Gallagher" on the outside and put the envelope into my backpack so I wouldn't forget it.

There was a knock on my door. "Come in," I said. Dad poked his head into the room.

"Dinner's just about ready," he said.

"I'll be right down" I said.

Dinner was already on the table when I got downstairs. Mom had made lasagna. It's this thing Mom does whenever one of us is upset—she makes our favorite food for dinner and thinks that fixes things. Like when Dad had a problem at his office, Mom made steak, or when I broke my arm last year, she made lamb chops. Lasagna was one of Julie's favorite meals. The food thing didn't really work on Julie, though. Whenever she was upset about school, she didn't eat much. I sat in my usual seat, in between Mom and Dad and across from Julie. Julie barely looked at me for the whole meal, and I knew she was still mad. When I'm done having an argument with someone, I just forget about it and move on. But Julie is different from me. She stays mad much longer. I thought about telling everyone about my idea for the jog-a-thon, but if Julie was upset, she would just tell me it was stupid, so I didn't say anything at all.

After dinner I helped clean up, and then Dad and I went into the den to watch television. Julie wasn't allowed to watch with us because she still had homework to do. She gave me a dirty look as she walked past the den to go upstairs. I sighed out loud, and Dad turned to me. "Everything all right, Katie-Katie?" he asked. He always calls me Katie-Katie. There's an old song about someone named Lisa-Lisa. Lisa is Mom's name and Dad used to call her Lisa-Lisa, so when I was little, I started calling myself Katie-Katie, and Dad just kept on calling me that. Mom didn't like being called Lisa-Lisa because the name of the song is actually "Sad Lisa." So Dad hardly ever calls Mom Lisa-Lisa anymore.

"I'm kind of tired," I told him. It was true. All of a sudden I felt exhausted.

"Why don't you go up to bed?" Dad said, and I nodded. I kissed him good night and headed upstairs.

I got into bed and tried to imagine how my meeting with Mr. Gallagher would go. I wasn't as scared since Jake would be there, and Mr. Gallagher had never found out that Jake had also been involved in the plot to steal Mrs. Brenneke's candy. Besides, everyone at school, including Mr. Gallagher, knew how great Jake was at track. I pictured us both in the chairs across Mr. Gallagher's desk from him. My head felt heavy and I closed my eyes, hoping everything would work out the way I wanted it to.

Suddenly Jake and I were on the island in the middle of the reservoir. I was sitting between the trees and Jake was walking toward me. I heard a low rumble. I scrambled toward the base of a tree to stand next to the trunk, and when I turned back, I couldn't see Jake. Everything was shaking and pieces of trees were falling down all around me. Then, as if I were suddenly up in the air and watching the island from a distance, I watched the entire island shake and disappear underwater. I knew Jake was still on the island. "Jake!" I screamed, and I opened my eyes.

Four

My face was hot and my heart was pounding, but I saw that I was still in my room. The bookshelves loomed large and dark but not at all scary. "Just a bad dream," I said to myself. I flicked on the light next to my bed. Someone knocked on my door and it opened before I even said, *Come in.*

"Are you all right?" Mom asked.

I sat up in bed and pulled my knees up to my chest. My hands felt sticky. "I'm fine," I said.

"I was just walking down the hall and I thought I heard something," she said.

I shook my head. "Maybe it was the wind," I told her.

"Maybe," Mom said. "But it doesn't seem too windy out tonight."

"It could have been Mooner, then," I said.

Mom nodded. "Do you need anything before I go?"

"No, thanks," I said.

"Okay, kiddo, don't stay up too late," Mom said.

"Fine," I said. I didn't tell her that I'd already been sleeping. I waited until she closed the door before I turned the light back out.

The next morning I rushed through breakfast so I could get to school early. I wanted to make sure I had time to go to Mr. Gallagher's office before homeroom. Mr. Gallagher's office is in a separate building from my homeroom classroom, across the parking lot where kids get dropped off by their parents or buses. It's a small building with just Mr. Gallagher's office and the nurse's station inside. The nurse's station is right past the benches when you first walk in, and you can go straight into it on your own, but it's not so easy to get to Mr. Gallagher's office. Across from the nurse's door, there's a counter that takes up the whole width of the room. One of the secretaries behind the counter has to let you in through a swinging door in order to get to Mr. Gallagher's office in the back.

I crossed the parking lot and hurried up to the building, but when I got inside, I slowed down. What if they wouldn't let me behind the counter to leave him a note? Would I be able to give it to them to take to him? Would they make me explain my whole idea before they agreed to take the note for him?

"Can I help you?" one of the women behind the counter asked. I think her name is Mrs. Sutton. I remembered that she was there the day Mrs. Brenneke sent me up to Mr. Gallagher's office, and I hoped Mrs. Sutton had forgotten about that.

"Yeah," I said. "I have a note I wanted to leave for Mr. Gallagher, if that's all right."

"Is it for the suggestion box?" Mrs. Sutton asked. She tipped the pencil that was in her hand toward a box on the far side of the counter.

"No," I said. "It's just a note. It's kind of personal."

"You can put it in his mailbox, then," Mrs. Sutton said.

"I don't know his address," I told her.

Mrs. Sutton smiled. "No, dear, not his home mailbox. All the teachers have mailboxes over there." She pointed her pencil again, this time toward the wall beside the nurse's station. "There's a box there for Mr. Gallagher, too."

"Oh, thanks," I said. I smiled back at her and walked over to the back wall. There were open mailboxes that looked like miniature cubbyholes against the wall. Each one had a teacher's last name printed across the bottom. I had never noticed them before, but I looked them up and down until I saw the one marked "Gallagher." I saw that there were a couple of papers already in his box, and I slipped the envelope I was holding between the papers so mine wouldn't be on top. I called "Thanks" to Mrs. Sutton again and crossed my fingers as I walked out the door.

Five

Usually I take all my books with me for all my classes, but that day I purposely went back to my locker between each class to check if there was a note on my locker door. Each time the front of my locker was bare.

I was already making up in my head how great the jog-a-thon would be, and now all I could think about was whether Mr. Gallagher had read my letter. Why did it feel like time was added to the day when you waited for something? A few years ago Aunt Jean and I made a peanut butter chocolate cake. I stood at the oven and flicked the little switch so I could see inside. Every minute or so I went back to flick the switch and see if the cake was ready. Aunt Jean laughed and said, "A watched pot never boils." I didn't understand what she meant at the time — I was watching cake inside the oven, not a pot. But now I stared at the clock and understood completely. The minute hand never seemed to move, no matter how long I looked at it.

At the end of the day I went back to my locker one more time before leaving, but there wasn't a note. I opened my locker and shoved my French books inside, and then closed it with a bang.

"Wow, are you okay?" I turned and saw Tesa next to me.

"Yeah," I said. "Sometimes I have to slam the locker or it doesn't shut all the way." I didn't want to explain why I was really slamming the door and what I was nervous about, because then I would have had to tell her about the jog-a-thon. Anyway, it had been less than a day since I'd left the note for Mr. Gallagher. Just thinking about that made me feel silly. I'm sure Mr. Gallagher has a lot of important stuff to do on Mondays, and he probably gets lots of notes from students. Maybe he hadn't even gotten around to reading his mail yet. Maybe he was in meetings all day and would get to it after school was over. "Are you walking home today?" I asked Tesa.

"No," she said. "I'm going to Sara's. I'll see you tomorrow, though, okay?"

"Yeah, see you tomorrow," I said.

Jake was at the other end of the hall by his locker, and I picked up my backpack and went over to him. "Hey," he said. "I was just gonna find you. I don't have track today. The coach has the flu, so if you want to go to your aunt's and talk about your project, I'm free." Jake thinks Aunt Jean is pretty cool too. He was even coming over for her birthday dinner in a few weeks. I was glad he wanted to go to her for help.

"Thanks," I said. "That'd be great."

"Yeah, I figured you'd want to," Jake said. "I told Doriane to meet us by your locker. She should be here any second."

"You asked Doriane?" I said.

"Yeah, we're in math together," Jake said.

"But, Jake," I said, "you promised not to tell anyone."

"I didn't tell anyone," Jake said. "Just Doriane. I thought we said last night that we'd include her. And anyway she's the reason you had this idea in the first place. If she hadn't brought that article in for current events—"

"Yeah, yeah," I said, cutting Jake off. It wasn't how it was supposed to be. After all, how would this be a project for the Dynamic Duo if Jake included Doriane?

"Katie, stop it," Jake said.

"No, really, Jake," I said. "It's great and all that Doriane's so smart and so sensitive but I don't know why you think we need her for any of this. You can hardly even hear her when she speaks. How's that gonna be helpful when we go to Mr. Gallagher?"

"Katie," Jake said, his voice low, "you need to stop it now."

Jake was talking to me, but all of a sudden I noticed his eyes were focused on something behind me, and I knew Doriane was there. I dropped my backpack and moved my hands to my face, just like a little kid. Like if I covered my face with my hands, Doriane wouldn't be able to see me. After a few seconds I lowered my hands and turned around very, very slowly. "Hi, Doriane," I said.

Doriane smiled the smallest smile I had ever seen. I hoped she wasn't going to cry.

"Don't pay any attention to Katie," Jake said. "She's a real jerk." Ordinarily I'd have been mad at Jake for calling me a jerk, but this time I looked at Doriane and sort of agreed with him.

"It's okay," Doriane said softly. "You guys can just meet without me."

"Doriane, seriously, don't pay any attention to her. She didn't mean it," Jake said. "Right, Katie?"

"Right," I said. "I didn't mean it at all. I'm just in a bad mood." It was kind of like how I could be with Julie—get into a bad mood and say things I shouldn't. It just usually didn't happen at school in front of anyone else.

"And you're sorry, right?" Jake said, prompting me. He was speaking to me like I was a baby, but I guess I deserved it. Saying you're sorry is the kind of thing that's easier to think than to say out loud. I never told Julie I was sorry the other night, even though I was. I nodded at Jake, but Doriane said she still didn't want to intrude.

Jake looked like he was ready to kill me. But he was the one who invited Doriane without checking with me. Besides, it wasn't like I'd hurt Doriane's feelings on purpose. Jake could have shouted *Hey, Doriane* over my head to give me a clue that she was there.

"You really wouldn't be intruding," I said. "You should come. We could use your help. I'm sorry about what I said before." I gave her a small smile and she nodded. I looked up at Jake to make sure he wasn't mad anymore. But he moved toward Doriane and I followed behind them down the hall.

It was strange to walk behind Jake like that—to see him walking with another girl. Jake and Doriane, Jake and Doriane. I rolled their names, together like that, around in my head. It didn't sound right; I was so used to thinking about Jake and Katie—the Dynamic Duo. We fit together. I walked faster to keep up with them.

"So, Doriane and I think we should come up with a plan," Jake said.

"I have a plan," I said. "I told you about it."

"Well, now there's three of us," Jake said firmly. "Doriane might have some ideas too." I could tell he was still mad about before. I wanted to point out that it wasn't my fault, but I couldn't really do that with Doriane right there.

"Jake," Doriane said, "this was Katie's idea. I think we should go with her plan."

"Well, I already left a note for Mr. Gallagher this morning," I told her. "I'm hoping he'll agree to a meeting so I can tell him about the idea. If he agrees to let us have it at the school, then we need to get the word out to all the students and everyone else we know."

"Just let us know when the meeting with Gallagher is and we'll be there," Jake said.

I had never heard Jake call Mr. Gallagher just "Gallagher" before, and I knew he was doing it to show off to Doriane. And of course he said "we," to include Doriane again without even asking me. But I didn't say anything about it. I just said, "I'll let you know."

"Katie thinks Gallagher might turn us down," Jake told Doriane.

"Oh," Doriane said, "he just can't say no. It's too important." She sounded like she really meant it.

We turned the corner onto Sage Drive, which is Aunt Jean's street. "Wow," Doriane said softly when we got to Aunt Jean's house. I turned to her and she looked embarrassed. "It's just so big," she said.

"I know," I said. "And my aunt lives here all alone." I reached across Doriane and Jake and pressed the doorbell three times.

"I can't believe you still do that," Jake said. I stuck my tongue out at him. "Baby," he said.

Aunt Jean opened the door. "Hey, Katie. Hey, Jake," she said.

"Hi," I said. "This is my friend Doriane."

"Doriane . . . the girl who reported on the earthquake. I've heard a lot about you. It's very nice to meet you," Aunt Jean said. "I'm Jean Daly."

"It's nice to meet you, too, Mrs. Daly," Doriane said.

"Oh, call me Jean, please," Aunt Jean said. "My mother-in-law is Mrs. Daly." I always forget that Aunt Jean has a mother-in-law and a father-in-law from when her husband was alive. I've only met them a couple times and they are very stuffy. I could see why Aunt Jean didn't want to be called by the same name.

"I hope it's okay that I came over," Doriane said.

"Of course," Aunt Jean said as she ushered us inside. "The more the merrier. I'm going to get some cheese and crackers to snack on, and you have to tell me everything that happened today."

"Nothing happened," I said as I followed her toward the kitchen. "I left a note for Mr. Gallagher but he didn't answer it yet."

"Well, don't worry about it," she said. "It's only Monday. And I got a few books for you this morning, so we can figure out the next steps even before you meet with Mr. Gallagher."

We settled in the den after Aunt Jean finished slicing the

cheese, which is my favorite thing to eat besides chocolate chip cookies. She showed us a pile of books she'd gotten from the library. "I've read through some of these," Jean said. "A lot of it doesn't really apply here. But there are some good ideas, like how to formulate letters and write up proposals. You can model your letters to the local businesses on the examples in this one," Aunt Jean said as she handed me a book from her stack. I opened it up to the table of contents. There was a whole chapter called "Letters, Proposals, and Grant Applications."

"Thanks," I said.

"And I've been thinking about the halftime show," Jake said. "I've got a lot of ideas for it."

"Great," Aunt Jean said. "Let's hear them."

"I definitely think we should see about having a band play. But not the school band, like Katie said. I think maybe a famous band."

"I don't think we'd really be able to get a famous band to Hillside," I said.

"What do you think, Doriane?" Jake asked.

"Well," she said softly, "I think Katie is probably right."

"Oh," Jake said.

"It wouldn't hurt to ask anyway, Jake," Aunt Jean said.

"Yeah," Jake said. "I'm gonna write a letter."

"I thought of something else," Doriane said.

We waited for her to say what it was, but she was quiet.

Finally Aunt Jean said, "We'd love to hear your idea."

"It's okay if you don't like it," Doriane said.

"Doriane," Aunt Jean said, smiling, "it may be the best idea yet, but we have to hear it first."

"Yeah, let's hear it," Jake said. I wished Aunt Jean hadn't said the part about Doriane's idea being the best.

"Well," Doriane said, "we keep saying how we should have businesses sponsor people. I was thinking we could give it a special name, like a 'Super Sponsor,' if a company or even a person wants to pledge a certain amount. Maybe we could even put a sign up thanking those companies at the race itself. Companies like to have their names up places, so it might get them to donate more."

"You're absolutely right," Aunt Jean said. "I read about that in one of these books. It's called signage." Doriane beamed back at her.

"You know," Jake said, "if those Super Sponsors sponsored people on the track team, we'd get a ton of money. I bet we could each run like a hundred laps."

"I was reading some articles on the Internet about what's happened in Mexico," Doriane said. "There's this hospital they set up for the orphaned kids. It's not a real hospital. They set it up in a warehouse or something, because the real hospital was destroyed. I bet they need the money there."

"I think that would be a great place to send the money," Aunt Jean said.

"Mr. Gallagher has to say yes," I said.

Aunt Jean suggested we get some other things done before we even met with Mr. Gallagher, like come up with a draft letter to potential Super Sponsors, and decide which local businesses and people to write to. We also decided to write up a sponsor sheet and present Mr. Gallagher with a list of ideas for the halftime show, besides the band. Aunt Jean and I looked at the samples in the library books and started dictating a letter to the Super Sponsors. Doriane took it all down. Her handwriting is small and neat, and she can write as fast as Aunt Jean and I can talk.

Doriane handed me the letter. I saw that she had signed it from all three of us and put my name first and her name last: "Sincerely, Katie Franklin, Jake Oxman, and Doriane Leib."

"Mr. Gallagher could still turn us down, you know," I said. "After all, he didn't even answer my note yet."

"He was probably just in a meeting," Doriane said. She seemed confident for the first time, and I started to believe it too.

It turned out that Doriane was probably right. When I got back to my locker after lunch the next day, there was an envelope hanging from it. I took a deep breath and pulled it down. The envelope wasn't sealed, but the back flap was tucked in. That's how Mom closes envelopes whenever she gives cards to Julie or me on our birthdays or Christmas. She does it because she hates the taste of the glue on the backs of envelopes. Maybe Mr. Gallagher felt the same way. I pulled up the flap and pulled out the note.

Dear Katie,

I would be happy to meet with you to discuss your idea. I am free Friday afternoon at 3:15. Please let Mrs. Sutton in my office know if you are able to stop by then.

Sincerely,

Joe Gallagher

Six

I read Mr. Gallagher's note again and again over the next few days, and decided it was a good sign that he'd used the word "happy" in his first sentence and also signed the letter with his first and last name. Not only that, he'd also used his nickname instead of writing out "Joseph." Usually teachers and principals don't even like kids to know that they have first names, let alone nicknames. I think it makes them feel more important.

On Friday afternoon I sat next to Jake on the bench outside Mr. Gallagher's office. Doriane was on the other side of him. I wished it were just Jake and me. It wasn't that I minded Doriane being there, but Jake was sitting just the tiniest bit closer to her than he was to me. It made me feel sort of small. Didn't he remember that I was the whole reason we were there? "Hey, Jake," I said, so he had to turn and look at me. But then I didn't have anything to say. Luckily that was when Mrs. Sutton's phone rang.

"Yes, Joe," Mrs. Sutton said, and I knew she must have been speaking to Mr. Gallagher. She paused for a few seconds, and then said, "Okay, I'll send them right in." She hung up the phone and looked up at the three of us. "You can come right back, kids," she said.

We got up, and Mrs. Sutton stood and held open the swinging door for us. Mr. Gallagher's office is in the back behind the secretaries' desks, and he stood up when we walked in, and shook each of our hands. When he shook my hand, he said, "That's a strong handshake." My dad says it's important to have a strong handshake, and I knew he would be proud. "Have a seat," Mr. Gallagher said.

We sat in the chairs in front of Mr. Gallagher's desk, and he walked around the desk and sat behind it. He didn't look mad at me at all, but I decided to say something nice just in case he was thinking about Mrs. Brenneke's chocolate. "Thanks a lot for meeting with us today."

"My pleasure," Mr. Gallagher said. "I was very impressed by your note. I understand you want to have a fundraiser here at Hillside for the victims of the Mexican earthquake?"

"Yes," I said.

"And these are your partners in crime?" Mr. Gallagher said, nodding toward Jake and Doriane.

Did he think Jake and Doriane had had something to do with the stolen chocolate? Doriane didn't have anything to do with it, and I didn't know he knew about Jake. "Not in crime," I said quickly.

"I didn't mean crime literally," Mr. Gallagher said. "It's just an expression."

"Oh," I said. "Right. Yeah, they're my partners."

"Okay, then," Mr. Gallagher said. "Your note said you had a lot of ideas, so let's hear them."

"Well," I said, "we thought we could have a jog-a-thon at Hillside."

"We could hold it on the track," Jake piped up. I didn't think it was right that he interrupted me, but we were in front of the principal so I let Jake keep talking. "Kids would get sponsored for the number of times they run around the track," Jake continued. "We even thought we could have businesses sponsor the kids on the track team for more money—you know, because the kids on track will run the most laps. That way we can raise even more money. Also, we thought about having a halftime show, like they do on TV. I'm going to make a list of famous bands and try to get one of them to play."

"Or we could have the middle school chorus or band, or maybe even the high school band," I said. "I don't think we could get a famous band."

"We could try," Jake said.

"Anyway," I said, "we want to have the jog-a-thon as soon as possible. They need all the help they can get in Mexico."

"You're right about that," Mr. Gallagher said. "But this is a very big project, and there aren't even two full months left of the school year."

I realized he was about to say no, which wasn't fair because the jog-a-thon seemed like the most important thing in the world. I had already imagined exactly how it would be, and now it was going to be taken away. The three of us sat quietly. Not even Jake could think of anything to say. Finally I took a deep breath. "Mr. Gallagher," I said, "we know this is a big project. But it has to be big in order to make any kind of difference, and we'll work as hard as we need to work to do it. They set up this hospital in Mexico to take care of the kids who are hurt, and it's not even a real hospital because the real hospital was destroyed in the earthquake. I think everyone should try to help out, including Hillside. If everyone tried to do something to help, then we could save a lot of kids."

"How much do you want to raise?" Mr. Gallagher asked.

"It has to be at least ten thousand dollars," I told him.

"That's a lot of money," Mr. Gallagher said.

"I know," I said, "but the article Doriane brought into class said that's how much it costs for just one kid's medical bills."

"I see," Mr. Gallagher said.

"Please don't say no," Doriane said. It was the first time she'd spoken during the whole meeting. Then she blushed, and said softly, "It's just that they need help there so badly. It's so important."

"You're right, Doriane," Mr. Gallagher said. "And I don't mean to stop any of you from doing things to help out. But you're talking about raising a lot of money in a very short period of time. I'm just not sure it's going to be possible."

"That's why we have the Super Sponsors," I said.

"Super Sponsors?" Mr. Gallagher asked.

"That's what we're calling the businesses or people who sponsor the track team. We figured they might be more willing to donate money if there was a special sponsorship level, and then we can reach our goal," I explained.

"Yeah," Jake continued. "Then we'll have signs printed up thanking all the Super Sponsors. It will be like advertisements at real sporting events. Businesses like having their names up everywhere."

"As long as it's okay with you, that's what we'll do," I added.

"Those are all very good ideas," Mr. Gallagher said. I could tell he was starting to consider our idea again, and I decided to show him something. I unzipped my backpack and pulled out my binder. The letter Aunt Jean and I had dictated to Doriane was right on top, and I took it out.

"We even brought a sample letter we wrote to hand out to

potential sponsors," I said. "See." I handed the letter across the desk, and Mr. Gallagher took it from me. I watched his eyes dart back and forth quickly as he read it, and then he looked back up at us.

"I see you've put a lot of thought into this," he said. He turned to me. "It's good to see you're putting all that energy of yours to good use, Katie." His voice sounded stern for a second, but then he winked. I thought that meant he was saying yes, but I wasn't sure.

"Does that mean we can do it?" I asked.

Mr. Gallagher bent his head in one long and deliberate nod.

"All right, that is awesome!" I said. I turned to Jake and Doriane and slapped them five each. Then Mr. Gallagher cleared his throat, and I remembered that I still had to act grown-up. "Thanks, Mr. Gallagher," I said.

"Thank you, Katie," he said.

"We can show you the sponsor sheets too. We made one up for regular sponsors, like our parents and friends, and one for the Super Sponsors."

Mr. Gallagher looked over everything we had and said we should make up packets to hand out to the potential sponsors, including a copy of the article that Doriane had reported on. He pulled out a box full of official folders with "Hillside Middle School" printed in silver across the front. "These should get you started," he said.

"Wow," I said. "Thanks."

"The three of you have a lot of work to do this weekend," Mr. Gallagher said. "We'll have an assembly Monday morning, and you're going to need to make up enough packets to hand out to the students who want to participate. I have a feeling that there will be a lot of them."

Things were working out just the way I'd wanted them to—even with Doriane there. Mr. Gallagher stood, which was our clue to leave. Jake pumped Mr. Gallagher's hand, and then I stepped forward to shake his hand again too. That made it seem like an official agreement. Mr. Gallagher told us to meet him ten minutes before homeroom on Monday so we could talk about the assembly. We walked out of his office. I used Mrs. Sutton's phone to call Aunt Jean. We needed someone to pick us up since the box of folders was too heavy to carry all the way home. Aunt Jean said she would meet us in front of the school in five minutes, and we went outside to wait for her.

"This calls for a celebration," Jake said. "What do you say, Doriane?"

"I don't know," Doriane said.

"Come on," Jake said. "Katie's aunt can drop us off at Round Table Pizza."

"Okay, I guess," she said. "You're coming too, right, Katie?"

I looked over at Jake. I couldn't tell if he wanted me to come or not. But it was my idea and we were supposed to be in this together. "Yeah, I'm coming," I said.

Aunt Jean drove up a few minutes later and dropped us off at Round Table Pizza. It's my favorite pizza place in Redwood City. Mom doesn't like it—she says it's the kind of pizza that only kids can like. She likes pizza with thin crust, which I hate because the bottom gets all charred and they don't put enough cheese on top. At Round Table, they put tons of cheese on their pizza and there are about a million toppings to choose from. Plus they have video games in the back, but Jake and I don't play those as much as we used to.

Doriane followed Jake and me straight to the table in the back where we usually sit. Doriane and I sat across from each other and Jake went to order the pizza and our drinks. He came back carrying a couple sodas and he slid onto the seat next to Doriane. I had a feeling he was going to sit next to her instead of me, but I was still kind of disappointed. I didn't say anything, though, because I didn't want Jake to call me a baby for not wanting to sit alone.

"Here," Jake said, sliding a glass of Coke toward Doriane. "I got you a drink."

"Thanks," Doriane said. She smiled up at him.

"What about me?" I asked.

"Sorry," Jake said. "I couldn't carry three glasses. I ordered one for you, but you have to pick up your cup at the counter."

So this is it, I thought. *Jake likes some girl and she likes him*

back, so he forgets all about me. In my head I pictured myself growing smaller and smaller, until Jake couldn't see me at all. I tried to talk, but I was too small for him to hear.

"Come on, Katie," Jake said. "Get the soda. We need to make a toast."

I got the cup and went to the soda dispenser. I filled it with Coke almost all the way to the top, and I turned around carefully so it wouldn't spill. As I walked toward the table, I saw Jake put his arm around Doriane's shoulder, just like a boyfriend would. Something inside my chest tightened. *What, are you jealous?* Jake had asked me the week before. What was wrong with me? It was just Jake, after all. He was my best friend; I'd never wanted him to be my boyfriend. I just didn't want him to stop paying attention to me.

"All right," Jake said as I sat down. "Now for the toast."

"A toast to Mr. Gallagher?" I asked. "For saying yes?"

"No," Jake said. "A toast to *us*. We're the ones who have to do all the work." He grinned at me, and I raised my glass. Maybe I was imagining everything. Maybe it would all be okay. Doriane and Jake raised theirs, too. "To us," we said all together. We clicked our cups together. A little bit of soda spilled out of my glass and onto my hand, but I didn't care.

Seven

I woke up extra early on Saturday morning. Doriane's father had said we could go to his office to make up the packets for the jog-a-thon. Even though we weren't going to his office until later in the morning, I was way too excited about everything with the jog-a-thon to sleep in.

My parents were already awake when I woke up—Mom never sleeps past seven, and she and Dad have a weekly tennis game Saturday mornings. They go to the tennis courts at Sage Park, which is at the end of Aunt Jean's street. It's supposed to be a private park for the people who live on Sage Drive, but Mom and Dad use Aunt Jean's name to be able to play on the tennis courts. I could hear them downstairs, and I figured it was a good time to tell them about the jog-a-thon, especially since I'd already told Aunt Jean, and Mom hates when Aunt Jean knows things about me first. I followed my parents' voices down to the kitchen. But by the time I got there, I knew I wouldn't get a chance to tell them about the jog-a-thon or anything else. Mom was already talking about two of her favorite subjects—Julie and school.

"Peter," Mom was saying, "I met this girl at the bookstore the other day and I think she could really help Julie. She's a student at Stanford, and she said she wants to get a job tutoring to help her out with some of her living expenses. I just think it would be wonderful for Julie to be around someone that studious and responsible, don't you?" Mom sounded so excited, you'd think she had just discovered gold in the kitchen cabinets. The thing is, Mom loves anything that has to do with Stanford. It's a college really close to our house, and you have to be smart to get into it. It's Mom's greatest dream that Julie and I go to Stanford. If Julie's tutor went to Stanford, Mom probably thought that would give Julie some advantage, even though I thought Julie and I were too young to worry about college. After all, we were both still in middle school.

"It would be great," Dad told her, "but that's *if* we could get Julie to agree to it, and that's a big if. I'm not sure we can make this work. Remember how she hated being tutored the last time we tried this?"

"We can't make this a choice for her, Peter. She's starting

high school in a couple years." Mom continued talking as she turned away from Dad and stood on her toes to reach the cereal boxes on the shelf above the fridge. "We can't just let things stay the way they are now. The work is only going to get harder. She'll hate school a lot more than she'd hate being tutored."

I knew the only way my parents could get Julie not to hate school was if they hired Madonna to be her tutor, and even then it might not work. "I don't think Julie wants a tutor," I said. Mom ignored me. Dad looked at me and shook his head, which meant I should be quiet.

"Do you want white toast or rye, Lisa?" Dad said.

Mom turned around to look at Dad. "You know I don't eat white bread," she said.

"Right," Dad said. "I forgot." Mom opened the fridge to get the orange juice, and Dad smiled at me. He always finds a way to change the subject when he wants Mom to calm down about something.

I got into the shower after Mom and Dad left. I used to always take baths, but I switched to taking showers in fifth grade. It makes me feel more grown-up to take a shower in the morning. Besides, everyone I know takes showers now. Well, except Julie. She still takes baths. She says she likes to "luxuriate." All I know is she takes a really long time to get ready in the morning and the bathroom smells like it's been flooded with perfume when Julie finally gets done luxuriating.

I decided not to make my bed because it was a weekend. Mom has a rule about us making beds. Julie and I don't really see the point because we just have to sleep in them anyway. So Julie got Mom to make this deal that we don't have to make them on the weekends because it's our time off. I'm glad I'm the younger sister—Julie already has Mom and Dad broken in for things like that.

My bed may have been messy, but my desk was completely neat. I had organized all my papers the night before, and I had everything we needed. I went through it again to make sure I hadn't forgotten anything—sponsor sheet, Super Sponsor sheet, and the letter to the sponsors. I had even typed everything up so it looked more official. I pulled my English folder out of my backpack, put everything inside it so it wouldn't bend, and then put the folder into my backpack. Doriane promised to bring a copy of the article she'd brought in for social studies, because that was going into the packets, too. I thought about calling her to remind her, but I didn't want to be too much of a pain. Besides, she was definitely responsible. I was even getting used to the idea of her helping out with the jog-a-thon.

There was still a lot of time left before Doriane's dad came. I would have played with Mooner, but she was still sleeping in Julie's room and it was too risky to go in there.

Julie would scream at me if I went in there and accidentally woke her up, and I definitely didn't feel like fighting. I thought about making my bed just to keep busy, but that seemed like a stupid thing to do, and it would only take up a couple minutes anyway. It wasn't like I was about to clean the whole house just to keep myself busy. Finally I decided to call Aunt Jean. I had told Doriane that her dad could pick me up at Aunt Jean's house because we had to pick up all the folders anyway. Her house was only ten minutes away so I certainly didn't need to get ready to go to her house yet, but I thought maybe I could go over there before it was time for Doriane and her dad to pick me up. I wasn't worried about waking Aunt Jean up. She wakes up early, just like Mom and Dad do. Maybe it's a grown-up thing. Maybe when I'm older, like around thirty, I'll all of a sudden start waking up early every day—not just on school days or when I have a lot on my mind. I guess you get a lot more hours in the day that way to get things done. I picked up the phone and dialed Aunt Jean's number.

Twenty minutes later I was ringing Aunt Jean's bell— three times, just like always. I was glad to get there early so Jake wasn't there to see.

Aunt Jean met me at the door. Her hair was wet from the shower. There were dark blue patches on the shoulders of her light blue shirt where the water had dripped down. "Come on in," Aunt Jean said. "I'll make you a waffle."

After I finished eating, we still had a lot of time before Doriane's father came. Aunt Jean and I decided to do some research and try to find the hospital in Mexico that Doriane had told us about. I sat down in front of Aunt Jean's computer and typed "Mexican Earthquake" into Google. Thousands of links popped up. "This is going to be hard to find," I said.

But since Aunt Jean works at the library, she knows how to research and is really good at finding things. We switched places; she sat in front of the computer and I stood behind her. After a while she found an article about a makeshift hospital for kids who were orphaned. "Look at this," Aunt Jean said.

I leaned over her shoulder to get a better look at the screen. Aunt Jean scrolled down to a bunch of pictures of the hospital. There was a photograph of the outside of the building, which didn't look very sturdy, and another picture of a bunch of kids lined up in front of a wall. The wall behind them was papered with pictures. The caption underneath said, "Orphaned children stand alongside photographs of their missing parents." I strained to see if Emily's family was in any of the pictures, but then I realized I wouldn't recognize them even if they were. There was another photograph of a girl holding up a drawing she had made. It wasn't a very good drawing, but I could tell it was supposed to be a picture of a woman—probably her mother. Maybe the earthquake had destroyed all the photographs.

"It's good you're doing something about this, Katie," Aunt Jean said. "I'm proud of you."

I stared back at the picture of the little girl. I knew we were doing a good thing by trying to help, but I didn't feel that proud. I sort of felt like I had done something wrong, and I felt bad about being annoyed with Mom and leaving her out of everything.

Suddenly there was honking from outside. "Wow, it's ten thirty already," I said. "That's got to be Doriane's dad."

"You better get out there before he honks again," Aunt Jean said. "Some of the neighbors might still be sleeping." She walked me to the door and I picked up my backpack on my way out. "Have fun," Aunt Jean said.

Doriane's dad's car was right out front. I saw Doriane and Jake in the backseat and waved. I was looking straight ahead at the car so I didn't see my parents walking up the block until I heard my mother's voice calling me. "Katie! Katie!" she yelled. She was so loud, louder even than Doriane's dad's car horn had been. I was sure everyone on the block could hear her. I thought about shouting to her to keep it down, but that would only have gotten me into trouble.

I stood by the car and watched Mom jog up Sage Drive toward me, her tennis racket banging against her hip. "Katie," Mom said, panting a little. "What are you doing here?"

"I have a project for school, and Aunt Jean let me store some stuff here."

"What kind of project?"

I knew I didn't have time to start explaining. Dad came up behind Mom. "Hey, sweetheart," he said.

"I've really got to go," I said. "Everyone's waiting for me." I nodded toward the car. Dad waved at Doriane's father. Mr. Leib waved back.

"I guess we can just ask your aunt about it," Mom said. I knew she was angry but I didn't say anything. I climbed into the car.

Eight

Dear Sophie,

You won't believe everything that has happened since my
last letter! I had an idea to have a jog-a-thon to help kids
who were in the Mexican earthquake, and I met with the
principal about it. Jake and Doriane came with me, and
Mr. Gallagher—he's our principal—said we could have the
jog-a-thon at Hillside! Over the weekend Jake, Doriane, and
I made up these packets with a bunch of information on the
earthquake and getting sponsors. We also had the idea to call
the jog-a-thon Emily's Run, because the article about that
girl Emily was the main inspiration behind the whole thing.

*Today we had this big assembly at school. Jake and I got
to stand up onstage with Mr. Gallagher. Doriane could
have come with us, but she was too nervous. Mr. Gallagher
told all the kids about the jog-a-thon. He handed out the
information packets and asked people to sign up for different
committees. It seems like everyone at Hillside is excited
about this. I totally knew they would be! We're going to have
weekly progress meetings on Fridays. I think a lot of kids will
come—practically everyone at the assembly today came up to
get an information packet. Even Julie did, and she's mad at
me. I hope that maybe she'll want to help with Emily's Run
and forgive me. I'll keep you posted on everything!*

Sincerely,

Katie

I realized that Julie would probably forgive me if I said I
needed her to take me to the mall to help with the jog-a-thon,
and I was right. She's nicest to me whenever there's something I need her help with—something that she can do better
than I can. After I finished my letter to Sophie, I went down
the hall and knocked on her bedroom door.

"I'm working," Julie said, which is what she always says
when she thinks that it's Mom at the door, so Mom will go away.

"It's me," I said.

"I said I'm working," Julie said, and I knew that meant she didn't want to see me.

"I need your help," I said. "Can I come in? Please?"

I heard Julie moving toward the door. She opened it a crack and stuck her head out. "What?" she said.

"I need your help," I said again.

"So you said," Julie said. "Are you going to tell me why?"

"I need to go to the mall," I said.

"You?"

"Well, I thought maybe the stores in the mall would want to help with Emily's Run, but you know them better than I do," I said. "Aunt Jean's books on fund-raising said it's easier to get money from companies when you have a personal connection to them."

Julie opened her door wider. "All right," she said. "Come in. What else does it say in Jean's books?" Julie started calling Aunt Jean just Jean last year. It reminded me of how Jake now said "Gallagher." I walked into her room. To myself, so softly that Julie couldn't hear, I breathed a sigh of relief.

We made a list of all the stores at the mall she thought would be good to get donations from. I couldn't believe how many stores she could remember off the top of her head.

I had asked Jake to come with us and he'd said he'd meet us in the food court of the mall on Saturday.

• • •

The next morning I was sitting with Julie at a table right by the pizza stand. It was too early for the pizza place to actually be open. The only food stand open was the one selling doughnuts. It was the second Saturday in a row that I had woken up early, but I didn't care. Julie said it was better to get to the stores early before the crowds, otherwise the salespeople would be too busy helping customers to concentrate on Emily's Run, which was officially set to be the Friday before Memorial Day weekend—just six weeks away. It was also the day before I was going to meet Sophie for the first time. She and her dad were going to be in San Francisco and come to Redwood City over the weekend. When I told Doriane that Sophie was coming, she couldn't believe it. "That's so cool," she said. "My pen pal hasn't written me back in months, so I stopped writing to her."

"Jake doesn't write to his pen pal anymore either, but Sophie and I still write each other all the time," I said. Jake rolled his eyes. I knew he thought having a pen pal was dumb and old-fashioned. He always made fun of me for sending Sophie actual letters instead of e-mails. But Doriane didn't seem to agree.

"You're so lucky," she said. Her voice sounded kind of sad, and I knew she wished her pen pal would visit her too. I didn't care if Jake thought the whole thing was stupid. I was so excited to meet Sophie in person. It was coming up so soon, and that meant the jog-a-thon would be here even sooner. I imagined other kids were probably spending the weekend getting their parents and friends to sponsor them. Mr. Gallagher also said he would contact the high school to see whether we could use their track, since the high school bleachers were bigger. All the students who were participating were in charge of getting their own sponsors and helping get Super Sponsors signed up. I wondered if anyone else had thought to come to the mall.

I rubbed my eyes and looked around for Jake. "He's late," I said to Julie.

"Not really," Julie said. "You were just in such a rush this morning that we got here early. I'm going to get a doughnut. Do you want one?"

I was still a little too tired to eat, so I shook my head. Julie got up to get her doughnut. I put my elbows on the table, leaned my head against my hands, and looked upward. There's a skylight above the food court just like in Aunt Jean's kitchen. There were clouds passing above us, but I knew it was probably fog and that the sun would come out soon.

The glass from the skylight was made up of a bunch of panels that came together in the shape of an upside-down *V*. The glass looked clean, and I wondered how they did that. Someone must have climbed up onto the roof to get it so clean. I wondered if there was an extra long squeegee that they could extend across to the glass. If they walked out on the glass, would they fall through? What if there was an earthquake while they were cleaning? I'd never thought about it before. But since you never know when an earthquake is coming, I knew there could be one right then, while I was sitting there under the skylight and Julie was off to the side buying her doughnut. We probably wouldn't even have time to dive under the tables. We would just look at each other and scream, and the glass would come down and kill us both. That must have been what it was like for people in Mexico. They were just going about their day like it was any other day. They had no idea what was about to happen to them, and even if they'd known, they couldn't have done anything to stop it. I squeezed my eyes shut. "Please don't let there be an earthquake today," I said to myself.

"Hey, Katie," Jake said. "Earth to Katie." I opened my eyes and there he was, standing right in front of me, with Doriane. Even though I hadn't invited her, I wasn't really surprised to see her. "You know you were just talking in your sleep," Jake said.

"I was not," I said.

"Oh, yeah? Then how come your lips were moving just now when you were sitting by yourself with your eyes closed? Just ask Doriane—she saw it too."

I looked over at Doriane, who shrugged. "I really wasn't paying attention," she said. I stood up from the table.

Julie walked back over to us with a half-eaten doughnut in her hand. "Anyone want the rest of this?" she asked.

"I'll take it," Jake said. He was about to take a bite, but then seemed to think better of it. "Doriane, you want it?" Doriane shook her head. Jake opened his mouth wide and shoved most of the doughnut into it.

"That's rude," I said.

"What?" Jake asked. It was hard to understand him because his mouth was full, but I knew what he was trying to say.

"What if I'd wanted some?" I wasn't even in the mood for doughnuts, so I guess it was stupid to make a big deal out of it. I just wanted Jake to think of me, too.

"Sorry," Jake said. He held out the rest of the doughnut. It was the tiniest bite in the world.

"Never mind," I said.

"Suit yourself," Jake said, and he popped the last morsel into his mouth.

I turned and saw Julie looking at me funny, almost like she felt sorry for me. I couldn't be sure, though, because Julie never feels sorry for me, but I decided not to ask her about it. I really wanted to get out of the food court anyway. I felt better when we walked into the main part of the mall where the stores were. There weren't many windows, but there were a lot of doorways to go to in case the ground started to shake. I stopped being mad at Jake and started getting excited again.

We had talked about what we needed to ask the people who worked in the stores. Of course the first thing was to ask the stores to be Super Sponsors. But sponsoring the track team could cost a lot of money, and Julie said that probably not every store would want to do that. So we thought of other things people from the stores could do. Julie said she would ask the salespeople she knew to sponsor her individually. Then Doriane said we should also ask them to put the sponsor sheets on their counters in case customers wanted to be sponsors too. We'd made up special packets for the stores that wanted to be Super Sponsors, and we had a lot of extra individual sponsor sheets with us as well. Julie was in charge of everything we did at the mall. She led us out of the food court and toward the stores so we could get started.

It was almost like we were ducklings and Julie was the mother duck. Julie walked in front, and we all followed behind her. I was behind Julie, and Jake and Doriane were behind me. *Waddle, waddle, waddle,* I thought. I turned around to make sure they were keeping up with us and saw Jake put his arm around Doriane's shoulder. I tried not to care and turned to catch up with Julie.

Our first stop was Julie's favorite store, Sally's Shack, which really isn't a shack at all. The mannequins in the windows all had on little black skirts and different tops. I recognized Julie's new skirt. Inside, the store looked like a disco. There was even a disco ball hanging from the ceiling and music playing in the background. Sally, the owner, was actually there, and she knows Julie well because Julie's in there practically every weekend. She came up and gave Julie a hug. "Sweetheart," she said, "I'm so glad you stopped by. There's a sweater that just came in that would look perfect with your new skirt!"

I knew Julie probably wanted to see the sweater, but she didn't show it. "I'm actually not here to shop today," she said. "I'm here with my sister, Katie, and her friends, and they have something they want to ask you."

I stepped out from behind Julie and shook Sally's hand, strong and firm. Sally pulled her hand away and shook it out. "That's some handshake," she said, smiling.

I hoped I hadn't gripped her too hard. I took a deep breath and started. "You know about the Mexican earthquake," I said.

Sally nodded. I went through the whole story. Jake stepped forward and interrupted me a couple times, but Doriane stayed quiet, as usual. She twirled her hair around her finger so tightly that the tip turned red. It didn't matter. By the time we were through, Sally had become our first official Super Sponsor of the day. Julie thanked Sally, and Sally hugged her again. Then she said, "I need to hug your adorable sister too!" She hugged me and said she hoped I would come back to her store again soon.

"So, what do you think?" Julie asked me when we'd walked out of the store.

"She's so nice," I said.

"You see," Julie said. "Shopping's not so bad."

We did the same thing at every store we went to. I was proud of Julie because she knew how to talk to the people in the stores and get them to listen. The other thing I learned was that shopping was hard work. I never thought of walking through the mall as good exercise, but my feet were killing me by the end. Maybe that's how Julie stays so skinny without ever doing sports. The people in the stores seemed pretty impressed. Most of them said they would mention it to their bosses. Julie kept a list of who said what, and who made what promise, and if there was anyone she could call back. I was disappointed that people weren't agreeing right away to sponsor us, like Sally did, but Julie had said this was how it would go. Four salespeople filled out sponsor forms and said they would sponsor Julie individually. Eight stores let us leave sponsor sheets on the counters in case customers wanted to get involved. The last store we went to, a place just called Shop! also agreed to be a Super Sponsor. As we walked out of the mall, I knew, overall, that the day had been a success. We headed home to ask our parents if their companies would be Super Sponsors too.

nine

Mom was waiting for us when Julie and I got home. We opened the door and she didn't look at me. She didn't even say hello. "You've been gone for hours," she said to Julie.

"I was helping Katie," Julie said.

"You have a test on Tuesday, Julie," Mom said firmly. "You're not going to leave this house again before school on Monday."

"Except to babysit Sascha tomorrow, right?" Julie said. Mom was silent. "Except for that, right, Mom?" Julie said. Her voice was too high all of a sudden and I knew she was about to cry.

"You shouldn't have left today if you had something to do tomorrow," Mom said.

"But, Mom," Julie said. "I can't just not show up. Sascha's parents will never let me babysit again!"

"Then you should've figured out your priorities ahead of time," Mom said. Julie turned and ran up the stairs. I heard her heavy footsteps as she ran down the hall, and then the slam of her door.

I turned to Mom. Of course she didn't care about the important thing I was doing for school. That was a priority too, wasn't it? More important than a stupid test Julie would do badly on no matter how hard she studied. "You know we were working on the jog-a-thon," I said. "It's really important."

"It's not more important than Julie's actual schoolwork," Mom said.

"Yes, it is," I said. "Raising money for kids who were hurt is more important than math or anything else at school."

"I'm the parent; you're the child," Mom said. "I know best."

"You don't even care about what I'm doing," I shouted. "You're just mad you found out about the jog-a-thon from Aunt Jean and I didn't tell you myself. You get all upset that I tell Aunt Jean things but then when I tell you what we were doing all you care about is Julie's dumb homework!" I thundered up the stairs just like Julie had a few seconds earlier and slammed my door as hard as I could.

● ● ●

Dad knocked on my door a little while later. I knew it had to be him. Julie was still shut up in her room and of course Mom didn't care enough to check on me. "Come in," I said.

"What's all this ruckus?" Dad said.

"She hates me," I told Dad.

"Who?" Dad said.

"Don't pretend you don't know," I said. "Mom!"

"She doesn't hate you," he said gently. "She loves you."

"She's mad at me," I said. "Just because I told Aunt Jean about the jog-a-thon first." I wished for the thousandth time that Aunt Jean were my mother, but I didn't say that out loud.

"Now you're being silly," Dad said.

"I am not," I said. The problem with Dad was he never stood up for me and told Mom she was wrong. All he ever did was sometimes try to change the subject. "Why should I tell her things instead of Aunt Jean if she's not going to care anyway? I bet she won't even end up coming to the jog-a-thon."

"Of course she'll be there," Dad said.

"Wanna bet?" I asked him. "She didn't even come to the talent show last fall. Remember? She always makes some excuse about Julie's schoolwork."

"Come on," Dad said, trying to change the subject, "let's go walk Mooner. I think I hear her whining."

"I don't feel like it," I told him. "I just want to be alone."

"Okay, honey," Dad said. He left me alone and I climbed into bed. I tried to imagine Mom coming to the jog-a-thon and cheering me on, but it's hard to picture something you know is impossible. So I just lay down on my bed and looked up at the ceiling—just plaster and paint and no skylight. There was no way I would be showered with broken glass if there was an earthquake while I was sleeping.

Jen

❋ ❋ ❋

Julie was yelling in the kitchen. I could hear her as I came downstairs to get a glass of orange juice, and I stopped in the hall just outside the kitchen. I could tell she was crying and it didn't seem right to go in there even though I really was thirsty. "You made an appointment with the Stanford nerd without even asking me," Julie said. "I can't believe you!" She had to be talking to Mom, but who was the Stanford nerd? It wasn't like Julie to make fun of someone like that. It must be someone she really hated. And then I remembered: Stanford. Mom's new and improved tutor.

Sure enough, Mom spoke next. "Julie," she said calmly, "don't call her that. That's a really terrible thing to say. Besides, you haven't even met her. You don't know a thing about her."

"But I know you," Julie said. "I know the kind of person you'd pick out. She'll have glasses and wear loafers and button-down shirts, and be the smartest and most boring person in the entire world. You always like people best that are the exact opposite of me."

"Oh, Julie, really," Mom said. "You know that's not true."

"It's totally true," Julie insisted. "You don't like me. You don't care about me. You don't care that I had things I was supposed to do today. Otherwise you wouldn't go around making plans for me like that."

"I'm your mother," Mom said. Mom thinks being a mother is a good enough reason for anything. I'll never say anything like that to my kids.

"You just can't accept that I'm stupid, can you?" Julie said. "You'll never accept me for who I am."

"You are not stupid," Mom said firmly. "You can do anything you put your mind to."

"You see. You can't accept it. And now you're ruining my life!" Julie cried. "You're going to make me lose my clients. Mrs. Watts is never going to trust me to keep a job again."

"Julie, you need to calm down," Mom said. "I spoke to Denise Watts myself. She's going to a friend's for lunch and she's only going to be gone for a few hours. She said it was fine for Katie to babysit this time."

Mom had come into my room that morning to tell me I had to babysit for Sascha Watts. I didn't think she should have made plans for me either without asking first. What if I'd had something important to do? I didn't really want to spend a whole day chasing after a three-year-old. But I didn't want to mess things up for Julie anymore than they already were, so I told Mom I would go. Mrs. Watts was going to pick me up in a few minutes and drop Sascha and me back over at their house.

The kitchen had become quiet. I swallowed, still feeling thirsty. My throat was dry because I hadn't had anything to drink at all yet, so I walked into the kitchen. Julie was at the table with her head in her hands. Mooner was next to her whining softly. She always cries when Julie is crying. "You all set?" Mom said to me as though everything were normal.

"I just wanted some juice," I said. Mom opened the refrigerator and I sat down next to Julie. I would have put my arm on her shoulder, but I don't think she would have liked that. I wanted to tell her that I was going to be the best babysitter I could be, so she shouldn't worry that Mrs. Watts would stop calling her. Instead I just sat there and drank the orange juice Mom gave me.

"Mrs. Watts will be here any second," Mom said.

"I guess I'll wait outside," I told her.

Ten minutes later I was in the front seat of Mrs. Watts's car. The inside smelled funny, sort of like baby powder. I looked over at Sascha in the backseat. She was in a car seat that looked like a booster chair—the kind they make for kids who are too big for baby car seats but too small for just wearing a seat belt. Sascha saw me look at her and turned away. It was going to be a long day. I sighed. I didn't mean to, but it just came out. Then I felt my cheeks turning red.

"Don't worry. Sascha won't give you any trouble," Mrs. Watts said. "She promised to be a very good girl. Right, Sasch?" Sascha didn't answer. "She may C-R-Y a little when I leave," Mrs. Watts continued. "Don't take it personally. She's always fine as soon as I'm out of sight."

We pulled up in front of the house. Mrs. Watts helped Sascha out of the car and led her over to me.

"The door's open now, but lock the door behind you when you get inside," Mrs. Watts said. "The emergency numbers are all by the phone in the kitchen." She held Sascha's hand out to me. "Okay, Sasch, you be good with Katie. I'll be back soon." Sascha gripped my hand and we watched as Mrs. Watts got back into the car. As soon as she started to pull away, the wailing started.

I crouched down toward Sascha. "Don't cry," I told her. "We're going to have fun!" I tried to sound confident, but Sascha didn't seem convinced. She continued crying. It wasn't loud, just long and steady. She cried and cried as I pulled her toward the house and locked the door behind us.

I didn't know what to say to a crying three-year-old. "It will be okay," I said. "Your mom will be home soon." I thought to myself that it wouldn't be soon enough. "Do you want to color?" I asked. She sniffled and shook her head. "Do you want me to read to you?" I asked, and Sascha shook her head again. She was almost not crying anymore. She took in a deep breath, the kind you take when you're trying to catch your breath after too much crying. She made a funny ehh-ehh-ehh sound as she breathed in, like a car that won't start. We stared at each other for a few seconds, and her breathing became more and more normal. "We can do whatever you want to do," I told her. Sascha rubbed her stomach. "Are you hungry?" I asked.

Sascha nodded.

"Do you want cereal?" I asked, and she shook her head. "Toast?" She shook her head again. "Peanut butter and jelly?" I suggested. Sascha shook her head again. "Well, what do you want?" I asked. Sascha shrugged. Julie told me once that Sascha didn't talk much, but I didn't know that meant she would be silent.

Sascha walked toward the kitchen, and I followed her. She got to the refrigerator and tugged at the handle with both hands, but it wouldn't open. "Here, let me help you," I said. I reached above her hands and pulled the door open. She looked up at me as though she were impressed by my strength, and I smiled. Maybe this wouldn't be so hard. People liked me at school—I could get a three-year-old to like me. "Anything in here you want?" I asked.

Sascha stepped in front of me and pushed open the

refrigerator door wider. She took a long time looking over all the choices. I started to worry about the fridge door being open for so long. Mom always tells us if we hold the door open too long, all the food will get spoiled. What if all the cold air escaped and all the Wattses' food went bad? I didn't want Mrs. Watts to get so mad that she wouldn't ask Julie to babysit again. "Come on, Sascha," I said. "What do you want?"

Sascha looked up at me and shrugged. It was going to be a long day. I sighed again. Sascha sighed too.

"All right," I said, peering at the shelves in the fridge. There were cold cuts in labeled plastic bags. "How about a turkey sandwich?" I suggested.

Sascha shook her head.

"Salami? Roast beef?"

She shook her head again.

"What about this?" I said, pointing to the hot dogs.

She moved her head from side to side.

"Let's see," I said. "What's in here? Oh, cheese. You want some cheese?" I waited for her to shake her head again, but she didn't. "You want cheese, Sascha?"

Sascha nodded. I couldn't believe it. I had begun to think that it would be impossible for her to move her head up and down instead of shaking it from side to side.

There were four different kinds of cheese in the cheese drawer—cheddar, American, and two other kinds that I had

never had before, Brie and Havarti. "Do you want this one?"
I asked, picking up the cheddar. Sascha shook her head.
"How about American cheese?" I asked. Sascha nodded and
smiled. She had really tiny teeth and there were big gaps
between each tooth. I wondered if her teeth would always
look too small for her mouth or if, when she got her permanent teeth, they would be the right size and fill up her mouth.

"All right," I said, finally closing the refrigerator door.
"Do you want just some pieces of cheese, or do you want
cheese on a sandwich?" Sascha didn't answer. I realized I
had to ask yes or no questions. "Do you want me to put the
cheese on bread?" She nodded. "Should I heat it up, like a
grilled cheese?" I asked, and she nodded again.

I pulled a plate out of one of the cabinets. There was a
bread box on the counter, and I opened it and pulled out a
couple slices of white bread. Aunt Jean sometimes makes
me grilled cheese in a frying pan. She spreads butter on the
outsides of the bread so it gets nice and crispy. I loved the
way the crust was crispy and the inside was all melted, but if
I made it that way for Sascha, there would be a greasy pan to
clean up, and I really hate cleaning. I decided to just make her
grilled cheese in the toaster oven. She wasn't even four years
old yet, so I didn't think she would know the difference. She
watched from the doorway as I put a slice of cheese on each
piece of bread and put them in the toaster oven. The toaster
was unplugged, so I plugged it in and pressed the button

down. The coils on the inside of the toaster turned red as they heated up. "Just a couple more minutes," I told Sascha. "Why don't you go sit at the table? I'll get you some juice."

She turned and walked toward the table, and I went back to the refrigerator. I had just pulled out the bottle of apple juice when I noticed the smell.

I turned and saw the smoke coming out from along the edges of the toaster oven. I reached over to turn the toaster off and flip it open. The bread was blackened. I knew Sascha wouldn't eat it, and I didn't want to risk trying to make another grilled cheese in the toaster. I was trying to figure out what else I could give her to eat when the smoke alarm went off. I guess the smoke from the toaster had drifted up to the alarm. It was a horrible sound, like a high-pitched scream, and I hadn't been expecting it. The bottle of apple juice slipped out of my hand and onto the floor. Luckily it was a plastic bottle so it didn't break, but there was juice everywhere. "Oh my god!" I cried, and then I clapped my hand over my mouth. I turned toward the table to look at Sascha, but she was gone.

I felt my heart pounding inside my chest. *Sascha's fine*, I told myself. She probably just got scared and ran down the hall. I turned back toward the toaster and pulled the plug out of the wall. Then I opened all the windows in the kitchen to get the smoke out. The alarm was still shrieking. I spotted it high above the doorway next to the oven. There was no way I could reach it to turn it off. Maybe if I waved something in front of it so the burning smell went away faster, then it would stop. I pulled a chair over from the table and stood on it, waving my hands wildly. It seemed to take a long time, but finally the alarm stopped. I took a deep breath. So much for a shortcut to making a grilled cheese. Now I had to find Sascha.

The problem with a kid who doesn't talk is that she doesn't answer when you call her. I walked down the hall yelling, "Sascha, where are you?" But she didn't answer.

I darted in and out of rooms as I walked down the hall. She wasn't in the den or the guest room. She wasn't in Mr. and Mrs. Watts's room or any of the bathrooms. At the end of the hall I found the room that had to be Sascha's room. It was painted lavender and there were pictures of unicorns on the wall. At the far end of the room was a canopied bed, the kind of bed Julie always wanted when we were younger. I had wanted bunk beds. I glanced around the room, but I didn't see Sascha. I was about to turn around and keep looking, but then I heard something. "Sascha?" I called. "Sascha, are you in here?"

There was a rustling from under the bed. "Oh, Sascha," I said. "It's okay to come out now. The alarm isn't ringing anymore." I moved toward the bed, but Sascha didn't emerge.

"Come on," I said. I got to the bed, crouched down, and pulled up the dust ruffle. There was Sascha curled up like a little ball. "It's okay," I told her. I reached out my hand.

Sascha's eyes were wide and watering. She seemed to be thinking about whether to trust me. I thought of the apple juice, drying and sticky on the kitchen floor, and wished she would hurry up. Finally, she extended her arm and I took her hand. I pulled her gently and she moved toward me, inch by inch. She moved slowly, slowly, and then she stopped. Half her body was out and half her body was still under the bed. "Just a little more," I said, and I gave a stronger tug. She didn't budge. Her eyes grew wider. "Are you stuck?" I said, and her eyes overflowed.

I pulled and pulled at her, but she was absolutely stuck. It didn't make sense. She'd gotten under there, so naturally she should be able to get out, but I didn't want to pull too hard because I might hurt her. I stood up and reached under the bed to try to lift it, but it was no use. The bed was much too heavy. Sascha started sobbing out loud. I wished Julie were there. I knew I needed help. I couldn't even call Julie because Mom would be there, screening her calls, and I would have to explain everything to her. Then she'd probably want to help herself, and I really didn't want her to come over. Jake might know what to do but he had track practice and a math test to study for. Aunt Jean was in San Francisco for lunch because once every other month she went to the city to have lunch with her husband's parents. I could've called Tesa or Sara, but I didn't really know them well enough to call them in an emergency. That's the sort of thing that best friends are for. I decided to call Doriane.

Doriane answered on the first ring. I had taken the cordless phone into Sascha's room, and I sat next to her head while I explained the situation to Doriane. "My dad's on his way out," Doriane said. "I could ask him to drop me off if you need help."

I wasn't sure what would get me into more trouble — having Mrs. Watts come home while her daughter was still stuck under the bed, or having her come home and find me there with a friend. Maybe Doriane could leave before she even got home. "All right," I said. "Come over."

It seemed like forever before the doorbell rang, but I knew it had only been a few minutes. Doriane lived pretty close by. I got up and went to answer the door. "I'll be right back," I told Sascha. She was still crying, so I wasn't sure she even heard what I said. Doriane was standing on the front porch. "I'm never babysitting ever again!" I told her, and I led her back to Sascha's room.

"Hey there, Sascha. I'm Doriane," Doriane said softly. It was actually her normal voice, but Doriane said everything softly. "We're going to get you out of there." I doubt Sascha even heard her because she was screaming so loudly.

Doriane and I tried to lift the bed together, but even with two of us, it was still too heavy. She bent down to pull on Sascha like I had, but Sascha stayed stuck and kept wailing.

Doriane stood back up. "Maybe we should pull her together," I suggested.

"We need to calm her down first," Doriane said. "She starts kicking whenever you pull on her, and that could make her more stuck. Besides, if we pull on her when she's fighting like this, she could get hurt."

"Well, she's never gonna stop crying while she's stuck like that," I said. "Maybe we should put butter or oil or something on her. When Julie got a ring stuck on her finger, Mom put cooking oil on it and it slid right off."

"Yeah, but Sascha's wearing a T-shirt," Doriane said. "I don't think the oil would work on her shirt like that."

"So, what should we do to calm her down?" I asked.

Doriane knelt back down on the floor. "Hi, Sascha," she said. "It's me again. Doriane. You know, I have a brother named Avi Benjamin. He's three years old. Are you three years old? Are you this many?" Doriane held three fingers up toward Sascha. "Or maybe you're this many?" Doriane said, holding up four fingers. Of course Sascha didn't answer, but Doriane kept talking. "Are you this many?" she asked, holding up five fingers. "You can't be this many! That's a whole hand." Sascha looked at Doriane's fingers. She was still crying, but she seemed to not be crying quite as hard.

I bent down next to Doriane. "I didn't know you had a brother," I said.

"I do," Doriane said. She kept looking at Sascha, even

though she was talking to me. "He's actually my half brother. We have the same dad, and his mother is my stepmother."

"Oh," I said. "Do you have any other brothers and sisters?"

"Nope," Doriane said. "It's just Avi and me. I babysit him a lot. And you know what, Sascha, he really likes this song about eating spaghetti. Maybe you know it too." Doriane tipped her head so she was right by Sascha's ear, and she started singing. Her voice was practically a whisper. At first Sascha kept crying, but after a couple verses, she stopped so she could hear Doriane's voice. And then the most amazing thing happened: Sascha started singing right along with her. I could hardly believe it. How could Doriane get her to sing when I hadn't even been able to get her to talk? "Okay, Sascha," Doriane said after the song ended, "stay very still just like that. Katie and I are going to get you out now." We each took an arm and pulled, and this time Sascha slid all the way out.

"Doriane," I said, "you're a genius!"

"Not really," Doriane said, blushing. "I just know a lot about kids." She turned to Sascha. "You were so brave," she told her. Sascha reached out to hug her, and Doriane put her arms around her.

"Sing again," Sascha said. Doriane smiled and started singing the spaghetti song, and I went into the kitchen to clean up the apple juice. By then the juice had dried up so the floor was really sticky. It would have been easier to clean a greasy pan. I got down on my hands and knees and thought about how Doriane would probably tell Jake all about what had happened, and then he would think she was some kind of a hero. I rinsed my hands off in the sink and dried them on a paper towel. Then I headed back to Sascha's room. Doriane was bouncing her in her lap.

"Hey," Doriane said. "Look who's back."

"Hey," I said. "So I bet you can't wait to tell Jake about all this, huh?"

"Yeah," Doriane said. "I'm supposed to meet up with him when he's done with practice."

"I thought he had to study after practice," I said.

"I know," Doriane said. "But I'm better at math than he is, so he asked me to help him."

I was better at math than Jake was too, and I'd helped him plenty of times before. But I could barely get Jake alone anymore. I leaned against the door frame. "You know, Doriane," I said, "there's something I think you should know."

"What?"

"You have to promise not to tell Jake I'm telling you," I said. "He'd kill me if he knew I told."

"I promise," Doriane said.

"Okay," I said. "The thing is, Jake really likes Lexi Moss." What was I saying? What was happening to me? The words were tumbling out of my mouth. "You know, she's the girl in social studies. The one who transferred to Hillside in January."

"I know who she is," Doriane said. "She's the pretty one with dark hair."

"Yeah," I said. "Anyway, Jake talks about her all the time." The truth was that Jake had never said anything to me about Lexi Moss. But even though I knew what I was saying wasn't true, I couldn't stop myself. It was almost as if someone else were talking, not me. "He's practically obsessed with her," I heard myself say.

Doriane lifted Sascha off her lap and stood up. "Oh," she said. She bit her lower lip and I thought she might cry. It's not like I wanted her to cry, but I knew that meant she was already starting to hate Jake.

"I think he might just be using you to make her jealous or something. I saw him do the exact same thing to this girl Erin at camp last summer," I said.

"I saw him talking to Lexi in the cafeteria the other day," Doriane said softly. "She was standing next to him in line, and he leaned over toward her. But I was too far away, and I couldn't hear what he said."

Probably he had asked Lexi to hand him a carton of milk or something like that, but I didn't tell Doriane that. "I hope you're not mad at me for saying something," I said.

"No," Doriane said. "I guess it's good that I know. I better get going, though. Sascha's mom will be home soon anyway."

"Is your dad going to pick you up?" I asked.

"I think maybe I'll just walk," Doriane said.

"Isn't it far?" I asked.

"Not too far," she said. "Anyway, I need some time to think."

"Are you still going to Jake's?" I asked.

"No," Doriane said. "I just want to go home."

Sascha and I walked Doriane to the front door. Doriane looked so small and sad. I wished I could take it all back. What was wrong with me? Sascha was quiet again. "Your mom will be home soon," I told her. "Why don't we watch TV while we wait?"

A few minutes later I heard Mrs. Watts's key in the door. "Hello," Mrs. Watts called. "How's my girl?"

"She was great," I said, thankful that Sascha didn't talk much.

"What did you do?" Mrs. Watts asked.

I was about to say *Nothing much*, when Sascha started speaking. "The alarm in the kitchen went off and Katie spilled the juice. Then I got stuck under the bed, and Katie's friend came over to get me out."

My mouth hung open. I didn't know what to say. I had ruined everything for Julie for sure. "Sorry," I said. "I was trying to make grilled cheese for her and the toaster started smoking."

"Don't worry about it," Mrs. Watts said. "The toaster is

pretty temperamental. We keep it unplugged, but I should have told you."

"That's okay," I said. "I hope it's all right that I called my friend to help. She's very good with kids."

"Of course," Mrs. Watts said. She turned to Sascha, "Did you have fun today with Katie?" she asked and Sascha nodded.

"I did too," I said. It was true, mostly. I had fun the whole time until I said all that stuff about Jake to Doriane. I wondered if it was possible for Doriane to just forget it had happened. I tried to imagine things just going back to normal, like I hadn't said anything at all.

Mrs. Watts drove me home and paid me. I thought maybe I would buy something for Julie, and I ran upstairs to tell her I was home.

I knocked on Julie's door. "Yeah," she said.

"It's me," I told her.

"Come in," Julie said.

I walked into the room. Julie was stretched out on her bed. It didn't look like she was studying at all. "How was your tutor?" I asked carefully.

"I don't want to talk about it," Julie said.

"I'm sorry," I said. "Was she awful?"

"I said I don't want to talk about it," Julie said.

"Sorry," I said again.

"How was Sascha?" Julie asked.

I decided to leave out the bad parts. "She was fine," I told her. "Mrs. Watts said to wish you good luck on your test and she'll call you later in the week."

"I wish there would be an earthquake so I don't have to take this test on Tuesday," Julie said.

"Don't say that," I said.

"I was just kidding," Julie said.

"It's not funny," I said seriously.

"Okay," Julie said. "I won't say it again."

Eleven

The next Friday we had our weekly lunch meeting about Emily's Run. Mr. Gallagher had said we were all allowed to bring our lunches into the auditorium, even though there are signs up that say NO FOOD OR DRINK and on ordinary days you can get in trouble just for chewing a piece of gum in there.

I had told Jake that I thought we should bring something with us to thank everyone for coming, and we'd gone to Aunt Jean's to make chocolate chip cookies. I'd said he could invite Doriane if he wanted. I felt really bad about everything I had told her. But Jake had shrugged his shoulders and said he thought Doriane was busy.

"You made cookies?" Doriane asked when she saw us.

"Yeah," I said, trying to ignore the feeling in my stomach. "It was a last-minute thing." I shifted my weight because it was hard to balance the tray of cookies and my lunch at the same time. Doriane offered to carry my lunch for me.

"It's okay," I told her. "I can manage."

"I don't mind helping," Doriane said.

"Thanks," I said. I handed her my lunch bag. My stomach did another flip-flop and I thought I would drop the tray of cookies anyway. I gripped the sides of the tray tighter and walked into the auditorium.

"What's this?" Mr. Gallagher said when he saw.

"Cookies," Jake said from behind me.

"We wanted to bring something for everyone," I explained.

"As long as it's not contraband," Mr. Gallagher said. He peered down at me and looked stern.

"Of course not," I said quickly. Mr. Gallagher smiled, and I hoped that meant he had been kidding.

There were more than fifty kids at the meeting, including a bunch of kids that Jake and I were friends with, like Tesa and Sara and all the kids Jake knew from the track team. We had moved the chairs around so we were more or less in one big circle instead of all facing the stage. I put the cookies on a chair right in the center so people could take them whenever they wanted. Doriane had put my lunch on the seat next to her, like she was saving the seat for me, so I picked it up and sat down.

Jake sat in the empty seat next to me — not next to Doriane.

Mr. Gallagher cleared his throat loudly to get everyone's attention. My stomach still felt funny so I decided just to concentrate on Mr. Gallagher and not think about Doriane at all.

Things were definitely falling into place. The high school had agreed to give us their track. Some of the high school students had volunteered to work at the jog-a-thon. All the runners were going to wear cards around their necks, and each time they ran around the track, one of the high school volunteers would punch a hole in the card to keep track of how many laps they'd run. The more laps they ran, the more money they raised.

Mr. Gallagher asked for a report on the halftime show. "Well, I haven't heard back from either of the bands I sent letters to," Jake told him.

"What bands are those, Jake?" Mr. Gallagher asked.

"Oh, two great bands," Jake said. "You might not have heard of them, but kids love their music. One is called Dozer. The other one is Razor's Edge. I wrote them all about Emily's Run. I think we should hear back soon."

"Cool," I heard someone say from the other side of the circle.

"I was thinking more about the high school band," Mr. Gallagher said. "I know the Hillside band and chorus groups didn't want to perform because they wanted to participate in the jog-a-thon, but a couple of our eighth-grade band members were going to contact some of the ninth graders who are now in the Redwood City High School band to see if they can step in. Has anyone checked that out?"

"But, Mr. Gallagher," Jake interrupted, "you said it would be okay if I tried to get a famous band."

"Yes, Jake," Mr. Gallagher said, "and I think your effort was great, but we also discussed that it would be a long shot. Since we haven't heard back from your bands, can someone report on the status of the high school band?" A couple of eighth graders raised their hands. I didn't know their names until Mr. Gallagher said, "All right, Eric and Bill, let's hear it."

"Okay, so we spoke to Matt Hogan, who was in the Hillside band last year and now he's in the high school band. Matt talked to his band members about the jog-a-thon, and they're totally in. They just need to know when and how long we want them to perform for."

Another girl raised her hand. "Yes, Ella?" Mr. Gallagher said. I thought it was amazing that Mr. Gallagher knew everyone's name.

"My sister's a cheerleader at the high school," Ella said. "I told her about Emily's Run, and she said the cheerleaders would be happy to perform too."

"This is all wonderful," Mr. Gallagher said. "I appreciate all your hard work. But now we have to get down to the most important part. I want to hear how the sponsorships are coming. Can I see a show of hands first from everyone who has gotten sponsors so far?" Almost everyone raised their hands.

"Good job," Mr. Gallagher said. "Now how many of you have gotten Super Sponsors?" This time only about fifteen kids raised their hands. "All right. That's great," Mr. Gallagher said. He bent toward the notepad in his lap. "I want to make a list of the Super Sponsors we have so far. That way we can get to work on the signage and also keep track of what companies have already signed up to do this so we don't duplicate our efforts. I'll circulate the list at the end of the day. So let's just go around the room. Katie, do you want to go first?"

I lowered my hand and listed the Super Sponsors we'd gotten so far—there were the two stores Julie had taken us to, Dad's company, and Doriane's father's company. Aunt Jean had even said she would be a Super Sponsor. "That's it so far," I said after I was done listing them for Mr. Gallagher. "But I'm sure Jake, Doriane, and I will get more." Jake hadn't even asked his parents yet, but he said he thought that each of their companies would be Super Sponsors. Aunt Jean was going to ask her husband's old company, and Julie said we could take another trip to the mall.

"Thanks, Katie," Mr. Gallagher said. I sat back while the other kids listed the Super Sponsors they'd gotten and Mr. Gallagher wrote it all down. I watched Mr. Gallagher's list get longer and longer. It wasn't just my idea anymore—the jog-a-thon was much more than just me. After we'd gone around the whole circle, Mr. Gallagher said we should take a few moments to think about other possible Super Sponsors to target in the next week so we could have more to add to Mr. Gallagher's list by the next meeting. I noticed that Jake wasn't writing anything down. Of course it wasn't like he was going to forget that he still had to ask his parents. But just in case, I wrote "Mr. and Mrs. O" on my pad, and decided I'd remind Jake later.

After a couple minutes we were all done with our lists. Mr. Gallagher told us to keep thinking about other potential Super Sponsors and to ask for his help if we needed it. "Obviously, we still have work to do, but this is a very good list so far," Mr. Gallagher said, holding up the list he had made of confirmed Super Sponsors. "So those of you on the track team who are here, I hope you are all practicing your long-distance running." I heard some kids laugh and looked across the circle to where some of Jake's teammates were sitting. "I do want to thank the track team," Mr. Gallagher said. "You're shouldering an important responsibility, and we're going to raise a lot more money because of you."

"No problem," Morgan called. I looked over at Jake. He loved pointing out to Doriane and me how important the track team was going to be, and I was sure he was thinking about all the money the track team (and he especially) would bring in. But Jake was looking at his lap.

Mr. Gallagher started talking about individual sponsors again. "This is the most important part, everybody," he said. "The individual sponsors are the bread and butter of this event. Please keep talking to your families about it. And for your friends who could not make it to this meeting, please fill them in. We have only five weeks left." I kept looking at Jake, waiting for him to look up from his lap. But he didn't. He shifted his weight in his seat and looked bored.

Our lunch period was almost over, and Mr. Gallagher wrapped the meeting up. He thanked everyone for coming and told us to have a good weekend.

There was a lot of noise at once as everyone stood up. Julie started to walk toward us, but I knew she was coming to talk to Mr. Gallagher and not me. He makes her check in with him every week to make sure all of her classes are okay. I would hate to have to meet with Mr. Gallagher by myself like that. Jake pushed back his chair as he stood, and it made an awful screeching sound when it moved against the floor. I thought we should probably stick around for a few minutes in case Mr. Gallagher wanted to talk to us, but Jake moved quickly toward the door. Doriane and I picked up our lunch bags and followed after him.

"Hey, Jake, wait up!" I called.

Jake turned on his heel to face us. "Can you believe Gallagher?" he said.

"What are you talking about?" I asked.

"He was just a complete jerk. I can't believe you didn't notice," he said. He looked at me like I was the dumbest person in the world. I hate when he looks at me like that. "You've turned into a complete idiot now that you're obsessed with making Gallagher like you. It's like you're a different person," he said.

"I didn't notice either," Doriane said. I nodded at Doriane, a silent thank you. Jake turned and started walking away from us again.

"Jake, come on," I said.

"You guys didn't even say anything when he just brushed me off like that," Jake said. "You could have at least said we should wait to hear back from the bands. Some friends you turned out to be."

"Aw, Jake," I said. "Now you're just being a baby."

Jake turned again. "What did you just call me?" I sucked in my breath. Jake looked back and forth from Doriane to me. "You two don't need me anyway," he said. He sounded like a baby again, but I didn't say it. "Forget it. Forget this whole stupid thing."

"What are you talking about?" I asked.

"I quit," he said.

"You quit Emily's Run?" Doriane asked.

"You guessed it," Jake said.

"You can't be serious!" I said. "I can't believe you would do this to Emily."

"Oh, don't be stupid," Jake said. "We don't even know Emily."

There he was calling me stupid again. If I hadn't called him a baby, maybe he wouldn't have done that. He certainly wouldn't have quit the jog-a-thon. This whole thing was supposed to be something we could do together, and now his back was to me, his shoulders were hunched, and he was striding down the hall. Doriane and I just stood there and watched him walk away. He walked quickly and didn't turn around to look at us.

"This is all my fault," Doriane said. She sounded like she was going to cry.

"No," I said. "It's my fault. I shouldn't have called him a baby."

"You don't understand," Doriane said. She sniffled, and I knew she was trying as hard as she could not to cry. "He kept asking me about meeting up this weekend. I didn't know what to say because I didn't want him to know that you'd told me anything, so I just kept making up excuses not to see him. But he kept on asking me, pretending that he really wanted to see me. It's not like I can tell him I'm busy every day for the rest of my life. So I told him I knew about Lexi. I said I saw him talking to her in the cafeteria."

Suddenly everything around me felt so big. I remembered how small Doriane had looked leaving the Wattses' house. That's exactly how I felt just then. "What did he say?" I asked.

"He said he didn't know what I was talking about," Doriane said. "But I saw him. I can't believe he would just lie to my face like that and keep trying to use me." Now she was really crying.

"Listen, it's okay," I said. "It's not your fault—you know that, don't you?" I said. Just then the weirdest thing popped into my head. In first grade we had to come up with adjectives for ourselves using the letters in our names. I made the *E* in Katie stand for "energetic." Now I thought the *E* should stand for "evil." But Doriane seemed to like me and she even seemed to believe me.

"Thanks," she said. "Do you think maybe we could do something after school?"

"All right," I said.

"I could meet you at your locker after last period," she offered, and I nodded.

Doriane was waiting for me at my locker at the end of the day. I started to walk more slowly. I didn't want to be around her just then. I didn't want to be around anyone. I just wanted to be home. "Hey, Katie," Doriane called out when she saw me.

"Hey, Doriane," I said.

I opened my locker and tried to remember what books I would need to take home with me for the weekend. It was hard to concentrate on homework when I had so much to think about.

"So, do you want to go back to Round Table?" Doriane asked. "I bet I could get my dad to drive us. He usually gets home early on Fridays."

I closed my locker and looked up at her. "I'm sorry," I said. "I know I said we could do something, but I think I'm just going to go home."

"You're mad at me," Doriane said.

"No, I'm not," I told her. "I'm just in a bad mood."

"I'm sorry," Doriane said.

"It's not your fault," I said. "But I'm not going to be any fun. Trust me—you won't even want to be around me."

"I don't mind," Doriane said.

Why was she making this so hard? "Listen, Doriane," I said, "no offense, but I really want to be alone."

"Okay," Doriane said softly. I knew I had said the wrong thing again and hurt her feelings. I didn't mean to sound angry, but everything I said came out wrong. Doriane turned to walk down the hall. Her shoulders slumped underneath her backpack.

"I'll call you later, okay?" I said. She turned around and shrugged, and then turned to walk the rest of the way down the hall. I turned back to my locker and packed up my backpack. My bag was heavy and I had to walk all the way back up the hill to get home. I walked slowly, so it took me a while to get there.

Twelve

Julie was already home when I got there. She used to always hang out with Val on Fridays, but Mom had decided that Julie should come home every Friday right after school. She thought Julie should do all her weekend homework before she went out with her friends or went shopping. I trudged upstairs and went straight to my room. "Dear Sophie," I wrote. "Everything is so messed up." I told her how mad Jake had gotten about Mr. Gallagher and how he'd quit the jog-a-thon, but I left out the part about Lexi Moss. Then I signed my name, "Sincerely, Katie," just like always. As I read over my letter, it occurred to me that I was one of the least sincere people I knew. I was always making things up in my head, and now I'd made them up out loud to Doriane, and look where it had gotten me. I put the letter into an envelope and put it into my backpack. Then I threw my backpack onto the floor. It landed against the wall with a thud. I liked the sound it made — heavy and angry, just the way I felt.

"Katie?" Julie called. She must have heard my bag when it slammed against the wall between our rooms. I ignored her and threw myself onto my bed.

"Hey, Katie," I heard Julie call again from the other room. "Come here!"

I didn't feel like going to see Julie. I didn't feel like seeing anyone. But I also didn't feel like shouting all of that to her. I heaved myself off of my bed and walked into Julie's room. "What do you want?" I said.

"Nothing," Julie said. "What's wrong with you?"

"Nothing," I said.

"Yeah, right," she said.

"Jake's quitting the jog-a-thon," I told her.

"Why?"

"I don't really want to talk about it," I said.

"Did you guys have a big fight?"

I didn't answer her. I leaned back against the wall and slid to the ground. "This isn't how it was supposed to happen," I said. "It just sucks. Now everything is ruined."

"The jog-a-thon won't be ruined," Julie said. "There was a ton of people at that meeting today. They'll pick up Jake's slack."

I didn't want to tell Julie that wasn't what I meant—everything between Jake and me was ruined, and it was all my fault. I had thought saying those things would make things go back to the way they were before—when Jake wanted me around and acted like my best friend. Now all I wanted to do was take it all back, but it was too late. "You don't understand," I told her.

"You know, sometimes you can really sound like Mom. You can't control everything and you need to chill out a little. The jog-a-thon will go on, even without Jake. And I bet you guys will make up soon anyway."

"I don't think we will," I said.

"Well, if it's meant to be, it'll work out. But, you know, I always thought something would happen between you and Jake."

"What do you mean?"

"I mean, it's just easier when your best friend is a girl. Do you have a crush on him or something?"

"No, of course not!"

"Are you sure?"

I took a deep breath in and held it for a few seconds before letting it out in one long sigh. Julie was looking at me, waiting for an answer. "Yes, I'm sure," I said finally. "But I just thought he would always be my best friend. I didn't think he would ever like anybody else as much as he liked me."

"You can't control people like that," Julie said.

"So does that mean you think I'm horrible?"

"No, you're not horrible," she said. "Look at everything you're doing for the Mexican earthquake. You wouldn't do that if you were horrible, you know?"

I nodded. I told myself it didn't matter about Jake and what I'd done. I'd just keep working on the jog-a-thon and I'd be a good person. "I'm just not going to think about Jake anymore," I told Julie. "Maybe I'll wake up and all of this will just go away."

"You can't ignore it," Julie said. "And you can't do anything to change it."

"Then what do I do?"

"You just have to accept that things don't always turn out the way you want," she said.

Thirteen

Once you say something out loud, you can't take it back, no matter how much you want to. The words just hang there in the air, so heavy and permanent it's almost like you can touch them: *Jake really likes Lexi Moss,* I had told Doriane. *I think he might just be using you.*

I thought about Julie saying that things wouldn't always work out the way I wanted, and I knew I had to call Jake. Maybe it wouldn't even be that hard. He didn't know I had anything to do with Doriane and Lexi Moss. Just because he was mad at Doriane didn't mean he had to be mad at me, too. Maybe I could cheer him up and it would all work out. Maybe I hadn't just ruined everything.

I dialed the Oxmans' number and Jake's mother answered

the phone. "Hey, Mrs. O," I said, "It's me, Katie. Is Jake there?"

"Hold on a minute," she said. I heard her call out, "Jake, Katie's on the phone."

Then I heard Jake's voice in the background. "I'm not talking to her," he said.

"Come on, Jake," Mrs. O said. There was a rustling noise. She must've covered the receiver with her hand so I wouldn't hear what Jake said. I felt my heart begin to beat even faster as I waited. It was probably only a few seconds, but it seemed like a long time before Mrs. O moved her hand and started talking again. "I'm sorry, Katie," she said. "He can't come to the phone."

Obviously she was lying. It wasn't "can't"; it was "won't." How could he still be mad at me about Mr. Gallagher? It didn't make any sense. After all, it's not like I could have made those bands write back to Jake. I wondered if Doriane had told him what I'd said about Lexi. Maybe that was why he was still mad. Maybe he would never pick up the phone when I called ever again. "Will you tell him that I called?" I asked Mrs. O, but my voice didn't sound like my regular voice. It was softer, almost like Doriane's.

"Of course," Mrs. O said.

I hung up the phone. My elbows were propped up on my desk and I lowered my head into my hands. Last year when Jake and I were playing Frisbee, he threw the Frisbee before I was ready and it hit me in the stomach, hard. I fell to the ground because I couldn't breathe. That's how I felt now, like the breath had been knocked out of me. I imagined Jake calling Doriane and telling her how I had tried to call him but he wouldn't come to the phone. Maybe they were talking about how much they hated me right at that moment. If they were, I deserved it—but I still wished Jake hadn't started ignoring me in the first place. I never would have made up that stuff about Lexi Moss. Then no one would be mad at anyone.

It was possible Jake still didn't know what I'd said to Doriane about Lexi, and that he was just mad about the meeting with Mr. Gallagher. There was only one way to find out—I had to call Doriane. It felt like something in my stomach was flip-flopping. Doriane's feelings were hurt too. I had messed things up with so many people. It wasn't supposed to be this way. Emily's Run was supposed to bring everyone together.

I didn't even have to look up Doriane's phone number anymore. I had called her enough times in the past few weeks that I knew it by heart, just like I knew Jake's. Her father answered the phone. "Hi, Mr. Leib," I said. "This is Katie Franklin."

"Well, hello, Katie Franklin," he said in a completely friendly voice. Would he have yelled at me if he'd known I had hurt Doriane's feelings? Would he have sounded different? I couldn't be sure. "I'll get Doriane for you," he said.

"Thanks," I said.

I heard Mr. Leib call to Doriane, and a few seconds later she picked up the phone. "Hi," she said.

"Hey," I said.

"Hey," she said.

"I'm really sorry about yesterday. I was in a bad mood, but I shouldn't have acted like that. I should have been more sensitive."

"That's okay," Doriane said. "I talked to my dad about it. He says sometimes I'm too sensitive."

"Really?" I asked. I thought it was strange, since Jake had seemed to like how sensitive Doriane was.

"Yeah," she said. "He said I should apologize to you for not realizing you needed space."

"Well, what does your mom say?" I asked.

"My mom left when I was very young," Doriane said quickly.

I had said the wrong thing again. "I'm sorry," I said for the second time in less than five minutes.

"That's okay," Doriane said. "I don't think about it as much as I used to. My dad's remarried now, and my step-mother's nice. And besides, now I have Avi, my brother."

I didn't know what to say, so I decided to change the subject. "Listen," I said. "Why don't you come over for dinner tonight? My parents are making this birthday dinner for my aunt. You remember her, right?"

"Yeah," Doriane said, "but I don't want to intrude."

"You wouldn't intrude," I assured her. "My aunt always says the more the merrier."

"Are you sure?" Doriane asked.

"Yes, I'm sure," I said in my most confident voice, even though I hadn't talked to Mom about it yet. But since she thought Jake was coming, she probably wouldn't mind if Doriane came instead. It's not like she would have to make more food.

"Well, okay," Doriane said.

"Great," I told her. "We're having dinner at seven o'clock."

After we hung up, I told Mom that Jake couldn't come over for dinner and asked if it would be okay if Doriane came instead, and she said of course. Mom had started cooking and wanted me to help even though that's usually Julie's job, but Mooner was whining by the door. "I think she needs to go out," I said. "She hasn't been out since early this morning."

"Well, I guess you're off the hook for now, kiddo," Mom said. "But check the mail on your way back in."

"Sure," I said. "I'm gonna see if Julie wants to come too."

"Please don't bother Julie," Mom said. "She might be working."

"I wasn't going to bother her," I said. "I was just going to ask."

"Katie," Mom said, "it doesn't take two people to walk the dog. Just go."

"Fine," I said.

"And take a sweater," she called after me. "It's getting cold."

Mooner and I headed outside and turned at the corner. I skipped down the block and thought about the present I had for Aunt Jean. Dad says the trick to presents is thinking of something that the person wouldn't buy for herself. He says Aunt Jean is especially hard because she already has everything. But I don't think it's so hard because I know Aunt Jean so well. Aunt Jean says she likes presents that make her remember the person who gave them to her. One year I got her a heart-shaped paperweight. Another time I made a papier-mâché frame for a picture of Aunt Jean and me from when I was a baby. This year I decided to get her a charm bracelet that she could wear every day and think of me. It was a good gift because I could keep getting her new charms to add to her bracelet. I had picked out three charms to start her off. The first one was a *J* for her first name. The second was a book, since she loves books and works in the library. And the third was the best one. I found a little charm in the shape of a girl with a ponytail hanging down her back, just the way I like to wear my hair. "I think Aunt Jean's gonna love it, don't you, Mooner-ballooner?" I asked.

Mooner didn't answer. She pulled me ahead on her leash like she was the one walking me.

"Okay, girl," I said. "I get it. One more lap around the

block and then we'll go wrap Aunt Jean's present."

Mooner and I rounded the corner and stopped at the mailbox at the end of our driveway. I looped Mooner's leash around my wrist and pulled the mailbox open. There was a catalog for ski clothes, one of Julie's fashion magazines, and a bunch of bills addressed to Mom and Dad. I started to sort through it so everything would be in size order, but Mooner was pulling at the leash again, ready to head back inside. "All right, all right," I said.

We headed back to the house. I closed the front door and unhooked Mooner's leash. She ran ahead of me into the kitchen to get a drink of water, and I followed behind Mooner and handed Mom the mail. "It's mostly for you and Dad," I said. "Julie got a magazine."

"Wash your hands," Mom said.

"Why?" I asked. "I'm not dirty."

"You were out with the dog," Mom said. "Now you're home, so wash up and peel the potatoes."

"Julie's home and she isn't helping," I pointed out.

"Julie is working," Mom said.

"I have work to do too," I told her.

"You can do it later," Mom said.

"I have to go wrap Aunt Jean's present," I said. I turned to leave the kitchen before Mom could stop me.

"Katie, one more thing," Mom called.

"What?" I said in an annoyed voice. I went back into

the kitchen. Mom held up a small blue envelope.

"It's a letter for you," she said. I started to take it, but Mom held it back. "If you're in too much of a rush to get upstairs, I'll just keep it here myself." It had to be from Sophie if it was in a blue envelope. She always wrote on blue paper with a matching envelope. I reached out to take the envelope again. Mom didn't let go of it right away, so when I took it from her, I had to tug a little harder than usual to get it out of her hands. Mom smiled like she was playing a game.

"Thanks," I said.

"You're welcome," Mom said, but I could tell by her voice that she didn't really mean it. I ran upstairs and ripped open Sophie's letter.

Dear Katie,

I am really excited to come to California! It's so cold in New York even though it's already the middle of spring. I can still see my breath in the mornings when I walk to school. Also, Haley is being more annoying than usual. I think she wishes she were going to California too. She's worried that she'll miss me when I'm gone, even though it's only a long weekend. Lately she wants to do everything with me. We don't share a room anymore, but she's always asking if she can bring her sleeping bag into my room and camp out on the floor.

The other night I said no, but she came into my room in the middle of the night anyway. I must have been asleep because I didn't hear her, but when I woke up in the morning, I almost stepped on her!

Anyway, I'm really happy to have a little vacation and also to get to meet you in person finally. And guess what! My dad said it's okay with him if I go to Redwood City a day early when he has to work. I know it's the Friday that you have your jog-a-thon, and I thought I could get a sponsor sheet from you and get sponsors too. Do you think that would be all right? I bet I could get a bunch of kids in my class to sponsor me, and also some of the people from my dad's office. I'll start asking people to sponsor me now, and when I get everything from you, I'll fill all the paperwork out so it's official!

I better get going now. My mom's calling me. She wants me to help Haley with her homework. She has to make a diorama about a book she read for school. Mom says I'm better at these things than she is so I'm the one who has to help Haley. Send me the stuff for the jog-a-thon when you get a chance. I'll see you in person in just a few weeks!

Sincerely,

Sophie

Fourteen

Aunt Jean and Doriane came over at almost exactly the same time. I was just shutting the door behind Aunt Jean when I saw Mr. Leib's car pulling up in front of our house. I waved to Mr. Leib. There was a woman next to him in the front seat that had to be Doriane's stepmother. Even though I'd never met her, she waved back. Doriane got out of the car. She was holding a bouquet of flowers in her arms. I watched her shift the flowers under one arm so she could close the car door. I held the front door open for her. "These are for your family," Doriane said, handing me the flowers.

"You didn't have to do that," I told her. Jake would never have brought flowers just because he was having dinner at our house.

"My stepmother is into stuff like that," Doriane said. "Besides, I wanted to."

"Hey, Mom," I called. "Doriane's here. She brought flowers."

"Well, thank you, Doriane. They're lovely," Mom said. She got a vase down from the top of the wall unit and put the flowers in the middle of the dining room table. They were yellow roses, and they happened to match the stitches on the tablecloth. The table looked really pretty. I had set the table, and Mom had let me put place cards like we were eating at a wedding. I sat myself between Aunt Jean and Doriane.

"So we have two of the three musketeers," Aunt Jean said when we sat down. "What's Jake up to tonight?"

"I don't know," I said.

"I don't know either," Doriane said.

I turned to look at Doriane. Her head was bent down and it looked like she was studying her hands, which were crossed on top of the table. Suddenly I felt like a horrible person all over again.

"How was school this week?" Mom asked. She said it like she was asking all of us, but I knew she just cared about Julie.

"Fine," I said.

"Boring," Julie said.

"Oh, Julie," Mom said, shaking her head.

"Tell me about the meeting with Mr. Gallagher yesterday," Aunt Jean said.

I started to tell her that it went really well, but Mom interrupted me. "I didn't know you met with Mr. Gallagher," she said.

"We have a meeting every Friday," I said. "Not just me. Everyone who's involved in the jog-a-thon goes."

"Did you go too?" Mom asked Julie. Julie swallowed a bite of chicken and nodded.

I turned back to Aunt Jean. "Anyway," I said, "you should have seen how many kids showed up."

"It was pretty cool," Julie said. Mom was sitting next to Julie, staring at the side of her face, but Julie looked straight across the table at Aunt Jean and kept talking. "At first I just expected the kids we knew to come, but all these other kids have been coming to the meetings too."

"It's too bad we can't bring all the money we raise to Mexico ourselves," I said.

"I'd love to go to Mexico," Julie said. "We could wear sarongs, sit by the beach and get really tan." Leave it to Julie to turn a trip to Mexico into something fashionable.

"I wouldn't let you go to Mexico now," Mom said. I wondered if she meant she wouldn't let us go because of the earthquake or because she didn't want Julie to miss school.

"Well, I'm proud of all of you, even if you never make it to

Mexico," Aunt Jean said. She put her hand on my shoulder. I was proud about the jog-a-thon too. No matter what I had said to Doriane about Jake, at least I was doing one good thing by planning a jog-a-thon to help kids in Mexico.

"Speaking of traveling," Dad said, changing the subject like he sometimes does so Mom doesn't get too worked up. "I was just saying to Lisa that I wished I had one of those jobs that send you to all different exotic places—you know, like Europe, Asia, or Africa. Or else one of those jobs that pay you a ton so you can travel all those places yourself." Dad laughed at his own joke. Mom laughed too, but no one else did. "Don't you think it would be great to be able to see the world, Jeanie?" Dad asked.

"Oh, I don't know, Peter," Aunt Jean said.

"If you could go anywhere, where would you go?" he asked.

"I haven't really thought about it," Aunt Jean said.

"Well, just off the top of your head," Dad said.

"I don't know. I'd rather talk about what the kids are up to," Aunt Jean said. She turned to me. We can read each other's minds sometimes, and I knew she wanted me to say something so Dad would stop bothering her.

"Well, speaking of traveling," I said. "Guess who's coming here for the jog-a-thon?"

"Who?" Aunt Jean asked.

"Sophie!" I said.

"Your pen pal?" Mom asked. I was surprised she had paid enough attention to me to even know who Sophie was.

"Yup," I said. "That's what she wrote in the letter I got today."

"That's so cool," Doriane said.

"I know," I said. I told them what Sophie said about the jog-a-thon—that if I sent her sponsor sheets she would get people in New York to sponsor her for running. "It's perfect because Mr. Gallagher was just telling us to get more sponsors in the meeting we had yesterday," I said. I didn't mean to sound like a show-off, especially because I knew Doriane's own pen pal didn't even write to her anymore, but I was really excited.

"I can't wait to meet her," Aunt Jean said.

"Me too," Doriane said.

"We could go to the post office in the morning to send everything to Sophie and then stop by the mall afterward, if you want," Julie said.

"The post office is closed on Sunday," Mom said. "And, Julie, you have Stephanie coming."

"Who's Stephanie?" Aunt Jean asked.

"The Stanford nerd," Julie said, lowering her voice. The way she said it made "the Stanford nerd" sound like a kind of disease.

"Oh, Julie, you could just call her Stephanie already," Mom said. "She's lovely, she's really good to you, and you're making so much progress!" Mom turned to Aunt Jean. "You should hear what Stephanie says about Julie. She absolutely raves about Julie's potential. I always knew Julie could succeed in school if she put her mind to it. Stephanie says Julie reminds her of how she was at this age, and now she's at Stanford! I'm so happy I found her."

"God, Mom, chill out," Julie said. I remembered how she had told me to chill out the day before when we were talking about Jake. Was it really because I sounded like Mom, or was it something that Julie said to everyone? I'd have to pay more attention.

"But you should be proud of yourself, Julie," Mom said. "Doesn't it feel good to be doing so well?"

"Maybe," Julie said. "But I'm cooped up all the time now. I barely have a life anymore."

"Oh, that's not true," Mom said. "It's just that school is a very important part of your life. And you know you can go out as soon as your work is done."

Julie pushed her plate forward. "Whatever," she said. "May I be excused?"

"No," Dad said. "Your aunt still needs to open her presents."

"Oh, really, Peter," Aunt Jean said. "Nobody had to get me anything. You know in some cultures the person celebrating the birthday has to buy presents for all her friends?

From now on that's what I want to do for my birthday."

"Don't be silly, Jeanie," Dad said. "We like getting you things. But funny you should mention other cultures. . . ."

"What are you talking about?" Aunt Jean asked.

Dad bent down and lifted up a present that had been in a small pile by the side of the table, but I wanted Aunt Jean to open mine first. I couldn't wait. "No, Dad," I said. "She has to open mine first. It's the little box in the red wrapping paper."

Dad bent back down. He rifled through the pile as though he were having trouble finding my gift. I knew he was just fooling around. Mine was the smallest box so it was right on top. "Are you sure it's here?" he said.

"Yes, I'm sure," I said.

"I hope I didn't lose it," Dad said.

"Come on," I said, feeling impatient. "Stop goofing around."

"You hear that, Doriane," Dad said as he sat back up and handed me the box. "My daughter just called me a goof. My very own daughter."

"That's because you are," Aunt Jean said. We all started laughing, and Mooner barked.

I handed the box to Aunt Jean. "Open it," I said.

Aunt Jean tore off the wrapping paper. "Oh my," she said softly. She pulled out the charm bracelet and fingered each charm gently. "This is beautiful," she said. "Thank you so much." Aunt Jean put her arm around my back and squeezed me to her.

"You're welcome," I said. Aunt Jean held up her hand and I fastened the clasp of the bracelet. It fit her perfectly.

She opened Julie's present next. It was a scarf, but not the kind you wear to keep warm. It was too thin and glittery for that. It was more like a fabric necklace that you loop around your neck. "I feel so glamorous," Aunt Jean said.

"Okay," Dad said. "Now mine." He held out a pile of presents all wrapped in matching paper. I counted the presents in the pile. There were six total. If Aunt Jean was so hard to shop for, then how did he come up with six different things to get her? "These are from Lisa and me," Dad said.

I had no idea what Mom and Dad had gotten Aunt Jean, so I was almost as excited to see her open their presents as I was to see her open mine. "Hurry up," I said. She pulled the paper off the first present. "It's a book," I said. I was kind of disappointed. Aunt Jean works in a library. It wasn't that hard to figure out that she likes books.

"Not just any book," Dad said. Aunt Jean turned it over, and I leaned closer to her so I could read the title: *A Sophisticated Traveler's Guide to Europe*. It seemed like a ridiculous gift to me. Why would Aunt Jean need a book about Europe?

"Subtle, Peter," Aunt Jean said. She sounded upset, but Dad didn't seem to notice.

Aunt Jean opened the rest of her presents. She smiled to be nice, but I could tell she didn't mean it. The next two presents were also books. One was about England and one was about France. Then there was a leather case that sort of looked like a wallet. The last two presents were games you can play on a plane—travel Scrabble and something called Magnetic Sudoku, which I'd never heard of. "It's a numbers game," Dad said.

"Thank you," Aunt Jean said.

"The passport case is the real gift," Mom said. She picked up the thing that looked like a wallet and flipped it over. "See, it has your initials. But you can exchange the books for other ones if you decide to go somewhere else. I picked these because I've always wanted to go to Europe."

"Lisa picked it out," Dad said. "She thought it might inspire you to finally treat yourself to a great trip."

It figured that Mom had picked it all out. She always thought she knew what was best for everyone, even if they didn't want it themselves. Aunt Jean didn't say anything. I knew she didn't want to go anywhere. It was no fun to travel alone. I looked over at her. There was so much I wanted to say to her. I wanted to tell her that I didn't care how much money she had or what she did with it. Mostly I wanted to tell her how happy I was that she stayed right here in

Redwood City, right near me. I didn't need her to travel anywhere. If she went somewhere else, she might like it better
and decide to move away. I didn't know what I would do
without her. Of course Mom would never understand that.
Stay here forever, Aunt Jean, I thought as hard as I could. I
hoped she was listening.

Fifteen

It had been more than a week since Jake and I had stopped speaking. He seemed so far away. I made myself think about the jog-a-thon so I wouldn't feel so bad about Jake, but then I started to get nervous that things wouldn't get done in time. What if we didn't have enough sponsors? What if we didn't have enough runners? What if it rained?

"But it never rains in California in May," Doriane told me. I had called her because I knew she would be thinking about the jog-a-thon too. Doriane was always scared about things. If she was relaxed about rain, then there couldn't be any reason to worry. So why didn't I feel any better? Maybe Jake was right; maybe I was turning into a different person. I used to think I was friendly and likeable, but now I felt weird and mean. I got up from my desk and looked at my reflection in the mirror on the back of the closet door. My hair was pulled back into a ponytail, just the same as usual. Some little wisps had escaped on the sides. They were a much lighter shade of blond than the rest of my hair.

"Katie?" Doriane said. "Are you there?"

I took a long, deep breath and closed my eyes, imagining the high school track with the sun beating down on it. "I'm here," I said. "And you're right. I shouldn't be worried about the rain."

Mr. Gallagher had said getting sponsors was the most important thing, so that is what I decided to concentrate on. I knew Sophie was already starting to ask people in New York to sponsor her, so I had to send her the information packet we'd handed out to everyone at Hillside. The Saturday after Aunt Jean's birthday, Dad drove me to the post office so I could mail the package to Sophie. Dad had worked late all week and for some reason Aunt Jean had been busy too, so the weekend was the first chance I got to go to the post office. I'd written Sophie a note explaining what everything was. "It's so great you can help because I've been so nervous lately and we need more sponsors," I'd written. But I hadn't told her what I was really scared about—that Jake would never talk to me again, that nothing would work out the way it was supposed to. I'd signed "Sincerely, Katie," at the bottom of the letter, and then I'd told Dad I was ready to go.

I was sending Sophie copies of sponsor sheets and Super Sponsor forms, and even the article about Emily that Doriane had found back in early April. It was too much to fit into a regular envelope but I would send it overnight so she could get it faster. Thinking about Sophie helped me forget about everything with Jake.

"It's too bad we couldn't go to the airport and find someone who was flying to New York. Then they could take the package to Sophie and she could get it the same day," I told Dad.

"That's a good idea for a business," Dad said.

"Hey, Dad," I said.

"What, Katie-Katie?" Dad said. He turned to look at me even though he was driving. Mom says you have to be careful when you talk to Dad in the car because sometimes he forgets to look at the road. He's never been in an accident, though. I think it's just one more thing that Mom likes to worry about. But even so, I waited until Dad turned back to the road before I kept talking.

"Do you think you need to do well in school to be able to run a business?" I asked.

"Are you planning on running a business before you finish sixth grade?" Dad asked, smiling.

I remembered the Dynamic Duo, but there was no way Jake and I were going to start a business now that he wasn't even speaking to me. "No," I said. "I was just wondering."

"Well, no, actually," Dad said. "I think there are plenty of good business people who didn't do well in school."

"Then why is Mom so worried about Julie all the time?"

"School is still important," Dad said. "It would certainly be easier for you and Julie if you did well in school. It's easier to get into college. It's easier to get a job. Not everyone can run their own business, after all."

"But Mom's so mean to Julie," I said. "It's not Julie's fault."

"No, it's not Julie's fault," Dad said. "But Mom's not being mean. She just wants everything to be okay. She gets worried when things are out of her control."

Like when Dad's not looking at the road, I thought.

We pulled into the parking lot of the post office. I gathered everything up and followed Dad inside. There was a line in front of the row of clerks. Dad says there's always a line at the post office. I hoped it would go quickly. I had a lot of work to get done.

"So who's paying for this shipment to the famous Sophie?" Dad asked.

"I thought maybe you would," I said.

"Is that what you thought?" Dad said.

"Please, Dad," I said. "You're my favorite dad in the whole world. Besides, it's for a good cause."

"You're right," Dad said. He ruffled my hair. "I guess I'll do it, but only because I'm your favorite dad."

It was our turn to go up to the clerk. I put all my papers on the counter. "I need to send this overnight to New York," I said. The clerk gave me a slip to fill out with Sophie's name and address. I didn't have to look up the address because I knew it by heart. It reminded me of how I knew Doriane's phone number by heart too. Just when I was starting to feel bad about myself, Dad put his hand on the top of my head. "My daughter is organizing an event in her school to benefit the Mexican earthquake victims," Dad told the clerk.

"How wonderful," the clerk said.

"It is wonderful, isn't it?" Dad said. He ruffled my hair again. I wasn't sure if it was because he was proud of me or because he thought I was a little kid. I hated when Dad treated me like a baby, but at least he thought there was a reason to be proud of me. He even got his company to be a Super Sponsor and he was paying for the package to Sophie.

Dad also said I could call some of his friends to see if they would want to be individual sponsors. He said he would help me make a list of all the friends of his that I knew. When Dad and I got home, Julie was studying with Stephanie in the kitchen. Mom says no one—not even Mom—is allowed to hang out anywhere near Julie when Stephanie is there. The problem is that the kitchen is smack in the middle of everything downstairs. Dad and I were banished from the kitchen, as well as the dining room and the den. He took his palm pilot out of his briefcase and we went up to my room and scrolled through his list of friends. I took a clean sheet of paper out of the top drawer of my desk and printed everyone's name and phone number as neatly as I could. In the end we came up with twenty-two people for me to call. I would just start at the top of the list and check off everyone's name as I went.

Mooner wandered into the room. "Hey, girl," I said. "I can't play right now. I have work to do." Mooner cocked her head like she was listening and whined softly, as if she knew exactly what I had said.

Dad sat next to me as I dialed. It was the middle of the day and a lot of his friends weren't home, but I ended up with nine sponsors. I left messages for the people who weren't home, and I figured I would get even more sponsors when they started calling me back. I hung up the phone after my twenty-second call and looked at the clock. It was three thirty-three. Dad said we should probably walk Mooner, but I still wanted to work on the jog-a-thon. "I guess it's just you and me, girl," he told her. After they left, I wandered downstairs. Stephanie usually left around three thirty, so Julie would be free. She had said maybe we should go door-to-door to get sponsors, like we did when we were little and sold cookies for our Brownie troop.

But Stephanie was still at the kitchen table with Julie, and Mom was there too. If Mom was there, then tutoring had to be over. I hovered right outside the kitchen, waiting for Julie.

Stephanie didn't look anything like I'd pictured when Julie had first described her. She had glasses, like Julie said. But she was also kind of pretty. She had really long hair pulled back in a braid. I could tell she wasn't wearing any makeup. Julie thinks everyone over thirteen years old should wear makeup. I knew that if Stephanie weren't Julie's tutor, Julie would have wanted to give her a makeover.

I shifted my feet and the floor squeaked beneath me. Mom turned her head toward me. "Katie," she said, "can we help you with anything?" She sounded like the assistant in Dad's office who always asks how she can help me when I call.

"I'm just waiting for Julie," I said.

"Julie's going to be a while," Mom said. "And after that she's going to be busy anyway." Mom spoke as though Julie couldn't speak for herself. I looked over at Julie, but she was looking into her lap. I just kept standing there, staring at Julie. "Anything else?" Mom asked. She sounded annoyed.

"No," I said. I went back upstairs to call Doriane and see if she wanted to come with me. But she said she had to babysit Avi, and actually she sounded relieved. I guess she's probably too shy to go door-to-door.

But I felt lonely. First Julie couldn't come, and now Doriane couldn't, and of course I couldn't ask Jake. Going door-to-door was exactly the kind of thing he would have wanted to do—he would have loved to impress all the neighbors. But instead I had to go by myself. I decided to concentrate on Sophie. The package was on its way to New York right at that very moment. I wondered what she was doing. Maybe she would start getting sponsorships before the package even arrived, or maybe she was too busy helping her sister with her homework. I bet Sophie's mom would never make her sit home all day long instead of being with her sister. It made me wish I had a different mother. I left the house and walked toward Aunt Jean's house. I could pretend she was my mother instead.

I stopped at a bunch of the houses in between my house and Aunt Jean's to try to get sponsors for the jog-a-thon. But as I continued down the street, I started having the same problem I had had making phone calls. Most people weren't home. I wasn't too upset about it, though. The people who were home were really generous, and I decided to share the sponsors with Julie. We could split it fifty-fifty. It was her idea, after all. By the time I got to Aunt Jean's, Julie and I had four sponsors each. I rang Aunt Jean's doorbell three times.

"Katie," Aunt Jean said as she swung open the door. "I didn't expect to see you today. What's going on?"

"Nothing much," I said. "Jake isn't speaking to me. I bet he's not even thinking about me. He won't even come to the phone when I call. Doriane is babysitting, so she couldn't hang out today. And Julie was supposed to help with the jog-a-thon today, but Mom won't let her out of the house."

"Sounds like a hard day," Aunt Jean said. She opened the door wider. "Come on in."

Aunt Jean said she would get me a snack, and I walked into the den. The television was on, but the volume was low. Sometimes she turns the television on just to have other voices in the house. I could tell by the program — some game show with the teammates all dressed up in all the same color — that it wasn't something that Aunt Jean had actually been watching, so I didn't feel bad about interrupting her.

Aunt Jean came back to the den with a slice of cheese and a glass of juice. I took the cheese and peeled off the plastic wrap. I began to fold it into squares. I like to fold it into as many squares as possible, and then eat it one little piece at a time to make it last longer. "So," Aunt Jean said. "I guess it's not your best day."

"I got a lot more sponsors," I said. I put the first little square of cheese into my mouth. It didn't taste as good as usual.

"Well, that's good," Aunt Jean said.

"I know," I said. "But Julie was supposed to help me. You know, just when there was something that Julie and I actually wanted to do together, Mom had to step in and ruin it."

"Your mom's making Julie work all weekend?" Aunt Jean asked.

"How'd you guess," I said glumly.

"Maybe you should talk to your mom," Aunt Jean suggested.

"I don't know," I said. "I don't think it would do any good." I didn't want to talk about Mom and Julie anymore. I wanted to just imagine Aunt Jean was my mother, and I stood up from the couch and walked across the room toward the window. Aunt Jean's computer and printer are right next to the window. I saw that the pictures of that makeshift hospital in Mexico were up on the computer screen. There were sheets of paper in the printer with the heading "Volunteer Information." I pulled the sheets out of the printer and held them up. "Is this for me?" I asked.

"Oh, no," Aunt Jean said quickly. "I thought I'd bring some information to the library."

"Oh," I said. "Sorry." I put the paper back on the printer tray.

"So, what about this stuff with your mom?" Aunt Jean said, reminding me.

"I don't really want to think about it anymore," I told her. "I think I'm just going to head home and see if Julie has stopped working yet. I'm giving her half of the sponsors I got."

Aunt Jean didn't even try to talk me into staying. "All right," she said. "I'll take you home." I climbed into Aunt Jean's car—"It's okay to be sad about your mom," she said. "But everything is going to work out."

"I'm not sad," I told her. "I'm so used to her being like this, I barely even notice it anymore." I was lying again, but I didn't care.

When I got home, I headed right upstairs to Julie. Her door was open, but she was in bed with her face to the wall. "Julie?" I said. She didn't answer right away. "Julie," I said again.

"What?" Julie said. Her voice sounded funny.

"You didn't miss too much today," I said. "So don't be upset. I went door-to-door like you said, but most people weren't home, and I'll share all the sponsors with you anyway."

Julie rolled over and sat up. Her face was red and blotchy and I realized she'd been crying.

"Are you okay?" I asked. But Julie didn't say anything. She stood up from the bed and walked straight toward me. I was still standing in the doorway, and Julie walked up so close that I stumbled backward a little. She moved her hand to the side of the door and pushed so it slammed in my face.

Sixteen

Dear Sophie,

Now Julie can't run in the jog-a-thon.

My mom hired this tutor for Julie named Stephanie,
but Julie calls her "the Stanford nerd" because she hates
her. Well, I don't think she hates her exactly. It's more
that she hates that Mom makes her get tutored. Anyway,
Stephanie found out about a program at Stanford for kids
with dyslexia—that's what Julie has. Of course Stephanie
told my mom all about it. And of course my mom thinks
that Julie has to be in it. There are special tests you

have to take to get into the class, and the first day of
testing is the day of the jog-a-thon. At first I didn't get
it. I mean, Stanford is a college. Julie isn't even in high
school. Besides that, Stanford is for kids who do really
well in school, and Julie doesn't exactly get all As. But
Dad says Stanford has a lot of different parts, including
an education part. So that's where Julie will be during the
jog-a-thon. She's not even speaking to me now. Actually,
Julie isn't speaking to anyone in my entire family. She
just gets up and goes to school, and comes home and goes
straight to her room and closes the door. My mom's all
upset because she thinks Julie should be excited about
the opportunity. She's convinced this will cure Julie or
something like that.

What makes it even worse is that Jake isn't coming to the
jog-a-thon either. I know I told you that already, but I really
hoped we would've made up by now. I'm still mostly excited
about Emily's Run, but it's hard to be excited when everyone
is fighting.

Anyway, I hope you got all the information I sent you, and
I hope you're getting lots of sponsors! I got your letter with
your hotel information. My aunt said she'll pick you up the
morning of the jog-a-thon. I know your dad has to work,

and that way you won't have to take a cab or the train by yourself.

See you very soon!

Sincerely,

Katie

I folded up my letter and put it into an envelope. Then I headed downstairs to ask Dad for a stamp. I had to pass by Julie's room on the way. Her door was closed, of course. I stopped right in front of it and thought about knocking, but I knew what would happen. She would just shout, "Go away!" like she always did lately. Then Mom would come up to hear what the fuss was about and tell me not to bother Julie. I think Mom pretends to herself that when Julie's door is closed, it means Julie is studying on the other side. But I was sure Julie was just lying there staring at the fashion posters on her walls. She hardly ever even came downstairs for dinner, even though Mom had made lasagna about a million times.

I kept moving down the hall and went down to the den. Dad was sitting on the couch reading the paper. "Hey, Katie-Katie," he said when he saw me. "What's going on?"

"I need a stamp," I said.

"Is that another letter for Sophie?" Dad asked.

"Yup," I said.

"She'll be here pretty soon," Dad said.

"Less than two weeks," I told him.

"You must be pretty excited," Dad said. He folded the paper and put it down on the ottoman. "What are the two of you going to do?"

"The jog-a-thon. That's why we had to send Sophie that package the other week," I reminded him. I was kind of annoyed. I expected Mom not to pay attention to anything I was doing, but Dad should have known better.

"Right," he said. "I knew about that part. What else?" He patted the seat on the couch next to him, and I sat down.

"I don't know," I said. "All I've really thought about is the jog-a-thon. You're going to leave work early so you can come, right?"

"I told you I would," Dad said.

"You'll be the only one of the family there," I said. "Except me and Aunt Jean."

"Mom wishes she could be there," Dad said.

"No, she doesn't," I said. "I told you she would find a reason not to come."

"Of course she wishes she could be there," Dad said. "But Julie needs her that day."

"Julie doesn't care if Mom is with her. She's not even

speaking to her," I reminded him. "She hasn't spoken to any of us in two weeks."

"I know," Dad said.

"It's not fair," I told him. "It's not even my fault."

"I'm sorry this is hard on you," Dad said. "But there's nothing I can do to change it."

"Yes, you could," I said. "You could tell Mom not to make Julie go to Stanford. She doesn't even want to go to Stanford."

"You're right," Dad said. "She doesn't. And you know I want Julie to be happy. But Mom thinks this will be a good opportunity for her. Julie needs help in school, and this might actually be good for her in the long run."

I started to remind Dad how hard we had all worked and how the jog-a-thon was important in the long run too. But Dad cut me off.

"I'm sorry, Katie," he said. "We've made up our minds."

I heard footsteps moving toward us from the hall, and I knew it had to be Mom. Julie was way too angry to just drop into the den to talk to Dad and me. Sure enough, Mom peeked her head around the corner. "What are you two up to?" she said.

I said, "Nothing," and at the same time Dad said, "Katie and I were talking about Julie's tests."

"Those tests are very important," Mom said. She turned to look directly at me and put her hands on her hips. It's like she's always ready for a fight even when I haven't done anything wrong. I thought maybe Dad would stick up for me or even just try to change the subject like he sometimes does when Mom is getting worked up about something for no reason. But Dad just picked his paper back up from the ottoman. I sighed loudly so he would know I was upset, but he didn't put the paper down again.

"I'm going to my room," I said loudly, and I stood up from the couch.

"All right, Katie-Katie," Dad said from behind his paper, as if everything was fine. Maybe he didn't even realize anything was wrong. He treats me like a baby sometimes, like I'm too young to know anything. And he sides with Mom about Julie needing more help with school. But if you ask me, sometimes Dad acts like he doesn't know anything at all. I looked over at him. He held the newspaper up so I couldn't see his face. Just the top of his head was visible. He's sort of going bald a little bit, so his forehead is longer than it used to be. The hair at the edge of his hairline is also a little gray. I thought he looked too old to be acting so completely clueless, and I waited a couple more seconds in case he looked up to see me. But his head stayed bent down toward the paper, and I turned to walk toward the stairs.

"Don't bother Julie when you go up there," Mom called after me. I didn't even answer her. My whole body felt hot. I stomped back up to my room and closed the door. I had forgotten all about my letter to Sophie. It was sitting on the couch in the den, but I didn't want to go back down and get it because then I would have to see my parents again. I would just wait to get it in the morning.

I tried to distract myself by thinking about the jog-a-thon, but I only felt worse. I had wanted to plan it with Jake and make everyone proud, but nothing had worked out the way I'd imagined it.

Every time I thought about the jog-a-thon, I remembered that Julie and Jake wouldn't be there. I saw Julie in the mornings when we got ready for school. Sometimes I would walk into the bathroom as she was walking out. But she would brush past me and not say anything, like I wasn't even there. It was the same way with Jake. Besides homeroom, we had one class together—social studies—so I saw him only in that one class and during our lunch period. In class he stared straight ahead at Mrs. Katz. He paid more attention to her now than he ever had before we were fighting. At lunch he would sit at the table with a bunch of kids from the track team, and I would sit with Doriane and a few other girls from my grade. Once I looked up and caught him looking at me from across the room. Our eyes met, but he turned away quickly and pretended that he hadn't seen me at all. Jake and I had never gone so long without speaking to each other. I bet he didn't even miss talking to me. He probably thought he was better off with his friends from the track team and decided he couldn't be best friends with a girl after all. Just like Julie had said.

Even thinking about Sophie didn't make me feel much better. She had written me back after I'd told her Jake was mad and had quit the jog-a-thon. I went to my desk to get her letter, and traced her handwriting with my finger. "I know how it feels to lose your best friend," she wrote. "But trust me—it gets easier. Just think about all you're doing for those kids in Mexico and how practically the whole school wants to help you." She had signed her name, "Sincerely, Sophie."

Sincerely. There was that word again. Sophie probably meant it when she said "sincerely." I put down her letter. If she knew the truth about me—that I was a terrible liar— then she would probably never write to me ever again.

I put Sophie's letter back on my desk, and I looked around my room to see if there was anything to do to distract myself. Everything I'd ever owned was there—the pictures above my bed, my books, my desk, my stuffed animals that I was really too old to play with but I didn't want to throw away. I thought about how things could be ruined so quickly and easily, in an instant, in ways you can't even control. The ground shakes and splits and swallows everything you ever had. There had been earthquakes in California before. If there were a big enough earthquake the next time, it could all be taken away from me, too, hidden in rubble. Emily hadn't lost her home, since she'd been only visiting Mexico, but she'd lost her family. They were there one minute, and then they were gone. Even her sister, Julie. "It's a random event," Aunt Jean had said. Kids at school used that word sometimes: How random, they said, when someone said something strange. "Random" meant "different, odd." But "random" could mean "dangerous," too.

There was so much to be scared of. I still have all my stuff, but there are so many ways to lose people, and things had been taken away from me too. It wasn't random—it was my own fault. I turned around and around—there was my bed, my desk, the photo collage of Jake and me, my closet full of clothes, including the hand-me-downs from Julie. I realized that, in my mind, the jog-a-thon wasn't just for Emily. It was for Jake. I had wanted it to be something we could do together. And it was for Julie, because Emily had lost her sister, Julie, and I still had mine.

That's when I remembered Julie's black skirt. It was the skirt she'd wanted to give to me weeks ago, and she had kicked me out of her room when I'd said I didn't want it. Somehow it had ended up in my closet. I knew that meant Julie had gone into my room when I wasn't looking, and I had pushed it toward the back, next to a couple of shirts and a pair of pants that had also been Julie's. I had never tried any of it on. Now I slid off my jeans and stood in front of the mirror. The skirt was made of a soft, stretchy material. I liked the way it felt—sort of like a sweatshirt but with more elastic. Maybe I should have listened to Julie all along—maybe Jake would like me better if I dressed the way Julie did.

I undid my ponytail and pulled on Julie's skirt, and then I turned and stared at my reflection. It's funny how the same clothes can look completely different on different people. I fingered the widow's peak on my forehead, but it didn't make me look pretty at all. I made myself start to laugh so I wouldn't feel bad that I didn't look a thing like Julie. I lay down on my bed in Julie's stretchy skirt and imagined waking up and looking like her.

That night I had the worst dream about the earthquake ever. It was the day of the jog-a-thon. I was there early to set up. Mr. Gallagher and I were the only ones on the track at the high school. Suddenly there was a loud noise, like a horrible crash. The ground was shaking. I crouched down on the ground just like I was supposed to, and brought my hands up over my head. I was staring at the ground beneath my feet, and I saw a crack running along the ground. I looked up, even though I wasn't supposed to, and the crack was spreading as the earth kept shaking. Then the ground split wide open and I was falling inside it. "Mr. Gallagher!" I cried. "Mr. Gallagher!"

"Katie!" he said. He appeared right above me. I was hanging on to the edge of the crack, and I looked up and reached out for his hand. But instead of giving me his hand and pulling me up, he handed me a bag of candy. It was the same bag of miniature chocolates that I had found in Mrs. Brenneke's drawer.

"Here," he said. "Mrs. Brenneke said you wanted this."

"No, no," I told him. But he wasn't listening. He was already walking away. I lost my grip as I called after him, and then I was falling and falling.

I woke up sweating. My body felt gross and sticky, and I stood up to change. My legs were shaky as I moved across the room. I turned on the light so I wouldn't feel so afraid, and I walked toward my closet to get a fresh shirt and a pair of sweatpants. I passed by the mirror and realized I was still in Julie's skirt. My eyes looked bigger, like they belonged to a whole other person. I stared at myself, and felt different and strange, kind of like when you say your name over and over again until you can't recognize it anymore. With my eyes so big and my hair all messed up from my sleep, the skirt kind of looked good on me. I wanted Julie to see me like that, looking sort of pretty, and I wished I could walk into her room and wake her up. But it was the middle of the night and Julie would yell and not look at me anyway, so I peeled off the skirt and pulled an old T-shirt over my head. I decided to leave the light on when I went back to sleep.

• • •

The next morning Julie and I walked past each other in the hall. She had a towel wrapped around her head and I could smell the sweet scent of her shampoo—it's called Sugar & Spice. I looked right at her, but she pretended not to see me. I wanted to tell her that I'd finally tried on her skirt. She would be so mad if she knew I had ended up using it as pajamas. Was it just my dream that I'd looked sort of good in it? I would have asked Julie about it if she were speaking to me.

Dad offered to drive me to school, but I told him I would walk. I was still mad at him about taking Mom's side. Besides, it's not so bad walking to school, since it's all downhill. When I got there, I saw Mr. Gallagher walking into his office. He waved at me when he saw me. I felt my heart start to pound because I remembered my dream from the night before. "It was just a dream," I reminded myself. "Mr. Gallagher is a perfectly nice guy. Julie always says so, and besides, he's been great about the jog-a-thon." My heart was still beating fast, but it wasn't because I was afraid of Mr. Gallagher. It was because some things were going to be up to me to change. Some things you can't control, like the slow rumbling of an earthquake, and some things you can. I had an idea.

I couldn't believe I hadn't thought of it before. If anyone could talk Mom into letting Julie come to the jog-a-thon, it would be Mr. Gallagher. He was the one who'd once said

Julie could be a normal kid in normal classes. Mom listened to him and trusted him. But I didn't have much time. I had to talk to him that day. As soon as my last class was over, I ran across the parking lot to Mr. Gallagher's office.

I ran so fast that I was panting when I got to his office. "Hey, Mrs. Sutton," I said in between breaths. "Do you think I could speak to Mr. Gallagher? It's kind of an emergency."

"Is it about the jog-a-thon?" she asked. I nodded. "Is it anything I can help with?" she asked. A bunch of the teachers and staff at the school were helping with the jog-a-thon. Mrs. Sutton was coordinating the refreshment stand. But I knew she couldn't help me with this.

"No, thanks," I said. "It's kind of personal."

"Have a seat," Mrs. Sutton said, motioning toward the bench across from her counter. "I'll give him a call."

I sat down and tried to catch my breath. The last time I'd sat on that bench, Jake and Doriane had been there with me. This time I was all by myself. Julie spoke to Mr. Gallagher on her own all the time, but that was different. She never did anything to get into trouble or make him angry. All she did was have trouble in school, and that wasn't her fault. I glanced at the empty space next to me on the bench. Jake wouldn't have come with me even if I'd asked him, and it wasn't the kind of thing I could ask Doriane to help me with. It was about the jog-a-thon, but it was also about my family. Doriane didn't really know about the stuff with my family. I hadn't known her long enough to tell her.

"He's ready for you, Katie," Mrs. Sutton said.

I took one last deep breath. It was time to face Mr. Gallagher, all by myself.

Seventeen

✳ ✳ ✳

Mr. Gallagher was sitting at his desk. He stood up when I walked into the room, and he held out his hand. My palms were sweating. I tried not to look obvious as I wiped my right hand on my jeans to dry it off. Then I took his hand. I knew my handshake wasn't as firm as usual, but Mr. Gallagher didn't mention it, and he didn't say anything about my sweaty palms. "Have a seat, Katie," he said.

I sat in the same chair as I had before. The other two chairs were empty. "So," Mr. Gallagher said. "You must be excited." I nodded. "I think it's going to be a great day," he said.

"I guess," I said.

"You know," Mr. Gallagher said, "when you first came

into my office, I didn't think you could accomplish something like this. You've come a long way, Katie."

I thought about when I'd stolen Mrs. Brenneke's candy. "I haven't changed that much," I said miserably.

Mr. Gallagher shook his head. "I mean it," he said. "I didn't think there was any way to pull an event together so quickly. But you were so enthusiastic, and I decided to let you go forward because I thought that it would at least be a good experience. And now look at you. . . . You've made Hillside history!" I shrugged. Mr. Gallagher stood up and came around to where I was sitting and sat on the edge of the desk. The desk was so much higher than the chair, and the way he peered down at me from above made me feel very small. "I'm proud of you, Katie. Most people your age are too focused on the little things in their own lives. In fact, most adults are too focused on their own lives to make such a difference. I think it's remarkable for a sixth grader to have done all this."

It's funny how sometimes when someone gives you a compliment, it makes you feel worse than ever. I felt my eyes grow bigger and bigger. There was a pressure behind them. I squeezed them shut and tried to make it all go away. But it was no use. I started to cry. "I'm not remarkable," I said. "I do a lot of things that I shouldn't. I'm really a terrible person."

"Oh, Katie," Mr. Gallagher said. He reached behind him

and grabbed a box of tissues. "That's just not true."

"It *is* true," I said. I took a tissue from him and held it over my eyes so I wouldn't have to look at him. "And now I'm crying."

"It's okay to cry," Mr. Gallagher said.

I shook my head. This wasn't how I'd planned to ask for his help. How could he be proud of a sixth grader who acted like a baby? I focused on the little things, just like everyone else, and now I was crying about them. I knew if Mr. Gallagher knew the truth about me, he wouldn't be so proud. He would go back to thinking I was just the bad kid who'd stolen Mrs. Brenneke's candy.

"Believe me, Katie," Mr. Gallagher said kindly, "you're not the first student to cry in my office."

"But I never cry," I said. I wiped my eyes, and then I looked down and folded my tissue into little squares like I did with the cheese at Aunt Jean's house. Then I realized Mr. Gallagher was looking at me, so I balled the tissue in my hand. It got shredded and sticky from my tears and my sweaty palms. "It's just that nothing is going the way it's supposed to. I've done horrible things. I've hurt people, and now it's too late to take it back. Even Jake is mad at me."

"It will be all right, Katie," Mr. Gallagher said. "I know it doesn't seem like it now, but friends fight and then they work things out."

"But I haven't even told you the worst part yet," I said.

"What's that?" Mr. Gallagher asked.

"My family doesn't care about the jog-a-thon at all." I told Mr. Gallagher about Stephanie and the tests Julie needed to take. "So now no one's even coming, except my dad," I said. "Doriane's parents will be at the jog-a-thon, and it wasn't even her idea. Her stepmother got a babysitter for her little brother so she could be there. But my own real mother has something better to do. She always thinks Julie's stuff is more important than my stuff. And Julie's so mad at me now that she won't even speak to me. We were getting along and now we're not again. I don't even really know why. It's not like I had anything to do with Stanford."

"It's difficult for Julie," Mr. Gallagher said. "She's jealous of you. Imagine how it must feel for an older sister to see things come so much easier to a younger sister."

"But it's not my fault," I said. "It's not fair. I want her to come to the jog-a-thon as much as she does."

"You're right, it's not fair. It's an important day and Julie should be there," Mr. Gallagher said. He handed me another tissue. I wiped my eyes and remembered how Doriane's father had told her she was oversensitive, but just then I understood how awful it is to feel helpless. I blew my nose and tried to stop crying. Mr. Gallagher stood and walked back over to the other side of his desk. He bent down to pick up the wastepaper basket and held it out to me. I dropped my dirty tissues into it.

"I need your help," I said. "Julie says you're a very help-ful person."

"I do my best," Mr. Gallagher said.

I took a deep breath. "Well, since you're a principal," I said, "I thought maybe you could call Stanford and reched-ule the tests. I told my mom she should do that, but she doesn't want to upset anyone at Stanford. She wants Julie to have the best chance to get into the class."

"I have a friend who's a professor over at Stanford," Mr. Gallagher said. "I can start with him and see if there's any chance at rescheduling those tests, but I need to speak to your mother first."

"I don't know," I said. I knew if Mr. Gallagher called Mom, she'd talk him out of it.

"Leave your mother to me," Mr. Gallagher said. "I think I know what to say to her."

"Thanks," I told him. It was no wonder Julie liked him. I knew he would take care of talking to Mom about every-thing, and maybe things would get better with Julie too.

But he couldn't help me make up with Jake. That was up to me to fix.

Eighteen

It's strange to wait and wait for something and then wake up one morning and the wait is over. The day of the jog-a-thon finally arrived. I let Dad drive me to school. I figured I should conserve my energy for the jog-a-thon. We walked out to the car and I noticed that it was misty out. There's always fog in the mornings, but the fog seemed a little thicker this morning. I could barely see the tops of the trees.

It was the Friday before Memorial Day, so we had a half day of school. But my morning classes seemed to last even longer than a full day of school usually did. I had French first period, and we were supposed to translate the sentences on the blackboard. I looked at the words on the board, but they didn't seem to make any sense. For the first time I understood what Julie must feel like—confused and over-whelmed. There was no way I could think about translating things when there was too much else to worry about. What if the fog didn't clear up? What if no one came? What if some-one got hurt? What if I finally met Sophie and she didn't like me? What if Doriane figured out I was a liar and told Sophie everything? I bent down and pretended to concentrate on translating the sentences, but it was useless. I just hoped Madame Saffron didn't walk by me and see my blank page.

After French came math and then biology. I watched the clock carefully during bio, because I was leaving halfway through class to go over to the high school. Mr. Gallagher had given Doriane and me special permission to leave early. I looked up and watched the clock change. Once it hit eleven thirty, I got up. My teacher, Mr. Rosenbaum, nodded at me as I walked out.

I hadn't seen Jake, except during homeroom. I heard a lot of kids talking about the jog-a-thon in between classes, so he must have remembered it was today. Doriane met me at my locker. I packed up my backpack for the weekend, and we walked over to the high school together. The sky was blue and clear. I looked up as I walked and stumbled a little.

"Are you nervous?" Doriane asked. I could tell she was nervous because she was playing with her hair again.

"Yeah, I'm nervous too," I admitted. It would have been awful if I'd fallen and sprained my ankle. Then I wouldn't have been able to run at all. I stopped looking at the sky and started concentrating on where we were going.

As we approached the high school, I saw our sign, flapping a little in the breeze. We had ordered it from Doriane's father's company: EMILY'S RUN—THE HILLSIDE MIDDLE SCHOOL JOG-A-THON. The names of the Super Sponsors were listed in smaller letters underneath. I saw the names of Dad's company and Doriane's father's company, and Aunt Jean's name. Signage, just like Aunt Jean had said. I hoped all the Super Sponsors would be happy with it.

Mr. Gallagher was on the track. He was talking to another man right by the bleachers. He looked up and saw Doriane and me and waved us over. "Katie, Doriane, this is Alan Manning. He's the principal here at Redwood High."

I shook Mr. Manning's hand. "Thanks for letting us use the track," I said.

"My pleasure," Mr. Manning said.

Doriane and I got to work. We had to set up the refreshment area and hang up a few more signs. Mrs. Sutton from Mr. Gallagher's office was at the refreshment stand already. We helped her unload the stuff kids had made. There were a lot of cupcakes and cookies. Doriane and I didn't really have time for lunch, but Mrs. Sutton let us each have some juice and a cupcake so we would have energy for the jog-a-thon. The runners would be getting free water, too. "Make sure you drink a lot of water, girls," she said. "I don't want you getting dehydrated when you run."

Before long, people started arriving. At first it was just high schoolers, who got out of class at noon. The high school has a requirement that the students do a certain amount of community service each year, and Mr. Manning was giving community service credit to kids who volunteered to help at the jog-a-thon, so a bunch of high school students were going to help out. I also saw members of the high school band off to the side. I could tell who they were because they were in bright red-and-white uniforms. Doriane and I kept looking at each other and shaking our heads. It was hard to believe that it was all really happening.

Finally the kids from Hillside arrived, walking over in one huge group. Some parents started arriving too. I saw Mrs. O come in and take a seat in the bleachers. I thought it was nice of her to come even though Jake wasn't running. I wondered where Aunt Jean was. She had driven into San Francisco to get Sophie almost two hours before. It shouldn't take so long to go from Redwood City to San Francisco and back.

"Hey, Katie," Julie called. I turned and saw her walking toward me. Julie's friends Val, Jennie, and Allison were with her. I was so happy to see Julie. Mom had announced a couple nights earlier that she had talked to Mr. Gallagher and had been able to reschedule Julie's tests. Mr. Gallagher's friend who was a professor had offered to come in on a Saturday and supervise Julie taking the tests so she could spend Friday at the jog-a-thon. "It's really the best possible scenario," I had heard Mom tell Dad before she had even told Julie and me. I was standing at the edge of the stairs, just out of their view, so I could hear everything Mom said but she didn't know I was there. "Julie will get to take the tests by herself, so she won't feel pressured by other kids around her. Besides, it's important that she go to the jog-a-thon." I heard Dad agree with her, and I ran upstairs to tell Julie. She was hiding out in her room as usual, and when I knocked on her door, she shouted at me to go away. But I went in anyway.

"Mom says you can come to the jog-a-thon," I told her. I was practically whispering. Even though Mom and Dad were downstairs, I was afraid they would hear me and then maybe they would change their minds.

"Give me a break," Julie said.

"No," I said. "I swear. I talked to Mr. Gallagher about it, and he must have talked to Mom, because I just heard her tell Dad that you were going."

Later that night Mom made the official announcement to Julie and me. But I sort of didn't believe it until I saw Julie actually walk onto the high school track the day of the jog-a-thon. She was in tight black running pants that came down to just below her knees. There was baby blue stitching on the seams of her pants, and her shirt was the same color blue as the stitching. Leave it to Julie to have the perfect outfit for a jog-a-thon. I didn't even know that she ever exercised.

"I'm glad you're here," I told Julie. I never really say things like that to Julie, and she looked surprised, but then she smiled.

"Me too," she said. "I'm sorry I've been so mean."

"It's okay," I said. "I know the school stuff is hard." I hoped she wouldn't be mad that I'd brought up school. I knew she hated that it was hard for her and not hard for me. "I mean, at least the tutoring stuff is almost over."

"Well, I still have to meet with Stephanie even after I finish the tests," Julie said. "But I guess she's not all bad. After the Stanford stuff is over with, she wants me to take her to the mall. She said I owe her, since she helped me with reading and all that, and she needs help with fashion."

"That's really cool," I said. "You're good at helping people with fashion."

"Thanks," Julie said.

I wasn't sure what to do next. It would have been too weird to hug her. "Have you seen Aunt Jean yet?" I asked.

"No," Julie said. "But look—there's Mom and Dad." I looked where Julie was pointing. Mom was holding her hand up to shield her eyes from the sun. She turned her head from side to side, scanning the crowd. I figured she was looking for Julie. She probably wanted to remind her about something Stephanie had said. I could tell when she spotted us, because she dropped her hand and began to walk more quickly toward Julie and me.

"Katie," Mom said, "I've been looking for you." Looking for me! I could barely believe it. "Aunt Jean just called from the car," Mom said. "She and Sophie ran into some traffic but they'll be here any minute. She didn't want you to be worried."

"Thanks," I said.

"Speaking of the devil," Dad said, "look. There she is. Jean! Jean, we're over here!"

I turned around and saw Aunt Jean, and the girl next to her who had to be Sophie. She was really tiny. I could hardly believe we were the same age. She was in a tank top and cropped pants like Julie's, except Sophie's pants were light pink and they weren't as tight. Her clothes looked great, although I bet she still shopped in the children's department. But her face looked exactly like the picture she'd once sent me. "Sophie!" I called out. I ran over to her and hugged her even though I was really just meeting her for the first time. It felt like I'd known her much longer.

"So this is Sophie," Dad said. "You know, you're quite famous in our house." Sophie blushed, but I could tell she was pleased.

"I like your outfit," Julie told her.

"Thanks," Sophie said.

"You must get the best clothes in New York."

"Yeah," Sophie said. "But actually this isn't from New

York at all. My grandmother got it for me in Florida."

Mr. Gallagher came over to say hello to my parents. "You have two wonderful daughters," he said.

"I know," Mom said. She patted me on the back.

"So, what do you think, Katie?" Mr. Gallagher asked. "Is today everything you hoped for?"

I looked around. There were Mom, Dad, and Julie, and Aunt Jean, and Doriane. Julie's friends were standing right by us, and beyond that were all my teachers and all the other kids I went to school with. Even Sophie was there. Almost all the important people in my life were standing there, all in the same place. But I wished Jake were there too, no matter how hard I tried not to think about it. I didn't know how to answer Mr. Gallagher. Luckily, Mr. Manning came over to say it was time to get started.

"Are you all set, Katie?" Mr. Gallagher asked. I was supposed to go with him to announce the start of the jog-a-thon. He had asked Doriane if she wanted to help too, but Doriane had said she didn't want to get up in front of all those people. But I wasn't scared.

"I'm all set," I said.

Mr. Gallagher and I went to the center of the track, where the podium had been set up. He welcomed everyone and talked about how important it was for Hillside to give to the kids who were in the Mexican earthquake. He spoke about Emily and the newspaper article that got it all started. Then he told everyone to run safely and drink a lot of water. I looked over at the crowd of students as Mr. Gallagher spoke. The track was packed. Almost everyone from Hillside was running. The track team wore special shirts with the names of the Super Sponsors listed on back. That's when I saw Jake.

He was standing next to Morgan wearing the track team's shirt. I tried to take a deep breath but it came out more like a gasp and Mr. Gallagher looked over at me. He just glanced at me for an instant, but I could tell he thought I was nervous about speaking in front of everyone. Mr. Gallagher put his hand on my shoulder. "And now I'd like to introduce one of our Hillside students, Katie Franklin." He stepped away from the microphone and lowered his voice to a whisper so only I could hear. "Knock 'em dead, Katie." I smiled at him so he would know I was okay and I stepped forward. I thanked all of the sponsors and then I paused dramatically, just like they do on television. "Let the jog-a-thon begin!" I yelled. There was cheering, and then everyone started running. I wanted to talk to Jake but I knew I couldn't. There were too many people, and besides, we wouldn't be able to run as many laps if we were talking the whole time. I spotted Doriane and Sophie jogging together, and I jumped off the podium and raced to catch up with them.

nineteen

* * *

By the time the halftime show started, I'd already run twelve laps around the track. Someone blew a whistle, and I heard Mr. Gallagher at the microphone again. "Let's take a break, runners," he said. He introduced the band and the cheerleaders. I headed over to the refreshment stand with Doriane and Sophie.

"Hello, Katie," Mrs. Katz said. She was helping Mrs. Sutton out with the refreshments. "What can I get you?"

"Three waters, please," I said. I figured it was important for Doriane, Sophie, and me to drink before we started running again.

"Here you go," she said.

"Thanks," I said. "Are you making a lot of sales here?"

"Oh, yes," Mrs. Katz said. "While you guys were running, the high schoolers and all the parents were buying up a storm. You guys are raising a lot of money today."

"Good," I said. I handed Sophie and Doriane their waters.

"I'm going to get a cookie, too," Sophie said, pulling a dollar out of her pocket. "Can I have one of the black-and-white ones?"

"Of course," Mrs. Katz said. She handed Sophie a cookie. "I don't recognize you. Are you in Mr. Bohensky's social studies class?"

"Oh, no," I said. "This is Sophie Turner—my pen pal from Pen Pals Across America. She came in from New York." I knew Mrs. Katz would be happy to hear about Sophie because she was the one who'd signed us all up for the pen pal project in the first place.

"Oh, how wonderful," Mrs. Katz said. She handed Sophie the cookie. "You must be pretty proud that your pen pal organized all this."

"I am," Sophie said. I felt my eyes start to well up just a little and I blinked quickly to make it stop. Sophie broke the cookie into three to split with Doriane and me, and we walked over to the bleachers together. My parents and Aunt Jean were sitting with Mrs. O. I heard Mom telling Mrs. O that the jog-a-thon would be good for our college applications, and I knew that Mr. Gallagher must have told her so. "These kids need to be well rounded," Mom said. "It's not just grades anymore." I decided not to worry about college today, and I popped the rest of my cookie into my mouth.

My mouth was full and it was hard to chew because I had eaten too much cookie at once. "Katie," Doriane said softly. She sounded worried. I didn't answer because I was trying to swallow, but I knew why she sounded scared. Jake was walking right toward us.

I swallowed hard. Now was as good a time as any to talk to him. "Hey," I said as he got closer. "We need to talk." Jake started to move past me like he didn't see me. I grabbed his arm. He looked from my face to my hand that clutched his arm, and for a second I thought he might hit me. I let go. "We really need to talk," I said.

I thought for sure that he was just going to keep walking away. But he said, "Okay."

"Let's go over there," I said. I motioned to the side of the bleachers, and Jake followed me. He stood in front of me, and behind his head I could see the cheerleaders standing in a pyramid. I wasn't sure what to say to him and I shook my head.

"What?" Jake said.

"I didn't think you were coming today," I said.

"I'm on the track team," he said. "The coach said we all have to run."

"Oh," I said. It figured he was there because he had to be, and not because he wanted to be. I heard the band in the background and thought about how Jake had wanted there to be a famous band instead. He was probably still mad.

"I guess Doriane's your best friend now, huh?" he said.

"Well," I said, "you weren't talking to me anymore."

"I know," Jake said. "I just hated to see you with Doriane so much. I really like her, and she made up some stupid reason for not going out with me. I guess maybe she didn't like me back. And you didn't seem to need me at all anymore. It was like you took her side and didn't care about anything I had to say anymore."

"Me?" I said. "But you were the one who liked her so much and started leaving me out of things. I had to be her friend just to see you."

"You were still my best friend," Jake said. "Anyway, you're still friends with Doriane now even though I'm not around."

"Well, you were right," I said. "She's really cool. But that doesn't mean I wanted to stop being your best friend. You're the one who stopped. It's like you didn't care about me at all."

"It's not like that," Jake said. He looked down and dug the front of his shoe into the ground. His voice dropped and he got quiet, just like Doriane did, which wasn't like Jake at all. "I care. I even got my parents to be Super Sponsors."

"But their companies aren't listed on any of the signage," I said.

"I know," Jake said. "By the time I asked them about it, the signs and T-shirts and everything had already been printed up. But they're Super Sponsors. You can ask them. You could even ask Mr. Gallagher."

"That's okay," I said. "I believe you."

"Anyway, it's been no fun without you," Jake said.

"It hasn't been that much fun without you, either," I said. "And I'm sorry about the band." I was sorry about a lot more than the band. I was sorry about everything with Doriane, and how awful I had been.

"That's okay," Jake said. "You were right. I never heard back from Dozer. I did get a letter back from that band Razor's Edge, and they said they couldn't do it. They sent me an autographed picture, though."

"That's cool," I said.

"Yeah," Jake said. "I'll let you have it if we can call a truce." He looked up from the ground and held out his hand.

"You mean you'll be my friend again?" I asked.

"Yeah," Jake said.

"Okay," I said. I took his hand and pumped it with in my firmest handshake. "You're still my best friend."

"You're still mine," Jake said.

"Come on," I said. "The jog-a-thon is gonna start again."

We went back over to Doriane and Sophie. Jake and Doriane eyed each other awkwardly. Mr. Gallagher got back on the microphone and told the runners to get ready.

"I'm going to leave you in the dust, Franklin," Jake said to me. He jogged back over to where the rest of the track team was waiting.

I thought about how Jake had tried to leave me out of things, and how I'd tried to leave Doriane out of things so I could have Jake to myself. Jake might have been my best friend, but Doriane was my friend now too. I had to make it up to both of them, not just Jake. Even if it was too late to take back what I'd said, I could still make it right. I turned to Doriane. "By the way," I told her, "Jake told me he still likes you."

"But what about Lexi?" Doriane asked.

"Jake doesn't care about Lexi," I said. "He really likes you." Doriane smiled. I knew she and Jake would probably be friends again. Maybe she would even be his girlfriend. And I knew that I would have to tell Jake and Doriane what I had done. We were friends, so I had to be honest. Things might not work out the way I wanted them to. Like Julie said, I'd have to accept it. Something started to swell up inside me. I was still scared but at least I was sincere. I looked over at Sophie and she smiled at me. Then the whistle blew, and we were off again.

Twenty

We were the last ones to leave the jog-a-thon, mostly because people kept coming up to talk to me. I shook everyone's hand. By the time everyone left, my hand was almost as tired as my legs. I guess that's what you get for having a firm handshake. But I didn't mind feeling tired at all.

The track emptied out slowly. Doriane and her family left to go home to her brother. The high school volunteers were cleaning up the bleachers and the refreshment stand. My parents said good-bye to Mr. Gallagher. I shook hands with him one last time. "Ready to go, girls?" Dad said.

"Yeah," I said. Sophie and I were going to go to dinner with Dad and Aunt Jean. Mom and Julie were going straight home, where Stephanie was meeting them. Julie had her first test at Stanford the next morning.

"We'll all go out Sunday night to celebrate," Mom said. "That's when Julie will be done with the first part of her tests. Sound good?"

"Yeah," I said. "Sophie will still be here on Sunday night. We can go to Round Table Pizza. You like pizza, right, Sophie?"

"Of course," Sophie said.

"I was thinking we could go somewhere nicer than Round Table," Mom said. "Maybe that place in Palo Alto with the outdoor garden that you like."

"Ah, come on," I said. "Round Table's the best. Right, Aunt Jean?"

"It's pretty good," Aunt Jean said. "But I won't be able to go with you. I'm sure you'll have fun wherever you go, though."

"What do you mean?" I asked.

"I'm going away," she said. "I leave Sunday morning."

"Where are you going?" Dad asked. He and Mom both started to smile.

"I'm not going to Europe, Peter, so don't get too excited," Aunt Jean said. "I'm going to Mexico."

"Seriously?" Julie said.

Aunt Jean nodded. "I'm going to go down there and volunteer at one of the children's hospitals. What do you think, Katie?" she asked.

"When do you come back?" I asked.

"I don't know yet," she said. I didn't say anything. "They need me. You know that. So it might be for a while."

"That's so awesome," Julie said.

"Thanks," Aunt Jean said.

"I guess we got you the wrong books," Dad said.

"I don't think I'm going to do much sightseeing while I'm there," Aunt Jean said. "But it will be nice to travel a little."

"I think it's great," Dad said.

"Well, I don't think it's so great," I said. I looked right at Aunt Jean. "What's wrong with staying in Redwood City? You're the one who said you were perfectly happy here!" I saw her face change and I noticed lines around her eyes that I hadn't noticed before. She opened her mouth to say something, but I didn't want to hear what she had to say. I just stormed off.

It's hard to storm off when you don't know exactly where you are. I had never been anywhere in the high school before besides the track, so it wasn't like I could go hide in a classroom or something. I wouldn't even know which building to go into. So I just headed toward the parking lot. Before long I heard footsteps behind me. Then I heard Mom's voice calling, "Katie! Katie, wait!" Of all the people in my family, she was the last person I expected to be following me. But I just kept going. I didn't want to listen to anyone. "Kathryn Lyn," Mom said. Now she sounded mad. I turned around and looked at her. "You can't just run away," she said. "That's not like you."

How would she know what was like me? She hardly paid any attention to me at all. But I stood and waited for her to catch up to me. I felt so tired. My legs were sore from running for so long. Maybe I would just go home with Mom and Julie. I could take a hot bath and luxuriate like Julie always did. I could watch the bathroom get all steamed up and forget about Aunt Jean and Mexico and earthquakes and kids I would never meet. "I just want to go home," I said.

"What about Sophie?" Mom asked. "She's your guest. You should at least go to dinner with her."

I shrugged.

"Come on," Mom said. "This is a great opportunity for Aunt Jean."

"Big whoop," I said. "Now you're gonna tell me that I shouldn't bother her or mess up her plans, because everyone is more important than me."

"That's not what I was going to say," Mom said.

"Whatever."

"Oh, Katie," Mom said, "you are so much like me." I rolled my eyes and turned away from her. What did Mom know about me? She barely ever paid any attention. "I think Julie takes after your dad's side of the family," Mom continued. "They spend most of the time just being sad about the way they are, without doing anything to change them.

You're not like that. You were born with determination."

"Oh, yeah?" I said, turning back to Mom. "Then how come you never tell me I can do anything I put my mind to? You always tell Julie. How come you never tell me?"

"Oh, kiddo," Mom said. "I guess I didn't tell you as much because I didn't worry about you as much as I worried about Julie. But I'm sorry. We're a team—you know that. And every player needs support. So I'll tell you now: You can do anything you put your mind to. Anything at all. You can change the world, if you want."

"It's not true," I said. "I can't even change Aunt Jean going to Mexico."

"Katie," Mom said, "you're the reason Aunt Jean is going to Mexico."

"So you're saying it's my fault?" I asked.

"I'm saying you taught her something the rest of us never could. When her husband died, she just stayed in that house for weeks. We couldn't get her to do anything. She didn't want to see her friends, or go anywhere, or even think about meeting anyone else. And now it's been years, and she still hasn't traveled anywhere or dated anyone. Then she watched you organize this jog-a-thon. You did it because something horrible happened and you wanted to do something positive to help. I think it gave her hope and taught her to be brave."

I thought about Jake and Doriane, and Mr. Gallagher, and all my dreams about the earthquake, and how afraid

I was about Aunt Jean leaving. Suddenly I understood why Mom acted the way she did about Julie's schoolwork. "Sometimes I imagine things the way I want them to be but it doesn't always work out that way," I said.

Mom put her arm around my shoulder and squeezed me to her, and I let her. It had been a long time since she'd held me like that. I was almost as tall as she was. "I'm still very proud of you," she said.

"You know what I learned?" I said to Mom. "I learned you can't fix everything. You can do your best and you can try to be brave, but sometimes things aren't going to be the way you want, and you just need to chill out."

"You're right," Mom said. "I'm learning it too. It's a tough lesson, isn't it?"

"Yeah," I said.

"Come on," she said. "Let's go find everyone. Julie and I have to get home to meet Stephanie, and I'm sure Sophie is waiting for you."

Twenty-one

✳ ✳ ✳

Dear Sophie,

I can't believe how fast the time went when you were here.
It felt like I was waiting so long for the jog-a-thon, and to
meet you in person, and now it's all over. Mr. Gallagher said
we raised more than twenty-four thousand dollars — that's
almost two and a half times our goal! And he said we can
make the jog-a-thon an annual event at Hillside, and each
year we'll raise money for a charity that really needs it.

A lot of other stuff has happened since you left. Jake is
friends with Doriane and me again. I didn't tell you before,

but the whole fight started because of me, and then I was really scared to tell the truth because I thought I would lose everything. After the jog-a-thon, I told them what I'd done. Doriane forgave me right away. She's really sensitive and understanding, but it was harder with Jake and he was pretty mad at me. Now things with him are getting better too. Sometimes it's hard to be patient, but it's worth it in the end.

Things are going well for Julie. She took all of her tests at Stanford, so she's really happy to be done with them! On the last day, Mom let me go to Stanford with her to wait for Julie. It's really cool there. They have tons of buildings, and even a tower. I think maybe I'll end up going to college there. I know a lot of kids want to go to college far away, but I think it would be nice to be so close to Redwood City. Especially since I might have a new cousin by then.

That's right—Aunt Jean went down to Mexico and she's helping out in the hospital. Her cell phone doesn't really work there. It's strange because I'm used to talking to her so much, but she's only been able to call us twice. There's one little girl named Maria who Aunt Jean has become especially close to. Aunt Jean says she's going to try to adopt her. I think it would be nice for Aunt Jean to have a daughter. Maria lost her family in the earthquake, so Aunt Jean is all she's got.

I know you can't control everything that happens, like the earthquake and what happened to Maria's family, but maybe Maria will have a happy ending too.

In the meantime, Jake and Doriane are sort of dating again. I'm really okay with it, though. I think that even after everything that happened, I'm still Jake's best friend. Julie's going to be taking classes at Stanford over the summer instead of going to camp. She was pretty upset about that since this year she was going to be a junior counselor, so to make up for it, Mom said we could spend a week in New York before Hillside starts again in September. You have to let me know when you'll be around, because I want to make sure we go when you're there.

Anyway, that's all that's going on here. I guess it's kind of a lot, but I like it that way!

Sincerely,

Katie

Look for Courtney Sheinmel's new book
All the Things You Are

For the past three years my best friend, Annie, and I have had the coolest tradition on Teacher Organization Day.

I guess I should explain what Teacher Organization Day even is: It's this random day at the end of September when classes are canceled and the teachers have a day to catch up on their work. I really don't get the reason for it; honestly, I think it's just an excuse for the school administration to have a three-day weekend. We go to a private school called Preston Day School. Tuition is pretty steep, which goes along with my stepfather's theory that the more you pay for a school, the more vacation days you get. He may be right about that—my stepsister and stepbrother go to public school, and they never have days off for things like Teacher Organization Day. Also, their winter and spring breaks are shorter, and their school gets out two weeks after ours does in June. But whatever the reason, I'm not going to complain about it. All that matters to me is that we have that Monday off.

So this is our tradition: My mom takes Annie and me to work with her. We've been doing it ever since the fourth grade.

I know it doesn't sound like much of a tradition. Actually, it probably sounds lame to hang out at the place where your mother works, and maybe that's how it would be if you were going to *your* mother's office. But my mom has a job where it's cool to go for the day—in fact she has the coolest job of all the parents I know. She works on the set of the soap opera *Lovelock Falls*. In case you haven't heard of it, Lovelock Falls is a made-up town, and the show is about all the people who live there. It's filmed in Manhattan, which is about an hour away from where we live. When we go, the crew totally treats us like we're celebrities ourselves. We get to go to the hair and makeup room and get made up just like the actors do, and then we watch the filming and the set changes. In between scenes the real actors come up and talk to us, and we get our pictures taken with everyone. They also have this area called Craft Services, where there's so much food you can't even believe it. Basically, any kind of dish you can imagine is there—including tons of desserts. I sort of wonder how all the actresses on the show stay so super thin, since they can eat at Craft Services all day long. But I think they have personal trainers.

Mom is a stylist on *Lovelock Falls*, and she handles the wardrobe for six of the women on the show, including the star, Ally Jaron. Ally plays Violet van Ryan. So far she's been almost murdered twice, been in a coma, and had four different weddings—two of them to the same guy. His character, Kyle Shepherd, has amnesia right now, so he doesn't even remember that she left him for the second time, right after she found out that he was a compulsive gambler and had gambled away most of her fortune. Violet also has ten-year-old twins, and one of them just came back from the dead. And she has a twin sister herself, but Violet's twin sister, Ivy, is evil, and Ivy got shipped off to an insane asylum last year.

Of course, Ally isn't anything like that in real life. Mom says the cast and crew of *Lovelock Falls* are like family, and she knows them all really well. I know Ally too, because Mom has worked with her for so long. Her house isn't too far from where my family lives, and I've visited her with Mom. When I had appendicitis last year, Ally sent me a care package filled with DVDs and magazines. It's not really intimidating to be around her, because she's so completely down-to-earth. She has two daughters, Madison and Nicole, who are super cute. They look so much like Ally that it's crazy—blondish hair and really wide blue-green eyes. They remind me of dolls. I've babysat for them a couple of times, and even though I don't think of Ally as a star, I have to admit that it was cool to see the inside of her house—maybe not as cool as getting to see where a movie star like Brody Hudson lives, but still. The table next to the couch in the living room has a bunch of framed pictures on it—pictures of Ally and her friends, who just happen to be famous themselves. And she has a huge walk-in closet right off her bedroom. There are all these photos on the walls of her dressed up in spectacular designer gowns.

Mom says Ally is a really easy person to dress because she has a great sense of style and everything looks good on her. In the scene she was filming that day, she was wearing a flowing dress that stopped just below her knees. It had a halter top—the halter part was crocheted, and then the bottom of the dress was sort of silky. It was a bunch of different colors that you wouldn't necessarily think would go well together, but somehow they just did. I think the truth is that my mom is really good at her job—she's just so stylish herself. She's personable, and she knows how to make people feel really good about themselves so they always like what they're wearing. Mom has even been nominated for a bunch of different awards for dressing the actresses so well. We have the nomination certificates framed in our den.

The funniest thing about the wardrobe on *Lovelock Falls* is that all the actors are always dressed up in really fancy clothes for their scenes, no matter where the scene takes place, as if at any moment they might need to dash off to a black-tie event. That day Violet van Ryan was at the hospital to visit her ex-husband—the one with amnesia. But she looked like she was ready to be a guest at a wedding. Annie and I were in directors' chairs just to the side of the set, so we had a good view. One of the crew gave us headsets so we could listen to the dialogue of Ally's scene.

"Well, Dr. Sparling, that is just unacceptable," Ally-as-Violet said. "I expect you to have a different answer when I come back tomorrow, or else I am pulling the foundation's funding of the new wing, and in case you don't know what that will mean for your son, I will tell you: It will be a disaster of epic proportions. It will change all—all the things you are." She turned around quickly and stormed off. Her dress swayed back and forth, the colors blending together just right. She looked glamorous and intense all at once.

"Cut!" the director said.

The scene was over, so Ally came over to us. "Hey, Carly," she said, hugging me hello.

"Hi," I said. "Do you remember Annie? She comes with me every year."

"Sure," she said. "Hi, Annie."

Ally extended her hand for Annie to shake. I happen to know that Ally doesn't like her hands. She thinks the veins in them make her look old. She taught me this trick that if you hold your hands so your fingers are pointed upward, you can't see the veins as well, and it makes your hands look younger. Annie shook Ally's hand. I could tell she was jealous that Ally had hugged me and not her. I know it's mean, but it made me sort of glad. At school Annie is definitely more popular than I am. She has this personality that just makes her stand out and sparkle. I'm lucky to be her best friend, but all the same it's nice to feel like the important one sometimes.

"How do you think the scene went?" Ally asked.

"It was great," I said.

"Are you sure?" Ally asked. "I screwed up a couple of the lines and I had to improvise." She seemed genuinely worried, even though she's been playing Violet van Ryan for years and years. She's really good at it, too. I think she's probably the best actress on *Lovelock Falls*.

"It sounded completely natural," Annie said. "It was just how I would have done the scene." Annie is actually in drama club at school, and every time we visit the set, she hopes she'll be discovered—like the director will decide that he really needs a twelve-year-old in a certain scene, and that Annie has the perfect look. She says a lot of really famous people got their start on the soaps. Whenever we talk about what we want to be when we grow up, Annie says she should be an actress and I should be a writer. Her plan is that I will be a writer on a soap opera, since I'm good at making up stories and I know a lot about the soaps, and I'll write her a really great part.

"Seriously," I told Ally, "you totally nailed it."

Ally ruffled my hair. "Thanks, girls," she said. "I've got to run—I have to make an appearance at a benefit downtown. I can't even remember if it's for the museum or the library. It's the third night in a row I've had one of these things. I promised the girls I'd be home in time to put them to bed, but I don't know if I'll really make it. You know, it's really hard to be a good mother. I look at how Leigh is with you, Carly. I just hope in the end I'm the same kind of mother she is."

I love when Ally talks to me like I'm her friend. "You're a good mother too," I said.

"My guru says I need to work on simplifying my life," Ally said.

Here's something else about Ally: You can't really know her without hearing about what her guru says. It's the one sort of weird thing about her. Her guru is this guy from India who teaches her about yoga and meditation. He says all sorts of things, like life is full of signs—you just need to watch for them—and there's no such thing as a mistake. I'm not sure I believe that last one; just last week I messed up on my math quiz even when I really knew the answer, and I certainly didn't do it on purpose. "Madison and Nicole are worried that if I simplify too much, they'll end up with fewer toys," she continued.

I smiled, because the girls have so many toys. It's practically a toy store at Ally's house. "Tell them I say hi," I said.

"I will," Ally said. "Come visit us soon—actually, maybe the weekend after next your mom can bring you by. I have a lunch thing, and I know the girls would rather play with you than tag along with their old mom."

"That sounds good," I said.

After Ally left, Annie and I headed back to my mom's office. Mom calls it her office, but really it's just a cluttered room that she shares with a few of the other stylists. There are racks of clothing everywhere, and labels taped to the hangers so they know who is supposed to wear which outfit in what scene. A couple of times I've seen actresses walking around Mom's office without clothes on. They don't seem to care who sees them, but I would definitely be more self-conscious. I'm kind of a late bloomer. I guess it's obvious even when I have clothes on that I'm totally flat-chested, but it's not like I ever want anyone to see it up close.

I pushed open the door to Mom's office. There was a rack of dresses right in front of the door—I couldn't see Mom through them, but I could hear her talking to Vivette. Vivette is the head stylist, so she's sort of Mom's boss, but she doesn't act like a boss at all. She and Mom are really good friends. Vivette and her husband, Ed, always come to our house for Thanksgiving. She makes a dish called three-cheese potatoes that is one of the best things I've ever tasted. It's why I really like Thanksgiving, even though the next day Mom and I always bring leftovers to my grandmother. She's in a nursing home. Mom actually visits Grandma every week, but she only makes me go with her once a month or so, and on special occasions, like Thanksgiving. It's really sad there. Once, Mom told me she hoped I would visit her often if she was ever in a home like that, and I got so upset because I didn't want to have to think about it: seeing Mom confused, sick, shriveled. It's true what they say about old people shrinking, because Grandma seems smaller every time I see her. She says the strangest things, too, which freaks me out sometimes.

"Leigh, I swear, don't worry about a thing," Vivette was saying. "I shouldn't have even said anything to you."

"No," Mom said. "This has gone on too long. Jonathan has no idea."

"You know this isn't the place to talk about this," Vivette said.

"You're the one who brought it up," Mom said. She sounded angry. Annie looked at me, but I just shrugged. We pushed our way through the rack of dresses. Mom had her hand pressed to her forehead. It was Vivette who noticed us first. "Hiya, Carly," she said. "Hi, Annie."

We said hi back, and right then Mom's whole face changed. She lowered her hand from her head and grinned. "Come on in, girls," she said, beckoning us. "I'm just about done for the day."

"Did you have fun today?" Vivette asked. She put her arm around my shoulder. When she does that—puts her arm around me, or gives me a hug—I feel like I'm being swallowed up. Vivette is really tall and broad. It's not that she's fat; actually, she's not fat at all, just muscular. Her shoulders are wide, like she's wearing shoulder pads, and she has thick wrists and ankles. My mom says Vivette is big-boned. I'm on the small side, like my mom. I've always been one of the shortest kids in my grade. Everyone says I have a gymnast's body, which is kind of funny just because I'm so completely inflexible. Anyway, I always feel like a really little kid when I stand next to Vivette.

"Yeah, of course," I said. "I love it here."

"Good, I'm glad," she said. "Listen, I have to get going. It was great to see you, girls . . . and Leigh, everything is under control." She kissed us all good-bye, and walked through the rack of clothes and out the door.

"What was that about?" I asked.

"What?"

"What you and Vivette were talking about?"

"Nothing," Mom said. She bent down to her desk and

scribbled something on a piece of paper: *Violet in hotel dream sequence*. Then she taped it up onto a hanger behind her—a crimson-red dress was hanging from it. It had an incredibly low neckline. Sometimes they have to put body tape on the dresses so they stay in place and the actresses don't accidentally flash the crew while they're filming. Mom turned back to me. "It was absolutely nothing. Are you two ready to roll?" Mom asked.

"Sure," I said.

Mom pulled our coats out of the closet. "God, I can't believe the three-day weekend is almost officially over," Annie said. "I really don't want to go to school tomorrow. Most of it's like a waste of time anyway. It's not like I plan to be a historian or a scientist or anything like that, so why do I have to learn about those things?"

"I suppose you never know when they will come in handy," Mom said. "You could sound very intellectual at a dinner party."

"But you don't need them here, right, Leigh?" Annie asked. My friends all call Mom by her first name.

"I haven't yet," Mom said.

"And this is really what I want to do," Annie said. "I want to be an actress."

"Well, whatever you grow up to be, I had to learn about history and science, and your parents had to learn about history and science—so maybe we just want you guys to suffer like we did," Mom said. It was a Mom kind of thing to say— when people are upset, she tries to be funny and lighten the mood. "Come on, let's get out of here and grab some dinner."

We went to a Mexican restaurant not too far from the set, and afterward we got Mom's car out of the garage and headed back up to Westchester.

Annie and I both live in Westchester County, just in different towns. Annie lives in Scarsdale, and I live in New Rochelle. I don't have any friends from Preston who live near me. There's just Amelia, who lives across the street, but she goes to public school. When we were little, our mothers were really close. They're not as friendly as they used to be, since Mom's best friend is Vivette. Still, I like Amelia, and being friends with her is convenient. We can hang out without needing anyone to drive us anywhere. (Although Annie's parents have a driver, so generally it's not a problem. She can get dropped off at my house whenever she wants.)

In the car on the way home Annie and I sat in the backseat, like Mom was our chauffeur. Annie was talking about her parents, who are way different from mine. They're really stiff, and sort of unapproachable. In fact their whole house is stiff and unapproachable. They actually have rooms in it that we're not even allowed to go into, because the furniture is so special and expensive. But sometimes, when Annie's parents are out and Annie's busy in another room, I go into one of the forbidden rooms and look around. I run my fingers along the silk on the couch, and feel the wood on the antique dressers.

"My dad said he'll be late all week, so I know my mom

will be in one of her annoying moods," Annie said.

I knew "annoying" wasn't really the right word for how Annie's mom would be. It was just code for how she'd be drinking. I've seen Annie's mother get drunk before—more than once. It usually happens when her dad is working late. Her mom sits at the dining room table with a bottle of wine and talks until her words are slurred.

Annie doesn't really talk about it. She's just got this weird thing with her mom: Sometimes she loves her and tries to be like her, glamorous and stuff, and sometimes she just hates her—mostly when she's drinking. I guess she can't really go up to her mom and say, "I don't think you should drink anymore." And she can't talk to her dad about it either. First of all he's not home that much, and second of all he's really intense and scary.

I just know, even though she doesn't say it, that it's easier for Annie when she stays at our house. Mom knows it too. "You can always stay with us if you want to," Mom told her.

"I wish I could," Annie said. "But my mom would never let me sleep over on a school night. She's got all these rules. It's so dumb—she's so into keeping up appearances."

I waited for Mom to say something to make Annie feel better, but all of a sudden there was a whooping sound and flashing lights behind us. Mom cursed under her breath and turned the knob on the car stereo. I hadn't even realized the music was on until then, when there was just silence.

"What's going on?" I asked.

"I don't know," Mom said. "I don't think I did anything wrong." There was something about the way her voice wavered that made me scared. We pulled to the side of the road. Mom pressed the button to roll down her window.

The officer leaned into the car. "Ma'am, are you aware you ran a stop sign at the bottom of the hill?"

"No, officer," Mom said. "I didn't see it."

"Can I have your license and registration please?"

"Of course, officer," Mom said. I watched from the back-seat as she reached for her bag. She pulled her license out of her wallet. "I'm really sorry, officer. This is my license. The registration is the glove compartment—one sec." She leaned over, popped open the glove compartment, and handed the registration over to him.

"Thank you," the officer said.

"I just can't believe I did that. I was in the middle of a very intense conversation with these two—which is a terrible excuse. I was trying to be a role model, but I guess I'm not setting a good example for them after all. Girls, do as I say, not as I do."

The officer smiled. "Don't be too hard on yourself, Mrs. Wheeler," he said. "I'll tell you what—I'll let you go with a warning this time. Just watch the signs and drive carefully, all right?"

"Of course, officer," Mom said. "Thank you so much." We pulled away slowly. Mom took a deep breath and let it out slowly, like she was still nervous about the whole thing.

"That cop car is always there," Annie said. "He's always trying to catch people. Our driver got a ticket from him a few weeks ago. My mom says the cops probably give out more tickets at the end of the month, just so they can meet their quotas."

"But it's the twenty-seventh of the month now," I said.

"He must have been in a good mood," Mom said.

"Maybe," I said. "I think there's just something kind of magical about you," I said.

"Thanks, honey," she said. She smiled and sounded like herself again. "That's why your faux pa married me."

Julia and Eliza have always been best friends . . . but everything is about to change.

From award-winning author

NORA RALEIGH BASKIN

EBOOK EDITION ALSO AVAILABLE

Simon & Schuster
Books for Young Readers

KIDS.SIMONANDSCHUSTER.COM